S C A T T E R E D
BONES
MAGGIE SIGGINS

bitlit

A **free** eBook edition is available
with the purchase of this print book.

CLEARLY PRINT YOUR NAME ABOVE IN UPPER CASE

Instructions to claim your free eBook edition:
1. Download the BitLit app for Android or iOS
2. Write your name in **UPPER CASE** on the line
3. Use the BitLit app to submit a photo
4. Download your eBook to any device

COTEAU
BOOKS

www.coteaubooks.com

SCATTERED
BONES

MAGGIE SIGGINS

Edited by Dave Margoshes
Book designed by Scott Hunter
Typeset by Susan Buck
Printed and bound in Canada

Library and Archives Canada Cataloguing in Publication

Siggins, Maggie, 1942-, author
    Scattered bones / Maggie Siggins.

Issued in print and electronic formats.
ISBN 978-1-55050-669-3 (paperback).--ISBN 978-1-55050-670-9 (pdf).--ISBN 978-1-55050-671-6 (epub).--ISBN 978-1-55050-672-3 (mobi)

    I. Title.

PS8637.I286S28 2016   C813'.6   C2015-908767-8
                                    C2015-908768-6

2517 Victoria Avenue
Regina, Saskatchewan
Canada S4P 0T2
www.coteaubooks.com

Available in Canada from:
Publishers Group Canada
2440 Viking Way
Richmond, British Columbia
Canada V6V 1N2

10 9 8 7 6 5 4 3 2 1

Coteau Books gratefully acknowledges the financial support of its publishing program by: the Saskatchewan Arts Board, The Canada Council for the Arts, the Government of Saskatchewan through Creative Saskatchewan, the City of Regina. We further acknowledge the [financial] support of the Government of Canada. Nous reconnaissons l'appui [financier] du gouvernement du Canada.

For my friends at Pelican Narrows

PROLOGUE

Summer, 1730

A SCORCHER OF A DAY. So hot that when you sat on the rocks your bum got burnt. The insects, though, loved the heat. Auntie patted smudge all over our bodies, but the mosquitoes still nipped and the deer flies bit deep, until our blood mixed with the dust and turned into mud the colour of rust.

We girls picked berries – the tart reds, the sweet purples, the sour russets, the big blacks. We laughed our heads off when the juice of the Dewberries shot into the eyes of our cousins. "*Maci-manchosis*, little devil," Auntie laughed as she grabbed my youngest brother, the naughtiest of us all, and tickled him until he pleaded for mercy.

Still, even in our glee, we felt the unease that was pricking at our camp. Our mother was nervous and cross. Not a hint of a smile on her usually sunny face. We assumed she was upset because our father was absent.

Each summer the men of our band of *Asiniskaw-itiniwak*, Rock Cree, loaded their canoes so high we were sure they would sink. After they waved goodbye, they travelled along the great river to Fort Prince William where white peddlers were waiting to greet them. There, the skins of silver and red fox, otter, mink, marten, fisher and, most important, the thick, glossy, black/brown beaver were traded for European tools, guns and ammunition.

Since the trip lasted many moons, our mother would goad our father, insisting he relished the break from his noisy children and nagging wife. But she loved the things he brought back – the sturdy needles, scissors and knives made of iron, the copper kettles, the glass beads which she used to decorate moccasins, bags, and belts. Once, the cargo contained a round glass mirror. Mother had laughed out loud. Reflected there were the deep dimples in her cheeks. How often had she been teased about those! And the tattoos her sister had painted with such precision, two straight white lines drawn on an angle from the corner of her mouth to her lower jaw. These she had especially admired.

Father and the other men were expected back any day, and we thought Mother might be stewing about this. Anything could have gone wrong: violent lightning could stab a canoe – in a wink all would be drowned; savage forest fires could suddenly ignite – all campers burned to a crisp; and, most menacing, a chance meeting with their long-time enemy, the Sioux. Now mercenaries who worked for the French, the Sioux were paid well – guns, ammunition, rum, tobacco, anything they wanted – to eliminate anyone doing business with the British, the *Asiniskaw-itiniwak* included. But it turned out that father's imminent return was not the reason for mother's distress.

Two elders, Nanahewepathis and Chachake, both noted medicine men with strong shamanistic powers, had been left in charge of our summer camp, although as mother said, Chachake was so old and fragile, he would provide as much protection as the pelican he was named after. Each chief was responsible for half of the sixty lodges which sat along the sandy, half-moon beach of Pelican Lake and scattered up the hill behind it. Nanahewepathis was our *mosom*, my mother's father, so naturally we were under his charge. Even in old age, he was a handsome man. His hair – black still, though speckled with white – was as thick as ever, braided into three plaits, two smaller ones falling at his ears and one down his back as thick as a moose's thigh bone. This was his pride and joy, his vanity. Mother spent hours applying bear grease to make sure it shone.

Chachake, on the other hand, was scrawny with a beak-like nose that resembled the beak of the bird that was his namesake. He was always forecasting disaster and searching for signs to back up his gloomy predictions – a red-winged blackbird lying dead on the ground meant nothing, but, according to him, two such corpses discovered on the same day signalled a winter so severe starvation was sure to follow. He got on our mother's nerves. "If the sun is shining, he will talk about the rain that is sure to fall. If it's raining, he will remember how it snowed last year."

That morning, very early, Chachake had banged on his drum and told everyone to gather round. His *pawachi-kan* – his guiding spirit – had visited him during the night and warned him that disaster was about to befall us. What the danger was, specifically, the spirit wouldn't say, but it would be calamitous. We must pack up and move that very day.

Since we were just settled in after months of winter travel, this would be a huge undertaking, and besides, the men were expected soon, maybe even the next day. How would they find us? So we asked what Nanahewepathis had to say about this. He shook his big head. No such dark scenario had visited his sleep and surely, if Chachake's dire warning was true, his *pawachi-kan*, his dream helper, would definitely have come to him as well. After all, his guardian spirit was cleverer and stronger than Chachake's.

The arguments volleyed back and forth. The two old men were respectful and courteous to each other, and, when the discussion did heat up, a resolution was quickly found. Chachake's entourage would relocate, Nanahewepathis's people, my family included, would stay put.

Later in the afternoon I strolled over to say goodbye to my favourite cousin, Wapun, a girl born at the exact time I was and lucky because of that. The celebration of our first blood-flow had just been held. Wapun's family had already dismantled their wigwam, the thin birch bark covering carefully removed, the long poplar poles taken down. These had been loaded in canoes, but most of their other paraphernalia – the silky bear-skin-covered eiderdown quilts, the pots, the kettles, the racks used to dry moose meat, the wooden cache where fish and other foods were stored – would be left behind. As soon as Chachake's *pawachi-kan* signalled that the danger was gone, his people would return. Wapun and I hugged each other goodbye, but we weren't too sad. We would be seeing each other soon.

Sitting around our fire that evening, we youngsters were eager to talk about the curious events of the day, but the stern and yet strangely nonchalant demeanour of our *mosom* signalled to us to keep quiet. Mother was more upset than I, the eldest of her four children, had ever remembered seeing her.

Recently, *Mosom* had taken special notice of me, his "cheerful black-bird." I was assigned to sleep in his wigwam and do his fetching – in particular to make sure that his *wikis*, dried rat root, was at hand when his rheumatism bothered him. "Soon a tall boy will take you away from us and then I will become a great grandfather," he said as he smiled at me.

"I will never leave you, my beloved *mosom*," I had answered, although I knew this wasn't true. I already had my eye on a certain beautiful boy.

That night, curled in my caribou bag, I fell into my usual deep sleep. As the first grey light appeared, I thought I heard a weird noise, a kind of deep-throated chant. It quickly ceased, and, thinking it was a dream, I fell back to sleep. A short time later I awoke to the terror that haunts me still, even now that my hair is white.

Standing in the middle of the wigwam was a tall, muscular man. Dark raven feathers shot out at the back of his head, green eagle feathers fell down his shoulders. His face was hideously decorated with black and white war paint, a whirl of blood red exploding on his forehead. A necklace of bones circled his neck. A leather loin cloth covered his private parts although I saw that enormous, telltale bulge protruding beneath it. In his raised hand he carried a curved metal knife. In a single, rapid motion, he grabbed my still-sleeping *mosom* by his hair, pulled his head back, and slit his throat.

Even now as I tell this story to you my beloved grandchildren, I still hear the dogs braying, the terrible human howls, the piteous pleading, the gun shots. A shadowy memory remains: of being roughly pushed from behind, of slipping in blood, of stumbling over mutilated bodies, young and old, babies even, all family of mine.

I was bundled into a canoe with the only other captive they took, a boy cousin about four years old, probably a replacement for a dead child of one of the chiefs. I put my arms around him, comforting him, trying so hard not to cry myself, not to throw up, not to faint.

As the convoy of six canoes travelled along, there was constant hollering amongst the war party. This grew louder and louder, back and forth from one boat to another. Since their language was foreign to me, I couldn't make out what they were saying. Finally, our steersman pushed backwards on his paddle and our canoe halted. My cousin and I were dumped on a reef. It was so small the water lapped at our toes. Then those brave, honourable warriors took off.

At first we were quite happy to have escaped what would have been a brutal life, particularly for me as I would surely have been made a sex slave – with revulsion in their voices, my people had sometimes talked about this horror. But as time passed, the panic set in. Slow starvation, exposure to the hot, hot sun, would be an even more hideous death then being shot or stabbed.

For a long time we sat on the tiny island, back against back, numb with terror. A group of solemn white pelicans sitting on a reef nearby peered at us, looking so sad, so sorry for us.

Evening approached. With our arms around each other, we tried not to think of the night spirits who would surely come to haunt us. Suddenly my cousin shouted out, "Look there!" Against a darkening sunset, in silhouette, a parade of canoes. We were frightened, sure that the Sioux had come back to kill us. But as the flotilla neared, the emerging shapes grew familiar. Quizzical voices shouted out. I jumped up and waved. Before I knew it, I was being held to my father's chest.

He wrapped me in a caribou hide, and packed me in his canoe beside him. As we lapped along, I couldn't stop shaking and sobbing.

v

He tried to comfort me by relaying some good news. My cousin Wapun was alive and well.

The day before the massacre, Chachake and his group had headed south on Pelican Lake, turning into a large bay into which a creek meandered from the interior. The able-bodied rounded up logs and felled trees, heaving them across the creek's mouth so as to hide the passageway – from what they weren't sure, only that that was what the chief insisted on. After that they travelled into the interior, paddling their canoes as fast as possible. By late afternoon they felt secure enough to set up camp. They devoured a meal, and, exhausted, fell asleep.

The moment Chachake awoke the next morning he knew that something dreadful had happened. Quickly he made his way back to the Pelican Lake camp. "What I saw was so hideous I thought I would die of sorrow on the spot," he told my father.

The only survivor was a young mother who sobbed out her story to him. When the attack came, she had plunged into the lake, right at the spot where spring debris – old branches, weeds, leaves – had accumulated. This provided her with an air pocket. She survived, but since her two children had been hatcheted to death, she doubted that this was any kind of blessing.

Not long after Chachake had discovered the massacre, the men of Pelican Narrows appeared, home at last from their trading venture. They had travelled from the north so they hadn't encountered the eastbound Sioux. Hours later, after the howls of anguish had finally subsided, the means of revenge was carefully mapped out. In his mind's eye Chachake could see clearly, like tracks in the snow, the exact course the Sioux had taken. Following it, that evening they found my cousin and I abandoned on our little reef.

After our rescue, our party travelled until it was quite dark. Then, leaving our canoes hidden in foliage, we quietly traversed a path that followed the steep bank above the water. When we finally spotted the fires of the Sioux camp twinkling in the black night, the young men wanted to attack immediately. They had to be held back.

Chachake silently signalled the place our party was to stop for the night. My cousin and I, exhausted by our ordeal, fell into a deep sleep, but at dawn we were awakened and led to a copse of white birch trees. "You are not to move from here," my father commanded, but it was an order we couldn't possibly obey. We hid in a clump of bushes high on a bank. From there we watched the drama unfold.

The Sioux seemed not to have noticed how the river had narrowed, how steep the banks sloped up on either side. They were surprised when the first gunshot rang out. The bullets had come from high up, across the bows of their canoes. They immediately fired back in that direction just as, from the rear, came a chorus of unearthly howls. A heavy volley of bullets and arrows followed. The river stained red with blood.

All the Sioux were killed except the headman – Chachake had asked that if at all possible he be captured alive – and a young relative who had served him. They were gagged, their feet and hands bound together behind them, then hurled into canoes face down.

Back at Pelican Lake, the young people, my cousin and I included, were not allowed to watch the revenge meted out, and over the years we were forbidden to talk about it, but the tale was too important to remain buried forever. I eventually was able to piece it together.

A log was laid on the shoulders of each victim, their arms strapped to it by leather thongs. The headman pleaded, "Do not kill me. I have many valuable gifts from the white man, tools and food, that I can give you."

"No," my father said. "You have inflicted a great horror on us and you will pay for it."

With sharp, sharp knives, the Sioux flesh was amputated piece by piece, slice by slice. Chachake, as old and feeble as he was, was particularly vicious, slicing off the nipples, then the penis, and then the testicles of each hostage. With a honking, vicious laugh, he called the dogs. They were to savour the blood as it dripped to the ground. The captives howled with pain until, at last, death intervened.

Once the act of revenge was finally played out, the women and children were attended to.

A large shallow grave was dug in the centre of a copse of trembling aspen on top of the hill overlooking the beach where the slaughter had taken place. The bodies were placed side by side, the children lying close to their mothers and grandmothers.

Since my *mosom* was a revered medicine man, his resting place was separate from the others. His thick braids, which had been chopped off by his executioner, were placed beside his body. On top of this mound were assembled the contents of his precious medicine bag — a raven's skull used to trick all manner of malevolent spirits; a crane's bill painted in bands of moss green, bright red, and midnight black which weakened the powers of the flesh-eating *witigo*; a hollowed bone of a swan used to suck diseases — boils, serrations, puss — from the human body.

On his chest was displayed his beloved stone pipe, presented to him years ago by a white man, a North West Company trader he had befriended. Arranged above his head were five eagle claws. These were used as counters in the games of chance he loved, for, if Nanahewepathis was anything, he was a gambling man.

There was one other who was so beloved by her people that she too was given a special, separate burial. She was dressed in a robe made of the softest deer skin over knee-high leggings; a cloak decorated with clusters of reddish/brown seeds; moccasins embroidered with glass beads and porcupine quills into small circles, triangles, oblongs.

Her beautiful necklace, the very symbol of how much her husband loved her, was given a place of honour. It was made from red and green and blue glass balls brought from the fur trading posts, hollow bones, spectral white and polished, from the shafts of duck and warbler wings, the legs of rabbits and the backbones of fish; and, her favourite, beads made of red pipestone — "blood of mother earth," she used to say.

Under her head was placed her birch-bark kit filled with her workaday utensils which she would need in the next world: a stone scraper used on animal hides; a steel-bladed knife with a moose-bone handle essential for butchering animals; an awl to punch holes in leather or birch bark; and a whetstone to keep her tools sharp.

In her right hand was placed her most precious possession of all – a lump of graphite, flat and smooth from years of use, found long ago on the banks of the great river. She had drawn divine images – animals, people, plants – sketching them on birch bark, tattooing them our bodies, etching pictures on rocks. They had astounded, amused and surprised.

I have prayed every day of my long life that the other-world spirits honour and love my mother as much as we did.

July, 1924

THE ARRIVAL
Friday afternoon

CHAPTER ONE

A SCORCHER OF A DAY, hotter than hell. Florence Smith has already gone for her swim, diving off Chachake Cliff into the refreshing waters of Pelican Lake. The boys cavorting on the beach nearby had burst into laughter. "Hippopotamus, hippopotamus, *wini-papam-tokowikakos*," they roared. They're obsessed with this creature, because they've been drawing pictures of it in Miss Wentworth's class. Florence doesn't mind; she's always been a big-boned, muscled woman, and these kids know how tough she can be. More than once, she's grabbed an ear, twisting, twisting until the victim yells out, "Sorry, Miss. *Namaw kitom katetin*," won't do it again.

It's 11:30 a.m., and since the store is shipshape, Florence decides she'll relax for a few minutes. She settles herself on her favourite log situated in front of the store where she has a good view of the lake; the birch tree behind supports her back. The two pugs, Artemis and Athena, sprawl at her feet. She pulls out her pipe, lights up, settles in for a long and leisurely smoke. But on the very first puff, the heavenly peace is shattered.

Florence has lived so long at Pelican Narrows that she can follow the bedlam's progress with her ear. The first explosion comes from the Northern Lights, Arthur Jan's fur trading post, located at the northwest limits of the settlement. Out for a walk earlier that morning, she spotted the manager of that establishment, that devious rat, Bibiane Ratt, hammering away at a loose plank on the store's dock. She scowled at him as she marched by; he gave her a raspberry. She pictures him now shooting off his beloved Spencer carbine.

The next outburst comes from the Whitebear compound located

up the hill from Arthur Jan's establishment. The chief's five sons have obviously fetched their rifles and are blasting away. That's where she was headed when she snubbed Bibiane. On her way to see how the dear old man was making out. She found him, wrapped in a blanket, sitting in his wicker chair on a rock overlooking the lake. He was humming Anglican hymns, but stopped and waved when he spotted her. His wife was nowhere in sight, so Florence was able to whisper to him, "I think of you every minute of every day." She loves Chief Cornelius Whitebear with a passion that she knows is ridiculous for a large, homely woman in her sixties.

Next comes an explosion further south. Thirty or so Cree trappers have emerged from their wigwams or log cabins, and at this instant are ejaculating as many bullets into the air in as short a time as is possible. Their kids, including those who think Florence is a hippo, are jumping up and down like grasshoppers.

Florence spots Father Bonnald pushing carrot tops into the rabbit cages located in the yard of St. Gertrude's Catholic Church. The priest is a little hard of hearing, so it takes a while before he realizes what's going on. Then he runs for his revolver, which he keeps under the bed, and joins the uproar.

Florence's husband Russell emerges from the house attached to the Hudson's Bay Company post. He's all spruced up, wearing his old naval jacket with two medals attached to the lapel and his captain's hat.

"They've arrived, Flo," he calls out.

"My heart's just a thumpin'," she replies.

Ignoring her sarcasm, he aims his rifle high into the sky and joins in the boisterous greeting.

The Anglican priest Ernst Wentworth refuses to engage in the uproarious welcome – he thinks that it's ungodly nonsense – but his wife Lucretia Wentworth comes running down from the vicarage. All week she's been babbling on about The Distinguished Writer, driving Florence and everyone else mad. "He really is *the* most famous author in the entire world," she told anyone who would listen, "His books have sold everywhere, millions of them." She has read both *Main Street* and *Babbitt* and thinks they are "the most brilliant literature ever produced by any writer at any time." Now she's chirping at Florence like an excited chipmunk. "Is he really here? I can't believe he'd actually come to this wretched backwater. I'm so embarrassed thinking of all the uncouth people he'll run into here. How will he be able to stand it?"

Florence controls an urge to take an axe to the silly woman's head.

Finally, around what is laughingly called The Island, travelling from the southwest, glides the caravan of four canoes, their Evinrudes purring like some kind of proud water cats, their Union Jacks and Stars and Stripes fluttering from the bows. As he does every year at this time, Russell Smith stands rigidly at attention, ready to salute the Canadian government's official Treaty Party.

Pelican Narrows, Saskatchewan, is now on full alert. The entire village, everyone, young and old, heads for the Hudson's Bay Company dock. The white people are eager to set eyes on the celebrated author about whom Lucretia Wentworth has jabbered so much, but the Cree know nothing of the American's eminence, and so care not a dog's fart. It's the government representatives they're happy to see, come to hand out treaty money.

Everyone watches as they disembark – officious Bob Taylor, the long-time Indian Agent; the physician, Douglas Mackenzie on Treaty Party duty for the first time and whom everyone calls Doc Happy Mac; the fur trader, Arthur Jan; the cook; the eight Cree paddlers; and the two paying guests, Dr. Claude Lewis, and his brother, the famous author, Sinclair Lewis. Who almost falls into the lake. After securing the dock with his left leg, he pushes too hard on the gunwale with his right so that the canoe drifts sideways while he slowly does the splits. One of the paddlers runs to his rescue, grabbing him around his skinny middle and bundling him onto land. After he has steadied himself, he straightens his back and strides forth, trying to ignore the crowd gawking at him.

A tent has been set up in a pretty grove of silver birch up from the beach, where tea chilled in an icebox and egg salad sandwiches will be served. The guests are about to make their way there when their travelling companion, Arthur Jan, comes beetling over. Ignoring everyone else, he eyeballs the Lewis brothers. "How would you fellows like to bunk at my place? It's not a palace but it's pretty clean. And the meals are a treat. I bet that you'd both enjoy a night in a real bed."

The Famous Writer looks tempted, but his brother pipes up, "Thank you most kindly, Arthur, but, as you are well aware, from the start of this trip, we've followed a strict policy of no special treatment. We're part of the Treaty Party and will live in whatever conditions they do."

Not at all cowed, Arthur replies, "That's understandable, I guess. But please accept an invitation to a small gathering at my place tonight. In honour of your arrival. It's not often that someone so famous drops into this neck of the woods."

Sinclair Lewis thanks him profusely; a delicious dinner *not* around a campfire would be heaven. As the writer turns and walks away, Florence spots Arthur folding into an obsequious bow, a mocking smile on his face. She feels like spitting at him.

She had planned to join the tea party but at that moment the Wentworths' daughter Izzy comes skipping by. Florence adores this eighteen-year-old. She's everything her mother isn't – sensible, kind, intelligent. "How you doing, my beauty?" she calls out.

"Just fine thanks, Flo. I'm on my way to watch the set up." Izzy is trying not to show how happy she is but Florence has a pretty good idea of why the girl's face is so flushed. She's eager to see caramel-skinned, honey-eyed Joe Sewap, the Cree boy she's fallen for.

"Okay, darling. Mind if I walk along with you?" Flo asks.

Arrangements have been made for the Treaty Party to pitch their tents on a flat stretch at the back of the Bay store. While the party is sipping iced tea, Joe and the other native workers put up the tents and move in the equipment. Izzy and Florence stand to the side, watching.

"What's that?" Izzy asks, pointing at a huge pile of canvas.

"That's a duffle bag, if you can believe it. Belonging to The Famous Author," says Cecil Ballendine, one of the more loquacious paddlers. He then proceeds to demonstrate an unbelievable number of buttons, flaps, straps, buckles, padlocks. "And this is nothing compared to the rigmarole that we go through at bedtime. Fluff up his eiderdown blankets, blow up his waterproof pillows, make sure the yards and yards of mosquito netting are pinned up around his bed. You'd think he was in Africa or somewhere tropical."

Once the tents are assembled, the firewood neatly piled, the latrine dug and the cooking area set up, the crew is free to go. Izzy quickly latches on to Joe.

"How's the trip so far?"

"Okay, I guess."

"What about The Great Writer? Everyone here is dying of curiosity."

"He's okay." Joe pulls a gadget from his pocket and begins separating its parts. "He gave me this. It's a knife, can opener, nail file, screwdriver, auger, pliers, and corkscrew, all in one. Haven't used it yet, maybe never will, but it was nice of him. Some people don't like him, but I do."

Izzy is amazed. This is not the taciturn, depressed Joe she has known in the past. He has spoken more than two words. Maybe he's beginning to feel comfortable with her!

"So, you translating for the Treaty Party today?" Izzy asks. What intrigues her most about this boy is his ability with languages. He can switch between Cree, English and French without batting an eyelash.

"Yeah, I get two dollars for doing it. Which is good 'cause my motor needs new plugs. The only problem is that sometimes I have to stop myself from punching the Indian agent in the mouth."

More words! An actual opinion! Izzy is in heaven. But then he abruptly walks away. "See ya later," he shouts over his shoulder.

"Isn't he a dreamboat?" the girl beams. "You've probably guessed, Flo, that I kinda' like him. But please, I beg you, don't tell my parents."

"Of course not. I promise, not a word."

At first Florence hadn't approved of Joe and Izzy becoming so friendly – life with a husband who was native would be so hard – but now she's changed her mind. They would make a divine couple, she's decided. But she knows that Izzy's father, the Reverend Ernst Wentworth, would have his daughter fry in hell until her skin crackled rather than have her marry an Indian.

Florence decides she had better see how the tea party is getting along and she walks over to the treed grove. The Famous Writer is holding forth, the crowd lapping up his every word. Florence can't help herself; she lets go with a honking laugh. This man is an idiot for sure. It's 80 degrees, but he's dressed in oilskin trousers and a heavy canvas jacket coloured brown and green, as a camouflage against God knows what, with huge pockets to store the game he never bags. He's also sporting thick, fleece-lined, 'self ventilating' gloves, a red woollen scarf around his neck, flannel socks and high-laced boots. Topping it all off is a wide-brimmed hat that makes him look like a debauched boy scout. That paddler, Cecil Ballendine, was wrong, thinks Florence. The Famous Author doesn't believe he's in tropical climes. He thinks he's in Antarctica.

Arthur Jan, his long pointed nose twitching, is shamelessly fawning over The World Famous Author. "You were such a trooper, such a sport on the long and dangerous journey," he mewls. Florence is reminded of Judas Iscariot before he betrayed Jesus. This performance sets her fretting again. It's been over two months and she still can't get the scene out of her head.

CHAPTER TWO

SHE HADN'T BEEN ABLE TO SLEEP. Reading the *Aeneid* hadn't helped, but she thought maybe a walk outside might. A remarkable aurora borealis was flashing in the sky and she decided to catch a better view by climbing the path up the steep hill behind the HBC store leading to a flat plain where the Cree graveyard was located. About halfway up, she heard the sound of metal, a shovel probably, crunching into the earth. Then she spotted two figures on top of the hill. Arthur Jan and Bibiane Ratt were digging furiously. Dozens of objects had already been retrieved and were scattered around them. Some had been placed on the ground, others were sitting along the trunk of a dead jack pine long ago felled by lightening. Florence could barely see them in the queer green light, but, after she crept a little closer, the shapes came into focus. Bowls, axes, knives, awls. And many other things she couldn't make out.

Suddenly Arthur Jan jumped up and yelled, "Son of a bitch! Ain't this a gem?" He began waving a long, narrow bone as though it were a band leader's baton. It glistened stark white in the beam of the Eveready flashlight which Bibiane had switched on. Bibiane laughed out loud. "What a clever chap you are, Arthur. I can see dollar bills flying into our pockets already. But wouldn't a spade speed things along?" Arthur nodded yes and, after thrusting his shovel into the dirt, Bibiane hurried off.

Arthur sat down, lit up his pipe, then reached over and carefully scooped up one of the objects. His back was to Florence so she was able to creep a little closer. By craning her neck, she could see the necklace, the red, green and blue glass balls and the blood-coloured pipestone beads. Arthur sucked in his breath. "Oh my God! What a beauty. What a precious thing."

Florence wasn't sure what to do. She was still hiding in the bush, but the night was cold and she was chilled to the bone. Also, she was a little afraid of what these men might do if they found her hiding there. Her bed suddenly seemed a wonderful idea and she snuck quietly away.

The next morning she returned to the grave yard, but there was not a sign of the previous night's activity. The curious objects had disappeared, and the spot where the Arthur and Bibiane had been digging looked as though it had never been touched.

Florence hasn't confronted either one about what she had seen. She's waiting patiently, for exactly the right moment.

ARTHUR JAN'S WELCOMING PARTY
Thursday evening

CHAPTER THREE

ARTHUR JAN HURRIES OVER to his trading post. He wants to make sure the unloading of his precious cargo goes well, but more, he's dying to tell his store manager, Bibiane Ratt, his thrilling news. The two go back a long way. They met years ago during a loud and vicious poker game at a La Ronge speakeasy, during which Bibiane pocketed an amazing amount of cash, not only from greenhorns, but also from the seasoned players, whites and Indians alike. Arthur caught how the half breed cheated: not only with the usual marked cards but, by performing audacious hand-mucks — switching one bunch of cards for another hidden in his Assomption sash. All with an impressive, steely-eyed calm. Arthur recognized him as a kindred soul, so uttered not a word.

Bibiane can count on his mother's side a French grandfather and an Assiniboine grandmother; his father's relatives were a mixture of Scottish, Métis, Ojibwe and Cree. 'Mixed blood" is how he refers to himself, but others are not so kind. "Mongrel," "cur," "mutt" – he'd been called it all, and suffered the beatings that followed. Which is why, Arthur thinks, he is so mistrustful and inscrutable, an outsider forever spying on the insiders. His kind of man.

Bibiane is easy to spot since, on this hot day, a bright red handkerchief has been wound around his head to soak up the sweat. Still, a bead or two trickles along the scar that cuts Bibiane's face in two – a memento of a long ago knife fight. He's kneeling in the flat-bottomed fishing boat, patching a leak. He looks up when Arthur calls out, "There you are, you old son-of-a-bitch."

Bibiane doesn't smile, but then he never smiles. He simply asks

"So how was the trip? Any luck?"

"Beyond our wildest dreams. I have much to tell, old chum."

The two men make for the store's office, and, before they sit down on the surprisingly elegant leather chairs, Arthur pours them both a whiskey. Then he settles himself, eager to relate what happened.

"The meeting in New York went beautifully. When I pulled off the covering and showed the agent the samples, I thought the man was going to faint. 'Incredible!' he bellowed. The bargaining that followed was still pretty rough, but we did good."

The two take a celebratory gulp of whiskey, and Arthur continues. "On top of that, I've come up with a plan to ensure it all happens. A brilliant one if I do say so myself. You know that American writer, the one I travelled with for all those interminable weeks? The guy that everybody is bowing down to as though he's a close friend of King Tut's?"

Bibiane nods yes, and Arthur continues. "You and I, we're going to have fun playing with him. He`s our ticket to the riches we both deserve."

The two clink glasses. "To our treasure," says Bibiane. He hesitates for a second, and then angles a leery eye at Arthur. "You'll make sure I get my share, won't you, Boss? Remember, I'm the one who found that christly mother lode."

"For heaven sakes, we're old friends, Bibi. How could you think I'd do anything but treat you well?"

CHAPTER FOUR

AS THE JUSTICE OF THE PEACE for Pelican Narrows, Arthur feels obliged to make sure things run smoothly for the Treaty Party, so he heads back towards the village centre. First though, he drops into Madeline Michel's crowded little cabin.

There was a time when he was enthralled with a tender Cree girl, but now she's a fat-assed squaw who harangues him mercilessly every time she runs into him, so you couldn't get him into her bed for love or money. Three of her children are his, he's acknowledged that. He drops off cash now and then and has remembered them in his will. But he has no real feeling for them. "Hi there," he greets them whenever he spots them. "Behaving yourselves?" They never utter a word, just stare at him with their big, doe-like eyes. It amazes him how Indian they look with their brown skins and midnight black hair. The only hint that British blood runs in their veins is their long, pointed noses. Madeline's a Catholic so they'll be shipped off to the new residential school opening in the fall. He can't say he's sorry; not being constantly reminded of past indiscretions will be a relief.

As usual, the shack is a muddle with all kinds of stuff strewn about. Dishes displaying relics of bannock spread with bearberry preserve sit on the table. A huge chunk of driftwood stands in the middle of the room; it looks as though one of the children is carving it into a bear's head. But nobody's around. Arthur assumes the family's gone off berry picking, or maybe they're lining up to fetch their treaty money. Wherever they are, Madeline's beady-eyed mother will be with them. She despised Arthur from the moment they were introduced. Well, the feeling's mutual.

He takes out two one-dollar bills and places them under a saucer.

Of course it would be cracked.

Madeline's place is situated in a neighbourhood that is called, ridiculously, The Bronx —Arthur's never been able to figure out why. He makes his way along a path that runs through the hodgepodge of three dozen cabins plopped down every which way like dominos gone crazy. They're pretty well all the same: one room, sixteen by twenty feet, made out of logs with sheets of tar paper covering the roofs. As well, there are a dozen wigwams scattered about. Each dwelling sits in a confusion of outhouses, storage sheds, dog kennels, fishing nets, traps of all kinds, drying racks for game, tools used for skinning moose, pots, axes, fishing rods. Arthur is inherently neat, and the jumble offends him. Still, he's been around Indians long enough to know that there is real order in the chaos: every piece of this flotsam and jetsam is essential to making a living.

These are temporary homes, camps really. The Cree travel through the fall and winter, hunting and trapping, returning in late spring to spend the summer months at Pelican Narrows. The kids run wild, swim, play games and pick berries. The women dry fish, tan moose hides, craft birch bark baskets, and gossip – boy, do they gossip. The men fish for pickerel, hunt ducks, and gamble. This goes on for hours, since in June the light doesn't fade until close to midnight. The teenagers, well, this is their big chance to sniff out the opposite sex, and that's about all they're interested in.

Although the Cree have been spending summers at Pelican Narrows for hundreds of years, there's still an impermanence about the place. Arthur thinks that if ever the fur-bearing animals are wiped out, as well they might be given the number of white trappers flooding in, the village will vanish into thin air. It wouldn't matter to him; he'd just move on.

The Treaty Party has arrived several days earlier than scheduled so that many families are away on berry-picking excursions. Messengers have been sent to fetch them in. In the meantime, the Indian agent, Bob Taylor, has decided to proceed with those present.

Everyone, except perhaps Arthur Jan, is frightened of this man. Even his appearance is menacing. He is short yet stocky with a barrel chest and muscular arms. Sinister black eyes. Bald except for a fringe above his ears. A sharply defined moustache and little goatee. Arthur thinks he looks a lot like Lenin.

The Peter Ballendine Band, named after its original chief, welcomed its first treaty party in the summer of 1900, and the ritual of this annual event established then has hardly changed in twenty-four years. A wooden table has been set up on the porch of the post office attached to the Hudson's Bay Company's store. The Indian agent — everyone calls him Taylor as though his first name, Bob, is too soft a sound for such a formidable man — sits at one end on the right, Arthur Jan as Justice of Peace in the middle, and Doc Happy Mac, who, has taken time off from inoculating the children to act as recording clerk, on the left. Behind Taylor stands Band Councillor John Custer. A wooden pipe is clamped in his mouth; he sports sunglasses; and, to emphasize the formality of this event, he is dressed entirely in black — a suit with baggy pants and out-of-shape jacket. A smart but crumpled fedora barely contains his long, wayward grey hair. The chief's medal of honour displaying the Dominion of Canada's crest is pinned to his chest. The actual chief, the beloved Cornelius Whitebear has sent his regrets. He is ill. Joe Sewap stands next to Councillor Custer. His job is to translate Cree to English and English to Cree. Waiting patiently in line down the steps and onto the path are the families.

As each is called, the head of household, his wife and children crowding behind him like a gaggle of geese, comes forward and hands Taylor a card. Most are ragged and greasy with age.

"Michael Bird, his wife, two girls and three boys," the Indian agent reads, and then barks, "Any births or deaths in this family?"

Joe Sewap translates smoothly, although he thinks it's ridiculous that, after twenty years as Indian agent, Taylor still doesn't know enough Cree to form a sentence.

"One boy drowned last summer," Councillor Custer answers.

Doc Happy Mac amends the records, and Taylor counts out seven piles, each with five newly minted one dollar bills taken from the stack of $1,500 sitting in the centre of the table. The money is passed to Arthur Jan who carefully counts it. "Correct," he announces, and the payment is handed over.

The proceedings run smoothly enough, although every now and then a case involving unusual circumstances breaks the pattern.

An elderly man shuffles forward and hands over a letter written by Father Bonnald on the family's behalf. Beside him stands his grandson who drools down his chin and sways incessantly from side to side. Taylor reads the document and then questions the old man through the translator Joe Sewap.

"You say this idiot is your grandson and that his mother died while giving birth to him?

Translation, then a nod of agreement.

"Why didn't you apply for his treaty money long ago?"

The grandfather says nothing, but stands motionless, his twenty-year-old grandson grinning and bobbing beside him.

Taylor eyeballs the two, his tone of voice growing even sterner. "It's through your negligence that this oversight has occurred. And now you and your priest expect the Canadian government to hand over the substantial sum of $120. I hardly think that's fair to the Canadian taxpayer. Do you?"

No emotion flickers on the elder's face.

"I'll take it up with the Department, but I can't promise you anything." With a backward wave of his hand the Indian agent dismisses the two.

Soon after, a man in his thirties dressed in heavy work clothes hobbles forward. He explains in accented but understandable English that he hasn't received his treaty payments for five years.

"And why not?" Taylor demands.

"I am a returned soldier, a sharpshooter with the North

Saskatchewan Regiment." He rolls up his trousers, exposes a leg criss-crossed with scars. "Wounded twice. At Vimy Ridge. Here on the ankle and here on the knee. I was in the hospital for a long time, and afterwards I needed to make some money. I have a family, you see. So, on my way home, I took jobs, anything I could get – helping with the harvest, working construction on the roads. I thought the government was sending treaty to my wife, but it never arrived."

"How are you feeling now?" Doc Happy Mac interjects.

"Okay, but my legs ache at night, and they're so weak that some-times I fall down. I don't know how I'm going to do on the trap lines. You know, in the heavy snow..."

The Indian agent abruptly butts in, "We won't go into that. I'll send a report to Ottawa."

Once all the payments have been made, the families scatter. With money in hand, the celebration can begin.

Arthur Jan races after the crowd, shouting out in a mixture of Cree and English, "Ladies and gentlemen, the Northern Lights Trading Post has just been restocked. The latest dress material! Wait till you see the new calico! Wonderful colours! Ladies' and men's hats. Ribbons and bows. All are on offer. Can you feel those dollars burn-ing a hole in your pocket? Come along. Bibi Ratt will be happy to serve you."

Out of the corner of his eye Arthur spots his competition, Russell Smith, the Hudson's Bay Company manager, staring at him. Arthur smiles and waves heartily. Russell is to Arthur as a mouse is to a lion.

CHAPTER FIVE

ARTHUR SUDDENLY FEELS DONE IN. The long, nerve-wracking journey, first to New York for his important business meeting, then the train ride across Canada babysitting The Famous Writer and his brother, and finally the arduous Treaty Party canoe trip to Pelican Narrows, have taken their toll. He climbs up the hill to his house, lets himself in, pours a whiskey, and says hello to his old friend, Reginald the parrot, sitting in his gilded cage. He is ridiculously fond of this bird, a gift from a lover he had met in a Moose Jaw brothel. Arthur makes sure that Reginald has water and seed, and then stretches out on the sofa on the screened-in veranda.

Oh how he loves this place. Given it's a twenty-minute walk from his trading post – even taking the shortcut through the grave yard – its location is a bit of a nuisance. It's situated directly north of the HBC store, and the Smiths, Florence in particular, have made no bones about it – they don't like him there.

But spread out below is that spectacular panorama. Nothing in the world is so beautiful, Arthur thinks, as Pelican Lake mirroring a glorious red/yellow sunset. He picks up a porcelain figurine sitting on the side table. It's about ten inches high, dressed in a yellow clown suit with bright red buttons. It has a mauve ruff around its neck and wears a pointed red-brown hat. It's stepping forward, its arm out-stretched as though to shake hands. With its pointed chin, long, pickle-like nose, heavy black eyebrows, and skinny moustache it bears an uncanny resemblance to Arthur himself, and this always makes him laugh. The character Pulcinella, from the Commedia dell'Arte, made in Strafford-le-Bow during George II's reign, it cost a fortune, but Arthur loves it. It's his favourite of all the beautiful things he has painstakingly collected over the years.

"I've come a long way from the haberdashery department of Debenham & Freebody," he says to himself. A long way from the workman's cottage in the old borough of Southwark, Central London, where he had grown up.

His father had been respectable enough, a skilled cabinet maker, but there were six sons in the family, so, although Arthur was a bright and industrious student, upper school education was out of the question. He showed more talent for chatting people up than handling a lathe, so a position was found for him as a stock boy at Debenham & Freebody. He was scarecrow-thin and slope-shouldered with crafty blue eyes and a pasty face, but he spent his evenings in the library pouring through newspapers and periodicals, teaching himself the fashion trade. Within a year he had been promoted to junior salesman in the haberdashery department. He still remembers with pleasure the striped flannel coats with patch pockets and brass buttons, the brilliant white shirts with their tall, stiff-winged collars, the polka-dotted silk ascots. It didn't take him long to evolve into a rakish smooth-talker who knew exactly how to please his customers.

One afternoon, a certain Mr. George asked, "Wouldn't you like to have tea?" "I'd be very pleased, answered the young clerk," and thus began his trade with older, wealthy men. Arthur was as manly as the next chap, but if these pansies wanted to bugger him, well that was the price he paid for a taste of the good life.

Mr. Leroy-Hutchins was his favourite. A dealer in smaller *objets d'art*, he'd take a piece out of his cabinet, and describe where it came from, how it was made. Arthur smiles now, thinking of one he particularly loved — a perfume bottle in a shape of a cat, the stopper a mouse in the animal's mouth. He loved to rub the glassy, white and gold surface, so smooth and cool to his touch.

"It's Chelsea porcelain ," explained Mr. Leroy-Hutchins, as he kissed Arthur on the neck. "Circa 1755."

Arthur had already sensed that he was in trouble, so he wasn't surprised when he was summoned to the boss's office. Private detectives had followed the young clerk to some of the finest hotels in London where he was regularly met by one or other of Debenham & Freebody's important customers.

"We're not running a depot for rent boys," thundered Mr. Peabody.

"Screw off," Arthur yelled, and ran out of the office before he could be fired.

When a grudge-bearing co-worker of Arthur's informed his parents, they were horrified. With five brothers just making their way in the world, a steamy sex scandal was the last thing they needed. How to get rid of the depraved thorn in their side? The propaganda pamphlets put out by the Dominion of Canada depicting golden wheat fields provided the answer. Arthur's father gave him 50 pounds and a third class ticket on the Pannonia, a steamship owned by the Cunard Lines. "See you don't disgrace yourself. Well, in that vast, cold country maybe it doesn't matter," were the pater's parting words.

Arthur arrived in Montreal in June, 1908, age twenty-two, cocky as a bantam rooster, ready to make his fortune. In an uncharacteristic flight of fancy, he chose the place with the most exotic name, Saskatoon, Saskatchewan, and boarded the next train heading west. He carefully selected his homestead – a quarter section of black/brown, supposedly fecund soil situated north of the infant city. But he quickly discovered that he loathed farming. Cutting down trees, clearing the land, seeding, harvesting – he detested it all. But what really got to him was the monotony, the tediousness of the same work performed over and over again like some dance from hell. On top of that was the unbearable loneliness. What did a former sales clerk of fancy men's goods have in common with a hardened wheat farmer? Even their daughters, longing for a good-looking young man with fine manners, felt uncomfortable when he chatted them up. Always, in the end, they rejected his advances.

Arthur hung on for three long years, built a shack on his land, and broke the required thirty acres. The very day he picked up his deed at the land office, he sold his farm to an American. For a handsome profit, thank you very much.

The one thing he did like about his new home was the boreal forest with its dark, foreboding spruce trees and many sparkling lakes. He wrote home, "The largest lake trout I caught was fifty-two pounds, but I heard of others to top that."

When the Paris-based trading company, Revillon Frères, offered him a job loading the scows that travelled the northern lakes, he enthusiastically accepted. By this time the effete Brit had developed into a man of sinewy muscle with a remarkable imperviousness to physical discomfort. "I'm no longer the skinny, little runt whose ears you used to box every day," he wrote to one of his brothers.

That first winter, Arthur met Bibiane Ratt at the La Ronge poker game and the two decided to team up. They naturally headed north into uncharted territory.

Reindeer Lake, 140 miles long with deep, clear water, dotted with thousands of islands, was still virgin territory for white trappers, and there weren't many natives there either. That first season, Arthur's and Bibiane's haul included beaver, mink, marten, lynx, red and silver fox. A lot of money came in, but it was dangerous work.

By midspring the ice was clear of snow, but overnight a storm had dumped another couple of feet on the lake. Arthur was mushing his dogs hard, trying to get back to the trading post before nightfall. Suddenly he spotted a couple of ducks swimming in open water just ahead of him. The dogs took after them. Arthur hollered at the team, but the lead wouldn't listen. He jumped off the sled and grabbed the reins, running alongside, pulling, pulling, praying the dogs would turn. Finally they did, making a sharp left, but although the sled turned too, its momentum carried it forward, toward the open water. Arthur managed to pull out his knife and severe the leads so the animals were freed, but the sleigh spun ahead, into the black hole. There was no way he would just stand by and watch his valuable cargo sink to the bottom, so he grabbed onto the toboggan. Suddenly he too was spinning, into the frigid water.

The more he struggled to climb out, the more the ice kept breaking, shards as sharp as glass ripping at his now gloveless hands. He was more indignant than frightened. Surely he was too young to die! God obviously thought so too, because just as Arthur was sinking for the third time, Bibiane Ratt's sled appeared.

The half-breed crawled slowly, carefully on his stomach towards the open water, until he was able to grab Arthur by his upper arms and allow him to wiggle his body, stiff from cold, up onto more solid ice.

"You and I, we surely are a team, Bibi," Arthur had gasped.

The near disaster taught them both a lesson — trading the tea kettles and steel traps which the Cree and Chipewayan hungered after for the furs the Indians caught was surely a safer way to make their fortune than trapping themselves. In 1913, Arthur decided to set up as a 'free agent', independent of the large companies. He chose Pelican Narrows as his home base because it was an important hub on the fur trading highway, with the Churchill River as its main artery.

Bibiane had attended an industrial school run by Oblates long enough to learn basic arithmetic and to read and write. And from childhood, he'd trapped with his Cree family so knew the business from the ground up. All skills which Arthur realized would speed success. The half-breed was invited to supervise the construction of the main building, a warehouse, a fish house and Arthur's lovely home. Bibiane did such an excellent job he was asked to stay on as manager of the Northern Lights Trading Post.

Arthur knew there would be competition at Pelican Narrows. The Hudson's Bay Company had been established there for years, but after he met milquetoast Russell Smith, he told Bibiane, "This will be a pushover. I'll have them out of business in no time." Except Arthur hadn't reckoned on Russell's formidable wife, Florence. He still doesn't know why, but to this day the Cree, at least the older ones, insist on doing business with her and her alone. Somehow she's mesmerized them, so that even the bigger advances Arthur offers doesn't tempt them. He and Bibiane have had to search out trappers in the outlying districts, north of the Churchill River, and this has been a costly pain in the ass.

Far into the bush they travel, the dog sleds loaded down with goods, visiting one camp after another, bargaining for the best skins. And twice a year, once with sleighs, and once with canoes, the pelts are hauled to the railhead at The Pas in Manitoba. There, the buyers from Montreal, Toronto, New York, St. Louis, Winnipeg gather to outsmart and outbid each other. If there is one thing Arthur is good at, it is haggling – he always gets the best price.

The fur trade is his main livelihood, but there are lots of other ways to make money – transporting goods to remote communities, prospecting, government jobs – he'd been made a Justice of the Peace five years ago. Most lucrative is the booze which flows from the still Bibiane has set up in a shed in the bush. Who cares if it is illegal to sell alcohol to Indians? They're human beings after all. Why shouldn't they indulge now and then like everyone else?

Arthur puts Pulcinella down on the table. 'That's how I could afford you, old chum. And all the other beautiful things in my life."

But it's not all about his swelling bank account. He's given a lot to this community of Pelican Narrows, not just through cash donations, although he's pretty generous there. More, it's his entrepreneurial spirit. He has no doubt that if this place has prospered, it's because of *his* business acumen.

He still feels a frisson of pleasure when he remembers the dinner at the Regency Hotel in Prince Arthur. Everyone dressed to nines, including himself. The Chief Justice, the Member of Parliament, the Anglican bishop, the elegant wives, clapping their approval as he accepted the plaque acknowledging "his enormous contribution to the development of the Great North." No question in his mind – he deserved it.

CHAPTER SIX

ARTHUR HEARS HIS HOUSEKEEPER, Mavis Custer, bustling about in the kitchen and goes to greet her. He lingers in the doorway a few moments contemplating this room which he considers one of his great accomplishments. There's a Victorian oak table with barley twist legs, and a French walnut buffet with swirling inlays. His set of Rose Bouquet bone china teacups and saucers are on display here. Today the sun is shining on them; Arthur thinks they are so pretty.

But don't let anyone say that he's only interested in antiques. A high society chatelaine couldn't be more up-to-date. This Hoosier cabinet, just arrived last month, is an example. It's truly a wonder, with separate bins for sugar, salt, and up to fifty pounds of flour with a built-in sifter. There's a pull-out work surface that's also a cutting board, a multitude of drawers for every imaginable utensil, shelves for dishes, glassware and mixing bowls, a coffee-bean grinder, a bread box, a spice rack and even an ant trap. Mavis is overwhelmed by the complexity of it all, and, to Arthur's annoyance, he's had to explain how things work many times.

"All ready for tonight's do?" he asks her. She nods yes in her usual surly, disrespectful manner. If she wasn't such a superb cook, he'd have gotten rid of her long ago.

Arthur's not sure who will come to his party. He's not well liked, he knows that. He usually doesn't give a damn, but tonight a respectable turnout is important to his plans.

The first to arrive is the competition. Actually, Russell Smith has been in the fur trade business for so long that he takes everything in his stride, doesn't worry at all about the cunning Mr. Jan or any other upstart rival. Besides, he adores Arthur's well-stocked liquor cabinet. Florence isn't with him. Arthur knows she despises him, but then he can't stand the fat cow either.

"Glad you could come, Russ. How's business?" he asks as he hands him a glass of whiskey.

'Pretty good. And you?"

Before Arthur can answer, there's a bang at the door. The second contingent, consisting of Bob Taylor, Doc Happy Mac and Claude Lewis, has shown up. The Indian agent, self-important as always, intones, "It's very kind of you, Arthur, to take the trouble to entertain our little group."

At the same time, Doc Happy Mac enthusiastically shakes Russell Smith's hand, crooning, "This is my first Treaty Party trip, you know, and I'm so very happy to make the acquaintance of interesting people like you." This instantly makes everyone feel at home.

A tall, good-looking, red-headed man, Douglas Mackenzie has acquired his nickname honestly. His broad, freckled face cracks into a grin at every opportunity.

The other physician, Claude Lewis, looks nothing like his famous sibling. Shorter, fatter and utterly ordinary. After solemnly acknowledging everyone present, he apologizes, "for my brother's tardiness. He's feeling a bit under the weather, but he'll show up shortly."

The next guests, Ernst, Lucretia and Izzy Wentworth, arrive, the Reverend ushering in his wife and daughter like a sheepdog nudging his flock. "Delighted to meet you both," he says, shaking hands with Claude and Doc Happy Mac. He smiles a solicitous greeting to the Indian agent. He has known Bob Taylor for years and has always been intimidated by him.

Lucretia was anxious about the invitation, and rightly so. Here is the host, looking at her as though he's going to eat her up, and she can't help but meet his gaze. She knew the situation would be embarrassing, but her husband had insisted. "After all, my dear, Arthur's a member of our congregation and his offerings are always generous."

And, of course, she's dying to meet The Famous Author on this his first night at Pelican Narrows.

Izzy Wentworth had no such qualms. She's never been shy, and tonight she's bubbling over with delighted-to-meet-yous. She kisses Russell Smith on the cheek. "So sorry Florence can't be here. I'll miss her terribly." But Izzy's even more disappointed when Arthur announces that Father Bonnald has declined his invitation. One of Joe Sewap's many jobs is to escort the old cleric on his rounds, and he surely would have accompanied him here. It will be a dull evening for Izzy without Joe in attendance, that's for sure.

"What lovely glassware," exclaims Doc Happy Mac, as Arthur hands him some sherry.

"From the Atelier of James Gilles, London, 1770."

The guests gape at him and the conversation rapidly switches to the more commonplace – the day's proceedings.

"You can say one thing for the Indians," said Doc Happy Mac, "they're honest as the day is long. One of the squaws walked right up and slapped down a ten dollar bill. She told us that her twins had died, and she was returning the money she'd got for them last summer. Can you fathom that?"

"That's one side of the story," Bob Taylor says. "But what about that old scoundrel who's been pocketing his daughter's treaty money for years? She married a nonstatus Indian, so isn't eligible to collect one cent. We finally discovered his theft." The Indian agent lifts his sherry glass in a salute to Arthur Jan. "Thanks to information provided by our kind host here." His voice grows sharp. "That fellow will pay the Department back the full amount or I'll see that he goes to prison. He must be made an example of, or every Indian in this country is apt to pull the same trick."

"There are sinners and saints wherever humans congregate," interjects Russell Smith. "But on the whole I'd say there is a lot more good than bad amongst our native population."

"Perhaps that's true," responds Taylor, "but given that their society is so primitive, and they're so childlike, do they even know the difference between right and wrong?"

"The thing I don't like," interjects Arthur, "is that we white people are always being blamed for what ails the redskin. They can be more savage to each other than a Brit or a Scot or even a Frenchman would ever dream of being. Do you ever hear about the famous massacre that took place here?"

His guests look as though they're genuinely interested, and Arthur is happy about this. He's obsessed with this story. Over the years, he has relentlessly prodded every old Indian he's come across for his or her version of events, and often, before he falls asleep, he mulls over the bloody details he has ferreted out.

"They reckon some sixty women, children and old men were butchered. Heads severed, breasts strewn on the beach, genitals hung on trees. The bodies were supposedly buried somewhere around here. I swear you can sometimes hear the ghosts moaning and crying."

"My Lord, what a ghastly tale," Claude Lewis calls out. "Did you discover a reason for the bloodbath?"

Russell Smith quickly butts in. "It can be traced back, as always, to the manipulations of the white man. The marauders were likely Sioux, who were well paid by the French to eliminate those doing business with the British. And at that time the Cree were allied with the HBC – the English in other words – so those poor women and children were considered fair game."

"It's proof of what I've always thought," interjects Reverend Wentworth. "The Indians are savages at heart. It makes my task even more essential, to preach the Glory of Almighty God and set them on the path to salvation."

Izzy feels her cheeks redden. She hates it when her father turns sanctimonious. Every Indian he's ever encountered he's seen through a haze of preconceived ideas – learned, she supposes, in divinity school.

"More like they'll turn your head around, and you'll end up beating drums," she shoots back, pretending that she's joking.

Arthur is trying to decide if the 'lunch' – fruit cake, cheeses, berry pie, coffee and tea – should be set out before the guest of honour arrives when Sinclair Lewis finally bangs through the door. Offering no apologies for being late, he yells out, "Hello everybody." Before the others can reply, he begins striding back and forth, peering at Arthur's pictures and *objets d'art*.

"Swell digs you have here, Arthur. Goddamn, look at this beauty!" he roars, as he spots a 60-pound sturgeon mounted on the wall. Arthur had caught it at Reindeer Lake. As Sinclair backs up to take it all in, he bumps into a commode and his elbow sends one of the Royal Doulton Toby Jugs – the precious Robin Hood – crashing to the floor.

"Oh, sorry about that," The Famous Author says, showing no genuine remorse at all.

Arthur's stomach heaves, but he utters not a word. Holding back tears, he picks up the pieces. Meanwhile, Sinclair continues to flap around the room, poking his nose close to all of Arthur's precious things.

Lucretia has been watching The Famous Writer's every move. His ugliness actually gives him character, she decides. "Like our Prime Minister King, revolting as a toad, but smart," she whispers to her daughter.

Izzy agrees. With his high, wide forehead, and his long face that narrows at the chin, The Famous Author reminds her of the tormented soul in Edvard Munch's 'The Scream', a reproduction of which had hung in her art class at school. His arms are so long that his wrists dangle down from the sleeves of his flannel shirt. His eyebrows are colourless and his hair, combed back slick to his head, has an unbecoming orange tint, like carrots. His bright-blue eyes are large, round and bulging. But it's his complexion which Izzy thinks is hideous. The sun has baked it a beet colour, the skin is still peeling, and the entire surface is riddled with red pustules and pock marks, with a scar jagging down his lower right cheek. During her last semester at school, Izzy had been assigned Mary Shelley's *Frankenstein*, and here, surely, is a living example.

After his whirlwind tour of Arthur's house, Sinclair flings himself on a couch beside Lucretia Wentworth. She smiles at him, "Mr. Lewis, everyone is dying to know how you and your brother came to join the Treaty Party. As I understand it, it's never been permitted before. Last year a famous Hollywood cinematographer wanted to film the expedition, but the bureaucrats turned him down flat."

"My dear madam," Sinclair says in a phony, high-pitched voice, "some fairies I know put the squeeze on your government, and voilà – permission was granted."

Claude Lewis is used to intervening whenever his brother makes fatuous remarks. "I'll let you in on the secret but it mustn't go outside this room. Sinclair has made the acquaintance, through his British connections, of a lot of top ranking Canadians. You probably have heard of the banker, Sir James Dunn? And Lord Beaverbrook? Isn't he the richest man in Canada? My brother has gone on motor trips with him."

Sinclair interrupts him. "Ah yes, Beaverbrook. A baldish, littlish chap, amusing and gay. We got along famously."

"At any rate," Claude continues, "strings were pulled, and the Department of Indian Affairs agreed we could come as long as we paid our own way. So here we are. It's been a long, hard journey."

"We wooed them though, didn't we, Claude?" Sinclair Lewis beams.

"You wooed them, brother of mine, not me."

And now I'll woo *you*, thinks Arthur. It'll be so easy to manipulate The Famous Writer. He knows this because he has travelled with him for the past two months.

Arthur was asked by the Canadian government to assist the two Americans on their journey westward. He agreed, and, after travelling from New York, was present at Winnipeg Union Station when the Lewis brothers arrived. So was a photographer from the *Free Press*, who snapped them as they stepped off the train.

Arthur had arranged everything nicely. An automobile with chauffeur had been hired for the brothers' use and, in Sinclair's hotel room, two big bottles of Scotch awaited him. The fur trader and the author connected at once.

Arthur could never have imagined anything like it. As they travelled west by train, the welcome for The Famous Writer became more extravagant, more hysterical. In Winnipeg, lunch with the mayor and 1,500 admirers at the Fort Garry Hotel. In Regina, a round of golf at a private club and a special concert by the touring Princess Pat band. In Saskatoon, a breakfast fête at St. George's Anglican Church, followed by an amateur theatrical – The Distinguished Writer fell asleep during act two. In Prince Albert a visit to the recently opened Federal prison was conducted by the warden, followed by a fishing expedition and then a turkey dinner put on by the Rotary Club at the Regency Hotel. Arthur thought that if Sinclair Lewis signed one more autograph, his hand would fall off.

Actually Arthur thought all the fawning and pawing was ridiculous. Before he joined the expedition, he had taken the trouble to read *Babbitt* and *Main Street*. Didn't these people realize that The Esteemed Writer had made his fame and fortune by ridiculing the wretched pettiness of their middle class lives? Apparently that was irrelevant. All that mattered was that Sinclair Lewis was an international celebrity bestowing his presence on the culturally deprived.

From Prince Albert they travelled to Big River, the end of the rail line and the start of the annual Treaty expedition. The party stopped for a day or two at every spot where Natives – Cree and Chipewyan – gathered for the summer. Doc Happy Mac provided their once-a-year check up. The Indian agent, who had done this job year after year, handed out the annual $5-per-person Treaty Money. All told the trip would take two months.

When the Americans met the Indian crew, they were sorely disappointed. Where were their buckskin trousers and feather headdresses? Claude had actually said, "You fellows look just like white men." And Sinclair complained all during the trip, "What's happened to the Noble Redskin? This bunch, they use Evinrudes on their canoes, eat soup from a tin, whistle tunes from Hollywood movies. And look at their clothes – all bought in a store. The only Indian thing about them is their moccasins. And, even with them, they wear wool socks." Arthur Jan had barely been able to stifle his laughter.

"And how did you get along on the rough part of the trip after Big River?" Russell Smith asks. This gives Claude Lewis the opportunity he's been looking for. His recitation of the treaty party's trials and tribulations is far more detailed than anyone wants to hear, especially since every person in the room, women included, has undergone far more onerous journeys. The guests begin to yawn but that doesn't stop Claude from jabbering on.

"My motor started okay but only on one cylinder. I changed spark plugs, but no use. Taylor here was anxious to get to the end of this big lake before nightfall, so he hitched our canoe to his and we all stayed together. But I was sure the sad boy to hold up the party. Then hello! Was I surprised! We had gone about two miles when all of a sudden the motor kicked in, good as ever…"

As the story drones on, Sinclair Lewis, standing behind the chesterfield where his brother is sitting, begins to perform an amazing pantomime. His long arms flail about as he pulls the motor's starter, changes the spark plugs, pours in gas, ties one canoe to another, while the expression on his face registers grief, shock, joy.

The guests hardly know what to do. They must be polite and listen to Dr. Lewis attentively, but how to stop from bursting into laughter? Finally, Izzy can't contain herself and lets go with a loud guffaw. Claude whirls around, spots his brother, and yells, "Will you stop with your foolish nonsense, you nincompoop!"

Abruptly the Reverend Wentworth decides it's time to leave. "Past our bedtimes," he explains as he hustles his wife and daughter out the door. They're followed by Russell Smith, Doc Happy Mac and Claude Lewis. Bob Taylor and The Famous Writer, though, are steered towards the veranda where Bibiane Ratt is waiting. It's time for Arthur Jan to set in motion the first stage of his plan.

CHAPTER SEVEN

THERE ARE CUBAN CIGARS. And cards for poker. But more to the point, three bottles of single malt Glengoyne, The Famous Writer's favourite Scotch.

"A man after my own heart," says Sinclair, raising his glass to Arthur. "An intelligent man, a sensitive man, a man who knows how to throw a party." In half an hour one of the bottles is empty, another is half gone.

During the month-long trip along the Saskatchewan River, Sinclair had stayed "as dry as a cactus plant," as he put it. Indeed, the purpose of the trip, Arthur had discovered, was to get The Renowned Author off the booze. It was a strenuous way to sober up. He was so frail that he was obliged to sit on a rock while the others performed the hard work of setting up camp. He got so fed up with the same meal three times a day – fish or bacon served with bannock – that he pretty well gave up eating. The mosquitoes and black flies were attracted to him more than anyone else. As a kid he had almost drowned in the local swimming hole, and this made him so terrified of water that he was awkward and fearful climbing in and out of his canoe. He was lucky that Joe Sewap had been assigned as his steersman. If it hadn't been for Joe's quick actions, Sinclair would have ended up in the drink a half dozen times.

Having grown up in Minnesota, The Famous Author liked to think of himself as a man of the great outdoors. But, while he carried his rifle everywhere, he was an amazingly incompetent hunter. The only thing he bagged during the entire trip was a duck which had come to rest nearby. And he'd lost so many of his brother's trolling spoons that Claude had upbraided him, "You always were a damn poor fisherman,"

It's obvious that Sinclair is too fragile to complete the Treaty Party trip – there is another month of travelling further north through even more rugged terrain. If Arthur's plan succeeds – it includes offering up as much liquor as possible which he is sure will not be refused – The Distinguished Writer will abandon ship right here at Pelican Narrows. Arthur will step in and escort him on the journey by canoe to The Pas where the railroad line begins. From there, in the comfort of a first-class coach, he will make his way home to New York City. Given how famous he is, he'll have no trouble getting Arthur's precious payload through U.S. customs.

The poker game quickly devolves into a raucous argument between Bibiane and Sinclair. "Dempsey's the best. How can you think otherwise?" the writer declares. To emphasize his point, he staggers up and, weaving back and forth, begins punching the air with his fists.

"Yeah, I guess," yells Bibiane. "Sheath your fists in plaster of Paris, and you're sure to knock out anyone who gets in your way."

"That's a lot of rot!" Sinclair is still sparing with an invisible opponent. "People just trying to tear Dempsey down. Look at what he did to the great Firpo, the mighty Argentinean Bull. Floored him seven times in the first round."

"The guy came right back though, didn't he, eh? One punch and the great Dempsey went flying right through the ropes onto the laps of the sports writers. And if they hadn't shoved him back into the ring, he'd never have made the count of ten."

"The proof is in the pudding. Dempsey pummelled him to a pulp in the next round."

Sinclair begins to unbutton his shirt but, because he is so drunk, this takes some time. Finally his skinny torso is bared – Arthur thinks of a boiled turnip. He puts up his scrawny dukes and begins poking at the head of the still-seated Bibiane Ratt. Arthur prays that the half-breed doesn't lose his temper. He could kill the writer with one well-placed punch if he felt like it. Where would that leave their dreams? But Bibiane keeps smiling, waving aside the jabs as though Sinclair is a fly.

Finally, the author gives up. "Have I landed in a desert? I'm dying of thirst," he whines. Arthur gently pushes him onto a sofa and fetches his glass.

More scotch is being poured when there's a banging at the door and Reverend Wentworth walks in. "Oh God, what a nuisance!" whispers the fur trader.

"Mr. Taylor, you should be aware that our young men are at it again," the clergyman announces. "As the Indian agent, it's your job to put a stop to it."

Bibiane, Arthur, and Bob Taylor groan in unison.

"Come on, Mr. Famous Writer," says Arthur. "Observe how respectability is trying to worm its way into our little community."

They all march to Arthur's large warehouse located halfway between his house and his store. The night is so warm the door has been left wide open. There, looking as guilty as if they'd robbed a bank, is the cream of Pelican Narrows' young manhood. All hold billiard cues and are standing around a pool table which has been set up on top of two sawhorses.

Pushing his chest out as though he's Field Marshall Von Hindenberg, the Indian agent bellows, "Listen up! How many times have I told you bastards. Under the Indian Act, engaging in games of chance, including billiards, is strictly prohibited. I could fine each one of you twenty bucks right here on the spot."

"We weren't gambling, just having a game," explains Gilbert Bear.

"And beavers go to church," roars Taylor.

"I hate that bastard so much I'd like to carve off his skin inch by inch." Ezekiel Morin whispers this, but rather loudly. Arthur prays the Indian agent doesn't hear him.

Happily, Sinclair Lewis pipes up. "For Christ sake, Taylor, they're just young guys having a good time. I'll pay, if you're going to be miserable and fine them."

Taylor's mouth turns downward into a scowl. "In honour of your presence, Mr. Sinclair Lewis," he says, sarcasm rippling his voice, "I'll let the punks off this time. But no more breaking the law, do you hear? The whole lot of you are going to end up in prison one day, I just know it."

With that the Indian agent, dragging the Man of God along, bangs out the door.

Sinclair Lewis is delighted when Ezekiel offers him his cue. He chalks the tip, then leverages the stick behind his back. From this show-offy position, he spins the eight ball into the pocket at a remarkable ninety degree angle.

"That's how you play pool, my lads," he cries. "Come, Mr. Jan, let the old men show these young pups a thing or two. And while you're up, pour us a wee scotch."

"I've hooked him," Arthur thinks to himself. "Sinclair Lewis, The Famous Writer, is now twisting on my line."

THE CHILDREN'S PICNIC
Friday

CHAPTER EIGHT

IZZY WENTWORTH LIKES TO SPEND some time first thing in the morning talking with Annie Custer who, as a Cree elder and an aficionado of gossip, knows what's really going on in Pelican Narrows. There might be a word or two about Joe, music to Izzy's ears. Today, though, the housekeeper is too busy to chat. The soirée in honour of The Famous Writer is to take place that evening, and, no matter what, it must be a resounding success.

Standing with her shoulders thrown back, Annie barks a parody of Lucretia Wentworth:

"Today we must all pull together and carry out our duty with vigour. Forward to victory!"

Izzy salutes. "Yes, Ma'am!"

As Izzy sips her tea and nibbles at the bannock put in front of her, she thinks how lucky she is to have a good excuse to leave the battlefield. She only hopes her poor father has thought up an escape plan.

She bundles her papers together and walks out into the dazzling sunshine. It's 8:25 and already hot – in a few minutes the back of her blouse is drenched with perspiration. She quickly reaches the hut situated not far from St. Bartholomew's Anglican Church, opens the door, and, accosted by the stifling heat inside, stumbles back. "What a sorry excuse for a school house!" she thinks to herself, and not for the first time.

The Anglicans of the Peter Ballendine Band had, on more than one occasion, pleaded with the government to provide funds for a proper building. They were always turned down – "a ridiculous waste

39

of money," a bureaucrat in the Department of Indian Affairs had written – so the fathers had cobbled together this shack using pieces of plywood donated by the fur trading establishments. There is a window, but it's very small and doesn't open. On most days this isn't such a bad thing – it restricts the view, thereby lessening the pain of the Anglican scholars who would otherwise have to endure the agony of watching the Catholic kids cavorting on the beach outside. But today, a little breeze would be a godsend.

In a few moments, the children swarm in. Izzy loves their round, smooth faces, the remains of berry preserves still visible on their sweet mouths, their expressions so guileless.

"How do you do, Miss Wentworth?" each asks in precise, clipped English. This phrase had been rehearsed many times over.

Just as The Lord's Prayer is concluded, Gabriel Caribou rushes in, falling over the door step in the process. Late as usual because he's been scrounging in the bush, searching for treasures. Today it's a bat, frozen in rigor mortis, already stinky.

"A present for you, Miss Wentworth," the little boy beams. His grandfather, a long-time trapper for the HBC, knows English and has drummed it into Gabriel's head. "It's for your birthday, whenever that is."

Izzy thanks the child and puts the stiff lump in a box in the corner, as far away from noses as possible. She must make time for a lesson on the Little Brown Bat before she heaves it.

She's glad to see the children so chipper. Usually a holiday is declared when the Treaty Party arrives but, since there are in total only thirty-two days to teach these kids anything before the families move to their fall hunting camps, Izzy has ruled that the school must remain open. She thought that they might be downhearted, but, as they scramble to their places, they seem their usual enthusiastic, if unruly, selves. Except for a couple of the older ones. Isaac Morin in particular, glowers at her with sullenness in his eyes. She ignores him. Eventually the insult of being imprisoned inside on such a lovely morning will abate, at least a little.

The wobbly plywood desks rest on sawhorses; the chairs are wooden crates. There are no text books – the only supply the government has seen fit to provide is twenty dollars' worth of biscuits that were gobbled up long ago. Izzy receives a teacher's salary, four dollars a day, five days a week for two months, and with this she has bought pencils and workbooks, a small blackboard and chalk.

She tacks up a picture from a rotogravure on the wall, and, pointing to it with a ruler, she carefully articulates, "el-e-phant." The children have a difficult time getting their tongues around the word – there's no 'l' in Cree – and yell back what sounds like "en-e-fent."

Slowly and clearly she continues: "Now, boys and girls, let's take out our pencils and draw this magnificent animal. The pictures should be ready to show our guests when they arrive." Which, regrettably, she says to herself, will be soon.

The younger children enthusiastically bend over their makeshift desks and begin. The older ones take a little time, but soon their pencils are dancing as well.

At the private school that Izzy attended in Toronto, copies of the work of great artists hung on the walls, grouped neatly by alphabet – Rembrandt, Renoir and Rubens; Cezanne, Constable, Caravaggio; Van Dyck, Velázquez, Vermeer. There was never a shortage of supplies – easels, palettes and palette knives, all sizes of brushes –a special one made of goat hair was used for laying down a colour wash – acrylics, pastels, the right paper for water colours, canvases for oils. There were live models with, of course, not an inch of inappropriate flesh showing. Exhibits were arranged at which tea and sandwiches were served. Parents came from afar to lavish praise on their progeny. The work produced was often masterful and polished – the smile of the Mona Lisa as enigmatic as required, sweet portraits of favourite dogs and cats, bright autumn leaves in High Park. But Izzy has come to realize that almost every rendering of an elephant done here today will display more originality than anything she encountered during her ten years at Bishop Strachan School. True art seems bred in the bones of these barefoot children.

The drawings are being collected just as the delegation arrives. Indian agent Taylor, Doc Happy Mac, and the two special guests, Claude Lewis and The Famous Writer, crowd into the little room. Izzy's father, the overseer of the school, takes up the rear.

"I'm absolutely right, Reverend Wentworth." Taylor is continuing a conversation began earlier, completely ignoring the children. "These day schools are a miserable attempt at education. What the heck can the kids possibly get out of a couple of months of sitting in this poorly-lit shack? When the term's over, they'll speak hardly any English, never mind read or write it. And when they return next year, they'll have forgotten every damned word."

"They'd do a lot better if they had proper desks and not have to hunch over like Bob Cratchits," responds Ernst. "Some books, and pens and paper would help too. You know, we could have a year-round school here. If they could get their hands on some building materials, the fathers would put up a proper log cabin, and some of the mothers would stay behind to cook and house-keep for the children."

"They say that, but do Indians ever keep their promises? No, never. And I don't think it would be wise to leave squaws in charge of children who aren't their own. Anyway, the government would never appropriate the necessary funds. That's all there is to it."

Izzy has carefully drilled her students to yell out in English, "Welcome to Pelican Narrows, dear guests." Now she's afraid that the Indian agent's rudeness has intimidated them. But they are as cheery as usual, and even Taylor smiles a little.

Since it's assumed that a writer must know a lot about art, Sinclair Lewis is asked to judge the drawing contest. He perches on one of the rickety benches and begins to pore over the twenty-five submissions. Izzy can tell by his attentiveness, and his grin, that he appreciates what's in front of him.

"This is more a woolly mammoth than an elephant," he exclaims, holding up one of the masterpieces. "But it's a gem."

While Lewis is at his task, the others walk among the desks, inspecting the students' notebooks. Izzy knows they are a disaster – Taylor tut tuts his disapproval, like a snake among the lambs – but she can see the progress. Twelve-year-old Jacob Bear didn't know a word of English when classes started, and now he's created a paean to the Evinrude motor. It's full of cross-outs and spelling errors, but his ideas are there, clear and bright, and in a sort of English. And Laura Whitegoose, who could hardly add two numbers together a month ago, has proven to be a mathematical whiz. She has learned to multiply to the factor of ten; the time tables are all written down in her notebook, though rather raggedly, Izzy admits.

"What a mess these are," Taylor barks. "There isn't one example of legible writing in the whole lot. It proves my point exactly. These schools are a waste of tax dollars. If I were you, Miss Wentworth, I'd be furious at having squandered my time."

"Oh don't be so hard on the kids," Doc Happy Mac interjects. "You can't expect the Indian to become civilized overnight. A few more years and these children will be as white as you and I."

Izzy is grateful when, at that moment, Sinclair Lewis announces he has finished his deliberations. His lanky frame looms over the classroom.

"Boys and girls, you're going to think I'm a terrible judge. Having considered long and hard, I simply cannot pick a best picture. Really, they're all so good. So I declare that you are all winners. Prizes will be handed out this afternoon."

With that, the party of large men, mopping their brows, say goodbye. As he goes out the door, Rev. Wentworth whispers to his daughter, "It wasn't an overwhelming success, was it?"

CHAPTER NINE

THE CHILDREN SQUEAL with delight when Izzy holds up the story book. On the cover three tiny *omomikwesiwak* paddle a canoe. The kids love these ugly creatures who sit slouched over, their thick black hair falling forward.

"Why won't they let us see their faces?" Izzy asks the class.

"They're ashamed 'cause they don't have any noses," they shout out in unison.

"Now, listen, my *athikisisak*, my little tadpoles. You are to write down everything you know about the *omomikwesiwak*. The first one finished gets to read his or hers out loud."

Izzy made the story book herself, from sheets of brown wrapping paper glued at the sides, the pictures painted with the water colours she brought back from the east. The plot line, though, is Annie's. For years Izzy has sucked up the housekeeper's stories, like a humming-bird siphoning nectar.

Annie Custer was always the first person Izzy ran to when she arrived back in Pelican Narrows for summer vacation. She'd throw her arms around her, screeching, "Annie, Annie, I'm back. Can you believe it?"

Annie, who is reserved even for a Cree woman, was always taken aback by such an extravagant show of affection. But then, who wouldn't be captivated by this exuberant girl? And there was a certain satisfaction that the child was obviously happier to see the Indian housekeeper than her parents.

For Izzy, the summers she was allowed to spend at Pelican Narrows were glorious. At first the Wentworths were reluctant to let her roam about, but they soon realized there was no way they could contain her. She ran with the Cree children, barefoot always, sometimes naked as a piglet, gambolling on the beach, racing, fishing with little nets, and playing cowboys and Indians – she was always made to be a Mountie. She took part in all the games – snow snake, deer sticks, marbles, spinning stones, the coasting-erect race. She won as often as she lost, never mind that her opponents were mostly boys.

There were dolls – Izzy's from Eaton's Department Store in Toronto, the other girls' made from socks stuffed with rags. Seagull feathers were fashioned into hats. Doll play began with the babies swinging in their hammocks, their little mothers singing them soft Cree lullabies, but often ended with a bloody massacre by the Sioux which left the sock heads ragged.

Izzy learned to insult in Cree, *kispakitcon* – fat lips – and *makistikwan* – big head – being her two favourites, and to fight with her fists because there was always some kid who made fun of her pale complexion. "Fish-belly Izzy, fish-eye Izzy."

A few weeks in the sun and Izzy would turn almost as brown as her playmates, but her mother, watching from the rectory window, her mouth pinched in annoyance, could easily spot her. It was her curly, fiery-red hair as untameable as the girl herself, always escaping from the braids that had been so firmly knotted in place. In the evenings, Lucretia would yank the tight ringlets with a fine-toothed comb. "Where you got this unsightly bramble bush, I'll never know. No one on my side, that's for sure." Izzy's eyes would water, but she did not cry out, not once.

The girl's unruly behaviour was a disgrace, no question about that. Lucretia nagged at her husband until Ernst finally laid down some rules. Izzy was to spend three hours each afternoon in the rectory, studying Latin and scriptures, and, in preparation for her future, was to learn something about keeping house from Annie. This would have been torture for Izzy except the Cree woman's stories, told while scrubbing the floor, or preparing rice pudding, or washing the clothes, enthralled her. Annie became Izzy's confidant, so much so that Lucretia suffered twinges of jealousy, although she would never admit such a thing.

It was Annie who trained Izzy to hear the music in the Cree language.

"Listen for the birds," she would say. "Over there is *piskwa*, night hawk, there *misko-chachakwan*, red-winged blackbird, there *makwa*, a loon, and on that tree *ohoh*, well you know what that is – an owl."

"Please, Annie, let's do snow," Izzy would plead, and together they would recite, *kona* – big snow; *mispon* – falling snow; *saskan* – melting snow; *piwan* – drifting snow, *papeskwatatin* – snow drifts.

Annie loved to shock the proper white girl. "Name the places in English where you go to pee," she'd demand.

"Washroom, toilet, ladies' room, WC, water closet, powder room."

"In our language it's *misiwikamik*, plain old shithouse."

Before her marriage to Alphonse Custer, Annie had been a Ballendine. Her father, Peter, was elected the first chief when the band was established twenty-four years before and she liked to tell stories about him.

"He was a wonderful old bird. But strange. He maybe wasn't even Cree. Well, they don't know where he came from. My grandfather found him all alone on an island in Deschambault Lake. A young boy, and yet he smelled like some animal long dead, so they nicknamed him *Wichikis*, the stinky one. My grandfather thought he had buffalo on him, or perhaps it was because he ate so much raw fish trying to survive in that place. He either got lost in the bush, and his parents finally left without him, or they died from the white man's illness that was killing so many of our people at the time.

"He didn't speak our language so he couldn't tell us anything, and when he did learn Cree, he wouldn't talk about his family. Or maybe he didn't remember. Whatever happened turned him very peculiar. Elijah the prophet, some people called him. Was there moose over there? Yes, he'd nod, and off would go our hunters. And always they came home with something. For years there was no hunger in our camp because of him.

"When he was an old man, he used to say, 'If white men come to our land, there will be a lot of them. Life is hard now, but it'll be harder when the white man comes.' And, of course, he was right."

Izzy hated it when Annie talked about the harm her people had suffered at the hands of white trespassers. She knew it to be true, but she, Izzy, would have cut off her right hand before she'd hurt Annie, she loved the Cree woman that much.

"I'll take care of you, Annie. I'll never leave you," she'd say.

"Just wait until some handsome, fair-haired guy with blue eyes comes sniffing around. You'll be gone before I can wave goodbye."

The scholars are starting to wiggle in their desks which means their assignments are almost finished. Izzy isn't surprised that Angus Crane is the first to jump up. She loves this kid – he is so enthusiastic, bright and funny.

"Okay, Angus, tell us what happened."

The boy stands up straight, his paper held in both hands in front of him, although Izzy knows that only half of what he will recite will actually be printed on the page. He'll begin in halting English but quickly switch to Cree. Izzy doesn't interrupt him; it's the story that counts.

"There are these people who are this little" – the boy puts out his arm at waist level. "They live in rocks in lakes and rivers. They especially like waterfalls. They're called *omomik-wesiwak*. One summer day – it was very misty – my *mosom* was out in his canoe tending his nets. He was surprised that they were all tangled and broken, like some huge fish had been in there. But there was no fish. Through the fog he saw a little canoe – it was made of stone – with three little people inside. They saw my grandfather and began singing" – here Angus imitates in a high quivering voice – "'Pali, Pali, Pali.' Nobody knows what it means. Then they paddled their canoe right into the rock and were gone. *Mosom* left some fish right there and it disappeared. They probably ate it.

"My *mosom* still has some of their medicine. He keeps it in his trunk. It's all powdery, in different colours. He got it from the *omomik- wesiwak* who live in Reindeer Lake where the water is very cold and clear. They live on a big island there with a great, steep rock in the middle. If you leave a piece of moose hide about the size of a napkin at a certain place, and say out loud exactly what is bothering you or someone you know – pain in the leg, pain in the backside, pain in the head – you have to say the details. You come back in a few days, and a bundle of medicine will be waiting for you.

"But the *omomikwesiwak* don't like everybody, and if they don't like you, you're in big trouble. Last spring a white trader, his partner who's a half breed, and a Cree guide were trying to find the *omomik- wesiwak's* island so they could get their hands on the medicine. As they came near, three *omomikwesiwak* paddled towards them. The Cree guide grabbed hold of the bow of their canoe rough like, and yelled, 'Where you going, little people?' The half breed asked, 'What are you hiding there?' And the white trader, pulling a dollar bill from his pocket, said, 'Why don't you hand over those bundles of medi- cine? See, here's real money.'

"One of the *omomikwesiwak* looked at the Indian and said, 'You'll never see the wild roses bud again.' A second told the half breed, 'You'll never see the leaves turn yellow,' and a third shouted at the white trader, 'You'll never again see snow fall in Pelican Narrows.' And that is the end of my story."

Out of breath, the boy plunks himself down, and the others clap and hoot their approval.

Izzy is taken aback at Angus's tale. She's heard the gossip, and knows exactly to whom he is referring. The Indian guide is George Ballendine who, while out hunting the previous April, fell through the ice and drowned. The half breed is Bibiane Ratt and the trader Arthur Jan, both men still very much alive. But then the leaves are still green and there's no sign of snow.

CHAPTER TEN

THE TEACHER IS ANYTHING but a tyrant, so when the scholars' captivity has obviously become unbearable – even Laura Whitegoose pays no attention when asked to recite the eight times table – Izzy dismisses her class an hour before lunch. But she is disturbed by Angus Crane's story and decides she'll visit his family to warn them that the child is spreading dangerous rumours.

As she makes her way along the narrow, wandering path up the hill from Pelican Lake towards the encampment where the Crane clan have pitched wigwams and built a few cabins, she thinks that, even on this lovely day, a dark pall of heartache lies heavy over this place. The story Arthur Jan told last night of the massacre, for example. Izzy's heard versions of it many times, none more gruesome than that recounted to her by Angus and three of his cousins when one day she joined them for lunch. "They carved the captives' flesh with their knives, piece by piece. The dogs licked up the blood," Angus had explained. His enthusiasm for this lurid tale, verging on joy, upset Izzy.

As she approaches the Crane enclave, she steels herself. Desperation, darkness, degradation – she's feels this so strongly that she almost turns around and leaves. But no, she would be too disappointed in herself. If there's one thing she's proud of, it's her nerve to face whatever comes her way.

All day, every day, Angus's father, Frederick, sits on a tree stump near his shack, rocking to and fro, and whimpering like a frightened dog. It's obvious that he's reliving the terrible event that occurred three years before.

THE HUNTERS HAD CAMPED for the night and were just finishing their meal. Fred excused himself and headed into the bush for a pee. He had just unzipped his pants when he noticed a huge grizzly standing there, glowering at him – she'd been poking at a nearby ant hill. Her two cubs were beside her. He let out a terrified scream, but, by the time his companions got to him, the bear had taken his head in her hands and was eating his face, bones crunching like shattered glass. Frightened that they'd accidently kill their friend, the trappers tried ramming the animal with the butts of their guns. Fred shouted, "Shoot, shoot, I'd rather be shot than eaten alive." One of the men finally got close enough to the animal to take accurate aim, and hit her in the chest. The cubs were slaughtered in revenge.

Fred survived the ordeal, but just barely. His face is a hideous mess of corrugated scar tissue. His nose and an ear are missing. He is blind. But, most tragically, his mind has shattered.

Izzy gingerly approaches him. "How are you today, Fred?"

The man, whose eyes have been torn out, turns his head towards her, but no words escape his misshapen mouth. Nothing but a moan.

"See you later," she says, and turns towards the cabin, half-hoping her knock will not be answered.

Even before Fred's accident, his wife, Susan Crane, ruled the roost. Big boned, handsome, smart, she is a ferocious woman who will brook no hint of rebellion. Izzy once sat in on a meeting of Indian elders, a discussion of what should be done about Arthur Jan's illicit booze. Susan was in favour of punishing any boy or girl who partook of so much as a drop. A couple of old men were sympathetic – "They're just young bucks after all."

"So when they end up in handcuffs on their way to the white man's jail, you'll be satisfied," Susan had honked at them. Her tongue lashing continued until they slunk away.

When in a confrontation with Susan Crane, most people simply give up and keep their mouths shut. And she's ambitious, so ambitious. Her six sons, including mischievous Angus, will succeed, in the white world too. To make sure of that, she's had the family baptized in both the Christian faiths so that any opportunity for education can be grabbed hold of. Summer with Izzy and the Anglicans is fine, but what she's really counting on is the Catholic residential school that will start that fall. There, her boys will be whipped into shape, she's sure of that.

Izzy doesn't know what to think. Teaching the native kids to take their place in the wider world is necessary. Well, given her background how could she think otherwise? Yet her heart goes out to Angus Crane. How will such an imaginative child, bright and brash, survive the discipline of a boarding school? She knows what her father believes – Indians are savages without a culture or religion, to be moulded into an inferior rendition of white men. Izzy wonders if Catholics will be any more compassionate. She doubts it.

Nobody answers at the Crane cabin, so Izzy makes her way to the home of Angus's grandfather. Izzy is as intimidated by Peter Angus as she is by his daughter-in-law. At 67 he is still imposing – tall, broad shouldered, with a handsome head of black-grey hair which he wears in a thick braid down his back. He is a stern man. Izzy can't remember seeing even a twitch of a smile on his lips. At this moment he is sitting in a chair, dozing in the sun.

"How are you today, Mr. Crane," Izzy says, her voice full of apprehension.

He half opens his eyes, glances at her indifferently, and says nothing.

"I wanted to have a word with you," Izzy continues. "It's about Angus. He's spreading dreadful rumours about Mr. Jan and Bibiane Ratt. I don't think it's proper in this small village."

"It's true, so why shouldn't the boy talk about it? Those bastards will be dead and gone by winter."

Abruptly the old man closes his eyes and begins to snore.

At that moment, the bells of St. Gertrude's and St. Bartholomew's clang out announcing the start of the canoe races. These are a highlight of the Treaty Party celebrations that will go on all day. Izzy is relieved. She has her excuse to escape the Crane family's gloom.

CHAPTER ELEVEN

IZZY JOINS THE CROWD gathering on the beach to the west of St. Gertrude's Church. There's a pretty good view of the finish line from here. Maybe she'll be able to catch Joe's eye.

Each race will begin half a mile away, at the dock jutting out from Arthur Jan's store. The canoes will travel across Macaroni Bay, around the northern tip of The Island, towards the monitoring boat anchored about five hundred yards from shore. Through her binoculars, Izzy can make out two red flags flapping from its bow and stern, and the three observers, Councillor Bird, Dr. Lewis and his brother, The Famous Writer, sitting within. The racers will navigate past the monitors, and then continue north to the wharf at the Hudson's Bay Store.

First up is the girls' race. There are five canoes entered, each occupied by two teenage paddlers. The starting pistol has sounded a full ten minutes before they finally come into view rounding The Island. Once she spots them, Izzy is disappointed. "My goodness, they're hardly trying," she thinks to herself. As they approach the dock, there's not a bead of sweat on the foreheads of the front-runners; Juliette Bird and fat Grace Morin are barely panting. What kind of race is that?

At Bishop Strachan School, Izzy loved sporting games – tennis, basketball, lacrosse, track and field, softball, golf, it didn't matter, she did her best to lay to waste her opponents. She would have liked to take part in the race, show these girls how to use their muscles but, of course, no one thought to ask. It's as though she walks around in a bell jar, exiled in a society to which she would give anything to belong.

The two-paddler race for men is next. There are eight entries, all young men in their twenties, but by the time the flotilla comes into view Joe Sewap and his partner, Moses Rabbitskin, are so far ahead

of the others the finish is anticlimactic. Izzy is desperate to congrat-
ulate Joe but before she can get to him he's already on his way back
to Arthur Jan's dock, where the single paddler's competition is about
to begin. This will be the most exciting event of the day, primarily
because the top contenders are so evenly matched. The odds are
about even on Cornelius Ratt, Moses Rabbitskin and Joe Sewap.

Izzy's stomach is crunched in a knot, and it gives a twist again
when the racers finally round the tip of The Island. Cornelius has been
left behind – Moses and Joe are neck and neck. Both are standing,
their legs apart, their knees bent for balance, their paddles slicing
cleanly into the water, stroke after stroke, uniform and amazingly
rapid. Moses is shorter than Joe but heavier, barrel-chested, with bulky
limbs, a result of years of hauling freight. Joe is slender, his physique
more elongated, more elegant. He's wearing a singlet and Izzy tries to
keep her eyes averted from his muscular shoulders, slick with sweat,
sculpted as if by Michelangelo, but still she feels a lovely tingling in
the parts of her body she has been admonished never to think about.

On the community dock, Father Bonnald, Bob Taylor, and Russell
Smith are crouched down, their eyes riveted on the finish line.

The canoes streak past, then jerk to a stop.

As Joe and Moses sit panting, and the crowd collectively holds its
breath, the three judges argue among themselves. Finally the
announcement is made: Moses Rabbitskin has won by a quarter inch.
A cheer explodes from the crowd.

Russell Smith, on behalf of the HBC, presents the prize, a crisp
five dollar bill. A grinning Moses graciously accepts it, shaking hands
with the officials, blowing a kiss to his sweetheart, Agnes Highway.
Adoring fans crowd around him, patting, slapping, mauling, until Izzy
thinks he must hurt all over. Joe is standing alone. Only a couple of
people have come over to offer condolences. It's something she's
noticed before. He seems to be as ill at ease in this company as she
is. As much an outsider. When she thinks back, this was obvious the
first time they met – which may be why she was so attracted to him.

CHAPTER TWELVE

WHEN IZZY WAS IN HER LAST YEAR at Bishop Strachan, her grandfather urged her to enrol at Trinity College. "Study sports if you have to. If nothing else, you'll catch a suitable husband." Her parents had wanted her to attend Normal School. "You'd make a fine teacher," her father said. "And who knows, the Lord might whisper in your ear, and you'll follow in my footsteps. Marry a missionary, or maybe even become one yourself."

Izzy had choked at this suggestion, but promised she'd think about it.

That spring, the Bishop Strachan graduating class was invited to an exhibition of Canadian painters at Toronto's Arts and Letters Club. When her grandfather heard about it, he scoffed, "Not that bunch! Infantile mishmash. Give me a lovely Dutch riverside landscape or mellow, sheep-clad hills in Surrey, not some rock in the desolate north. I want calm and order, not chaos"

Certainly she'd been perplexed by the jangle of colour and swirling shapes. But there were two paintings that caught her attention – 'Autumn's Garland' by Tom Thomson and 'Winter Woods' by Lawren Harris. Izzy had experienced the shield country during those summers she was allowed to travel to Pelican Narrows, but here were tantalizing glimpses of how glorious it would be at other times of the year. Months later she would discover how savage the winter was. How the cold could bite and sting your eyes. But that May nothing could have stopped her. To her family's chagrin, she announced that she wanted to spend an entire year at Pelican Narrows. "Then I'll make a decision about my future."

September *was* glorious, and so different from the red-brown autumn in the east. The bright yellow elms and birches prancing in front of the stolid, dark spruce reminded Izzy of sassy girls out on a date with handsome, dignified young men. A wind one night sent the leaves spinning, laying down a carpet of gold so beautiful she walked around with tears in her eyes. The landscape teased her, enchanted her, and, finally, the forbidding night seduced her.

It was a thick, frightening dark, and, at first, she went no further than the outhouse. But the white birch, lit up by the moon, turned into sign posts along the trails which crisscrossed Pelican Narrows. She ventured further and further, jack pine, balsam fir, and white spruce looming above her like centurions. There was the pleasure of overcoming her fear — even as a child she enjoyed being reckless — but more it was the intoxicating combination of a dread that made her heart thump and a joy that made her laugh out loud.

One night, an astonishing aurora borealis flashed in the sky. Huge sheets of gauze in shades of blue, pink and mauve roiled in the heavens. Around them white, shimmering crystals, triangular and circular in shape, pranced like high-spirited demons. As she sat on a tree stump mesmerized by the spectacle, lines from her favourite poet, Gerard Manley Hopkins, came to her:

"The world is charged with the grandeur of God
It will flame out, shining from shook foil;
It gathers to a greatness, like the ooze of oil
Crushed."

At that moment there came to her an epiphany so potent, so irresistible, that it instantly transformed her. Her Creator was no longer the God worshipped by Hopkins or the other poets or painters or philosophers she had studied. Nor was it her father's, nor the Anglican Church's. The divine lay deep in this severe, punishing, yet mystical ancient landscape, in its lakes and streams, its marshes and rocky outcrops.

And, in Izzy's mind, this perplexing place, this other godliness, came to be personified by a Cree boy with strange eyes.

Izzy met Joe six months ago at a meeting of St. Bartholomew's bible study club. Ernst had decided that "touching the heart of the savage youth" was his most important mission, and he had painstakingly taught himself a kind of pidgin Cree hoping to communicate with his young parishioners. Lucretia, in one of her more practical turns, understood that plates of bully beef and beaver stew served up after the lesson were bees-to-honey attractions. The bible club turned out to be a surprising success.

On this freezing cold Epiphany, the young Anglicans were gathered in the front pews of the church. A marker had been placed in the Cree translation of their bibles at Luke 2:39-52, the story of Boy Jesus at the Temple. A rotogravure print of William Holman Hunt's rendition of the event had been pinned on a wall. This was a painting Izzy had always loved, the delicate young Christ, his worried but adoring parents, the rabbis so colourful, the temple so exotic. The Indian teenagers gawked at it, but remained expressionless.

Reverend Wentworth spoke Cree as though he were chopping cabbage, words spewing out in rapid succession. "Jesus was twelve years old. His parents came to Jerusalem for the Feast of Passover. Then Mary and Joseph left to go home. In a caravan with ..." He had no idea what the Cree word for camel was, or even if there was such a word, so he substituted horses. "They discovered that Jesus wasn't with them. They rushed back to the city. After three days of searching, they found him in the Temple. There he was, many years younger than you youngsters here, debating with the rabbis as though he was a scholar."

At this point, Reverend Wentworth stretched up his arms, his palms raised towards Heaven, his eyes shining. In English he proclaimed: "And all who heard him were amazed at His understanding and His answers." The Biblical scholars stared at him mesmerized. He could have been a magician pulling rabbits out of a hat.

During the lesson that followed, Izzy spotted Joe Sewap sitting by himself near the back of the church, seemingly engrossed in every word uttered by her father. That he had come to the Anglican Church was a surprise, because first, he had been baptized a Roman Catholic, and second, he had an unusually close connection to St. Gertrude's – his mother, Sally Sewap, was the priest's housekeeper.

After the lesson, Izzy's father made a point of going over to him. "You're Joe Sewap, aren't you? I'm Reverend Wentworth and this is my daughter, Izzy."

Joe nodded to Izzy, but said not a word. In fact he turned his back on her. Cornering the clergyman, he proceeded to lay out his interpretation of the scripture.

"Okay, so Jesus impressed the rabbis. But what about his parents? They must have been worried sick, him disappearing like that for days. What kind of true Christian boy would do that?"

Ernst was taken aback – no Indian had ever challenged his theological interpretations before – and proclaimed with the unctuous condescension his daughter hated, "I'm sure He was torn between obeying his heavenly Father and minding his earthly father. But, after all, He was going about God's work, so any thoughtlessness towards his parents can be excused."

Interjecting before the scriptural debate could continue, Izzy asked Joe, "How come you know so much about bible stories?"

"Made to listen to them before I could talk. But actually I've always liked them," he replied.

"Come back and visit our little group any time you feel like it," Ernst urged.

But he never did. Izzy was sorry about this because already she was intrigued by him. For one thing, he was so peculiar looking. His complexion was light for a Cree – Izzy thought of honey – his cheek bones sculpted and high, his hair the usual brown-black. But it was his eyes that were so odd – the colour of orange marmalade with gold streaks riddling the iris. Over the next months she spotted him at different places around Pelican Narrows, in the fish-gutting shed cleaning turbot, along the trail cutting kindling, at the lake carving out chunks of ice which he would then bury deep in the ground for summertime use in Father Bonnald's icebox. He'd nod at her, but never spoke.

Finally, they ran into each other at Gertie Linklater's cabin. While her family was away trapping, the old woman had contracted bronchitis, and it was obvious that she was fading. Since she had professed both Anglicanism and Roman Catholicism as her one true religion, Izzy and Joe had both been sent to her cabin with bowls of soup and Christian messages.

"She seems a little better. She has a bit of colour in her cheeks," Izzy said pleasantly.

"You think so? Looks like death warmed over to me," he replied.

How could you help but fall in love with someone that bluntly honest?

During her years at her private, girls-only school, Izzy hadn't had much to do with the opposite sex. Her doctor and dentist were male, of course, but, since she was so healthy, encounters with them were infrequent. Her father was part of her life, but for only a couple of months each year. Her grandfather, at whose home she resided, spent most of his time in his study, and when he did emerge, he'd ask, "And the lessons today. How did they go?"

"Bellum, the Latin word for war," Izzy would recite. "Bellum, bellum, belli, bello, bello, bella, bella, bella, bellorum, bellis, bellis."

"Wonderful! And today's translation?"

She would shout out, Horace, *Satires* 1.6.65-92; or Cicero, *In Defense of Marcus Caelius Rufus*; or one of Catullus' poems.

He would nod his head in approval and disappear into his den once again.

At school there were a few male teachers. Mr. Klein, "a Jew" as one of the girls had sniggered, taught history, and Mr. Davey's speciality was mathematics, but Izzy couldn't remember ever having spoken a word to them outside the classroom. Mostly she daydreamed during their lectures — a spectacular basket she had scored in the last game between Bishop Strachan and St. Mildred's; the smell of bacon in the morning — Mrs. Aitkins, her grandfather's house-keeper made only porridge, not something Izzy relished — and, most often, the coming summer at Pelican Narrows.

So the adult males in her life, as far as Izzy could perceive, had had no influence on her at all. And the young men she met, well, they were a pathetic bunch.

Tea dances were held in the Bishop Strachan auditorium so that the senior girls could become acquainted with the opposite sex, but these were painful affairs — pimply-faced boys from one private school or another, smiling stupidly and holding out their sweaty hands, their eyes pleading not to be rejected, not to be humiliated.

Izzy was pretty enough to escape being relegated to the unhappy wallflowers clustered in the corner, but, after the chitchat which went on during the breaks between the foxtrot, the Charleston and the tango, Izzy's partner would most often fade into the crowd. There was nothing cute or coy or silly about her — she made it a point of *not* going out of her way to please — so she was hardly the belle of the ball.

In her last semester she did acquire a beau of sorts. Beefy, blond, slow-moving Timothy Clark was the scion of a wealthy family that owned an automobile brake factory. What she found most attractive about him was his new Chevrolet, a birthday present from his father. When he called on her at her grandfather's place, the old man would look dubious — was this proper behaviour for a young lady? He wasn't sure. But, oh well. "Have a nice evening," he'd say, as he shuffled into his study.

Sometimes Timothy took her out for dinner at Luigi's Spaghetti House, and that was certainly a welcome change from Mrs. Aitkins' cooking. He'd mumble all through the meal, mostly about horse racing to which he seemed addicted. Whenever she ventured an opinion or introduced a topic of interest to her, he'd yawn, his eye lids beginning to droop.

Sitting side by side in the front seat of the Chevy, they would buss lips in what Izzy supposed was a kiss, and fumble at each other's private parts, until he would suddenly announce that he had to get up early the next day. Was Izzy ready to be driven home?

Once, he began to unbutton her blouse and she thought, "At last, the real thing," but half way through, his head slid onto her shoulder. "So sorry, exhausted," he said, and fell asleep. A hard day at the track, Izzy assumed. Since graduation, they hadn't exchanged a word.

But now Izzy is truly in love, a mad, divine, all-consuming love.

She never stopped imaging what he was doing – feeding his dogs, hunting spruce grouse, gutting fish. On her night wanderings she connived to run into him on some dark path where she would dramatically declare her love. And was both annoyed and relieved when this never happened. During the day, she would hide in the bush behind the cabin he shared with his mother. She wanted only to catch a glimpse of him, nothing more. At least that's what she told herself.

She hardly ate, and Annie scolded her. "You're nothing but skin and bones. How is *Witigo* supposed to make a meal of you?"

Usually a fanatical reader, she barely picked up a book. She stopped playing the harmonium, or even listening to her favourite songs on the gramophone. Her mother said, "What's the matter with you? Oh, I know! Your monthly curse."

There was only one person in whom Izzy could confide her love for Joe, and that was Florence Smith. Izzy adored this big-boned woman, more muscle than fat, whose mind was like a large purse always over-flowing with queer ideas – for example her belief that the Greek gods were alive and well, and dwelling in the boreal forest, along, of course, with the Indian spirits.

One summer day when Izzy was twelve, she had been invited to go on an outing to collect medicinal plants in the forest and marshlands near Pelican Narrows with Florence and Sally Sewap, Father Bonnald's housekeeper – and Joe's mother, although at the time Izzy hadn't realized the significance of this. On that first trip, her sharp young eyes spotted, high on a rocky outcrop, a valuable *wikaswa*, wild mint used to relieve tooth ache. Florence and Sally admitted they would have missed it. From then on she was included in their weekly expeditions.

That Florence found the girl to be a delight was obvious, but Sally was much more reserved. Probably she thinks I'm a nuisance, Izzy thought. But then, just before she was to return to Toronto, Sally gave her a pair of gorgeous beaded moccasins which she had crafted herself. From that time on Izzy wore nothing else. On her return to school, she snuck them in her suitcase, but the rules permitted her to wear them only on special occasions, the Masquerade Party being one of them. Izzy dressed up like an Indian squaw and won second prize.

One day, Florence and Sally were up to their waists in the lake trying to yank an obstinate water lily from the mud. The root, when ground up, was used to ease headaches. Izzy was sitting on a rock nearby drawing a clump of wild roses in a notebook she had gotten for her birthday. When Florence emerged from the muck, she took a look at Izzy's art work and was astounded at how good the little sketches were. After that, she insisted that Izzy keep a pictorial record of the various plants they collected. With the help of a volume on Victorian botanical prints sent by her grandfather, the young artist would identify and label the samples. She branched into pastels and water colours. Her latest effort, 'Pink Lady's Slipper,' – called 'Moccasin Flower" by the Cree – was exquisite. Everyone said so.

"Izzy, you're a marvel," Florence exclaimed when she saw it. It was added to the collection of the girl's work which will eventually be sent to a publisher. For if Florence has a mission in life, it is to make sure Izzy's future is not dependent on the success of some man. Which is why, when Izzy confided her passion for Joe, Florence wasn't as sympathetic as Izzy thought she would be. She simply mumbled, "If this romance does develop into something, you'll have to tell your parents right away."

I will certainly do so, Izzy thought to herself. As soon as moose starts saying grace before his dinner.

CHAPTER THIRTEEN

NOW THAT THE CANOE RACES are over, everyone has moved on to other activities – except Joe. He sits on a log looking dejected. Izzy spots him, and gingerly walks over. "You put in a good race, Joe. Too bad you were cheated. I'd make an official complaint if I were you."

He smiles sweetly – Izzy is charmed. "It's not who wins the game, but how it's been played. Isn't that the rule we Christians are supposed to live by?"

What surprises Izzy is not that he's so forgiving – surely he doesn't believe that old cliché – but what he carries under his arm. It's a two-month old edition of Le Devoir. Probably it's Father Bonnald's; newspapers regularly come in his mail. Izzy is overjoyed. Joe can read and probably write, and that, in the struggle to come, will provide powerful ammunition.

The Great Writer has kept his word. With the help of that excellent organizer, Florence Smith, every jar, can, bottle of foodstuffs found at the Hudson's Bay post, at Arthur Jan's emporium, and in the Wentworth, Smith, and Bonnald pantries, has been rounded up. The Anglican scholars are to have a very special treat – an English picnic.

Makeshift tables holding all the goodies have been set up on a grassy plateau above the beach, but by the time the children scramble up the hill the lunch has been covered with tablecloths. The games come first. The tracks have been laid out, the pits dug, the poles set. Once the contestants are divided into age groups, the rules spelled out, and the admonishments about not being too rough made, a flurry of activity erupts – dashing, jumping, somersaulting, tossing horseshoes. A thousand bee hives would not have made more noise.

"Good thing Bob Taylor isn't here," Florence jokes. "Too much unbridled happiness for him. He'd close us down for sure."

There is order of sorts, with winner and losers, although Florence makes sure every kid, even the fattest and slowest, wins one bag of candy.

On one side of the grassy knoll, Izzy has set up an easel, and is making quick sketches, more cartoon than art, of the participants. These are a resounding success, each kid running off to show the portrait to friends, who all laugh their heads off.

Angus Crane, who has thrown himself into every activity, a tornado of joyous enthusiasm, hops up and down in line like a grasshopper. When it's finally his turn, he can hardly hold still long enough for Izzy to catch him on paper, and with this kid, she wants to do a good job. She also wants to gently admonish him for the tale he told that morning.

"Angus, dear," she begins. "You know that story about the three men who tried to steal the *omomikwesiwak's* medicine? Maybe it's not a good idea to say it out loud."

"Why? Everyone knows those guys are dead ducks. My Uncle Leonard says he'll kill them himself – with his hunting rifle – if they're not gone from here by the time the lake freezes over. "

Izzy recoils at this. Angus's uncle Leonard is one of the more approachable members of the Crane clan. She makes a mental note to try and pry out of him what's going on.

The most laughable event of the day, the three legged-race for adults, is announced. Just as the strips of cloth are being handed out, and legs are being bound together, Joe Sewap and Claude Lewis come walking along the path. Izzy wonders if Joe's been complaining about the results of that morning's competition, but no, they're smiling. Florence rushes over, "You boys have come just in time for the fun," she booms.

Thirteen-year-old Isaac Morin, the only truly surly boy in Izzy's class, has refused to participate in the games. He's been skulking about, mocking both the winners and losers, so now he grabs his chance. "Dr. Lewis, I'll bet you're fast as the wind, and Mrs. Smith, I've seen how good you swim. Very strong, very fast. So why don't you join the race?"

Izzy winces when Florence pipes up, "That sounds like fun," and marches over to an astonished Claude Lewis to have her right leg bound to his left.

"And what about you, Miss Wentworth?" Angus Crane calls out. "Wouldn't it be exciting..." Izzy realizes Angus intends to link her up with Sinclair Lewis, so she makes an instant decision. "I'll join in if Joe Sewap agrees to be my partner." A few seconds later she finds herself lashed to the limb of the man she adores.

Meanwhile, pretty Betty Bird has buttonholed The Great Writer and, surprisingly, he has agreed to team up with her. Now they're hobbling towards the start line.

The three teams ready themselves. The start-gun blasts. Off they go. Or at least try to. In about five seconds, Claude Lewis and Florence Smith tumble to the ground. They are both rotund, and coordinating their legs to march as one proves impossible. Like stout acrobats they roll, the doctor on top of Florence, then Florence on top of the doctor. Izzy hopes that neither sprains a limb.

Betty Bird and The Great Writer make a formidable team. At fifteen she is very swift – she's won all the races in her age group – so she can easily adapt to Sinclair Lewis's long-legged stride. They're off to a strong start.

Izzy and Joe stumble at first, but then quickly synchronize their movements. Izzy can feel his muscular hip against hers. Later, when she remembers this moment, chills will run down her spine. Right now, all she can think about is winning.

Only ten yards from the finish line, Sinclair Lewis, whose face is as red as beet, throws his hands up. "I'm finished," he gasps. "Can't go on." Then falls flat on the ground.

"Oh drat!" exclaims a chagrined Betty, and tumbles besides him.

Among cheers and applause the winners are presented with the first prize, a copy of *A Child's First Book of Verse*. Izzy and Joe bow their appreciation and everyone claps.

Izzy would like to manoeuvre Joe into some quiet place so they could enjoy a good laugh together, but The Famous Writer, recovered from his exertion, calls for silence.

"In honour of the Anglican scholars," he announces, and whips off the tablecloths. The picnic is exposed in all its glory.

There are plates piled high with sandwiches made with Florence's own bread, some filled with grape jelly, others with tinned ham. Canned tomatoes and pickles, radishes and lettuce, the latter two from Florence's garden, serve as the condiments. There's a huge potato salad and plates of Belvedere cheese, which the Indians don't much like and make a face at. For dessert, bowls of canned peaches and pears, and, best of all, sweet cakes with raspberry sauce.

The children are shy at first, slowly deciding what they want, and carefully placing these items on their plates.

"Gosh, I thought they'd be in there with both hands, gobbling like little pigs," says Claude Lewis.

"You will find, Doctor, that Cree kids are better behaved than most white progeny," Florence replies.

They sit in the sunshine enjoying the delicacies, the children sprawled on the ground, the adults in chairs that have been carried up for the occasion. Izzy's heart leaps when Joe parks himself beside her.

"Look in the bushes," he whispers.

She sees a dozen little brown faces peeking out. She laughs. "It's about time the Catholics have something to envy the Anglicans for."

Sinclair Lewis suddenly springs to his feet. "Ladies and gentlemen, boys and girls," he barks in a vaudeville voice, "It's show time!"

From behind a clump of birches, he pulls out the Wentworths' battery-operated gramophone. Angus volunteers to wind up the machine. Izzy carefully places the needle.

A scratchy rendition of *My Waikiki Mermaid* echoes through the boreal forest. The Great Writer's angular hips begin to sway back and forth, his right arm and then his left imitate an ocean wave; all that's missing is a grass skirt and a lei around his neck. Soon everyone, the scholars, Florence Smith, Dr. Lewis, Joe, Izzy, even the kids hiding in the bush, are doing the hula, sashaying like true Hawaiians gods.

It's a perfect ending to a perfect afternoon.

Izzy has promised her father she'd help translate during meetings with his parishioners and the Indian agent, so she has to unhappily says goodbye to Joe. As she wends her way down the hill, she spots Albert Jan walking quickly towards her. "Hello, Mr. Jan," she yells out. He looks startled as though she's an alien dropped from the heavens. He barely nods at her. With his skinny body, pointed snout and black beady eyes, he reminds Izzy of one of the ferrets found around Pelican Narrows that torture rabbits. He'd go for your jugular, that's for sure.

REVEREND WENTWORTH'S SUMMIT

Friday afternoon

CHAPTER FOURTEEN

ERNST WENTWORTH SITS FUMING. Now and then he lets go with an exasperated gasp, followed by a pitiful sob. For the umpteenth time he remembers the warning of Bishop Everett-Smith: "If God has called you to the mission battlefield, you will have great joy; if there is any other motive, it will be Hell." Obviously the Almighty has made a hobby of poking holes in his intentions because, during his twelve years at St. Bartholomew's, Ernst has suffered every sling and arrow the Devil himself tossed.

This morning had brought yet more humiliation, another defeat. He was making his monthly pastoral visit to the family of Harold Nistawepesim. As usual, babies, toddlers, aunts, uncles, grandparents, friends, all making a frightful noise, were spilling in and out of the log cabin. The older children were at school with Izzy. Harold was at the back inspecting his fish nets. In his usual cheery manner, he yelled out, "Glad to see you, Reverend Wentworth. Good news for you today. Father Bonnald came early this morning, and baptised our mosom and nokom into the Christian faith right here on the spot." Ernst almost choked. How many winters had he travelled in the most dreadful weather to the Nistawepesims' winter camp so he could comfort the old people and teach them the Word of God? How many gifts of warm underwear, tobacco and candies had he handed out to win them over to the love of Jesus? How many summer evenings had he sat with them patiently explaining the gospels' teachings, while they smoked their pipes, all the while glaring at him as though he was some alien from another world? They weren't ready to accept Christianity, that was made clear. So how come the

Catholic priest, who up to that point had not given a damn about these particular heathens, had arrived unannounced, and managed this miraculous conversion? Harold explained that the grandparents were tired of the religious people nagging at them. "So they thought, might as well get baptised, then they'll leave us alone."

At that very moment, Ernst Wentworth decided he had to take a stand. Sick onto death of the priest's dirty tricks, he marched over to the Indian agent's tent, and demanded a showdown. An astonished Bob Taylor promised that if Father Bonnald agreed, he would arrange a summit for later that afternoon. The little post office attached to the Hudson's Bay Company store was deemed neutral enough territory. Ernst realizes that he must carefully prepare for what he has wrought, and so secludes himself in the lean-to attached to the rear of the church that is laughingly called his study.

He is so tired of being bullied. Domineering men, so much tougher, self-assured and cunning than he, despots each and every one, have oppressed him his entire life. The first of these was that huge, jowly man, his father, a successful barrister famous for the patronizing, scathing manner in which he cross-examined his prey.

At six months old Ernst fell out of his crib and bruised his forehead. He cried as though his heart, not his head, was broken. Douglas Wentworth decided right then that his son was a weakling, a judgement from which he never veered. Ernst's mother was more sympathetic towards her third child, but she was so caught up in her multitudinous charities – the greatest moment of her life was when she was elected president of the Imperial Order Daughters of the Empire, Toronto branch – that she had little time for him. His two brothers, William and James, big, manly fellows, years older than he, were interested in only two things: playing polo and hunting down the opposite sex. They gave him about as much thought as they did the family's cocker spaniel – an absent-minded pat on the head on good days, a bad-tempered smack on his ear on bad.

He was handed over to the care of a nanny, good-natured Betty

Brun, a farm girl from Tweed, Ontario. She gave him the run of the family's Rosedale home, a grandiose pastiche of brick and stone, soaring gables, peek-a-boo porches, wide lawns both front and back. A perfect place for a shy boy to play.

His idyllic time with Betty ended all too soon. At age seven he was packed off to Upper Canada College, where he spent a miserable twelve years supposedly having his character moulded by an assortment of tyrannical teachers. He was not the worst scholar, but certainly not one of the brilliant set, as brother William had been. He played lacrosse and tennis decently, but did not shine as brother James had. He did take up a hobby though, grew passionate about it, and this turned his young years golden.

The clouds of butterflies floating like coloured confetti over the vast garden at the family's summer home on Lake Simcoe enthralled him. Here, at last, was something precious and beautiful that he could call his own. That he could master. He was judicious in the number and the kind of specimen he went after. And those he did net, he learned to mount properly. The corpse must be prepared quickly after death so as to remain soft and malleable. The pin must be thrust through very hard, very straight, right at the centre line of the thorax. The wings neatly, carefully spread. Twelve or twenty-four or thirty-six or even forty-eight of these beauties were then lined up in boxes and covered with glass. These were displayed on his bedroom walls. When every inch was covered, they were piled on the floor, one on top of the other, leaving only a pathway to the door. The maid complained that she spent more time dusting his room than any other in the house.

Ernst picks up the glass case on his desk. It's his very first collection. Each specimen is labelled neatly, printed in his childish hand: *Papilio Canadensis* (Canadian Tiger Swallow Tail), July, 1891; *Limenitis arthemis* (White Admiral), June 1893; *Chlosyne Harrisii* (Harris' Checkerspot), August 1893; *Celastrina argiolus* (Spring Azure), July, 1894; *Colias philodice* (Clouded Sulphur), July 1895; *Nymphalis antiopa* (Mourning Cloak), August 1891. Wherever he has travelled this treasure has gone with him – an everlasting tribute to the wonder of God's creation. Only, in this desolate place, it's turned into a bitter reminder of the sacrifice he suffers to perform The Almighty's work. Butterflies are so difficult to locate in the bush, and many of them are so ordinary looking, the pale Cabbage Whites, plain Brown Elfins, the ghostly Northern Cloudy Wing. He once came across a magnificent *Vanessa atalanta rubria* but such finds were rare. His heart broke when he realized that his passion was leaking away.

He returns the butterfly collection to its place next to the photograph of his parents. Both are gone now – his mother killed when she stepped in front of a tram as she was on her way to a meeting of the Women's Christian Temperance Movement, his father dead after suffering a massive heart attack during a ferocious argument with Sam Hughes, the Minister of Militia. Lifetime friends and debating partners – they were at university together – the two quarrelled over whether the Lee-Enfield should replace the Ross Rifle in the trenches of the Great War. Wentworth was for it, Hughes against it.

Ernst has never grieved much for the senior Wentworths. After all, they had hardly bothered with him. But today he feels a certain nostalgia. Maybe he shouldn't be so hard on them. The old man thought butterfly collecting an effete pastime, better left to fat ladies in large hats, but he always handed over the necessary funds for a deluxe net or the best kind of forceps. And his mother actually took the time to attend a presentation put on by the Toronto Lepidopterist Guild, during which he was named first place winner in the Young Collectors category. The trophy was even given a place of honour on the mantel in the living room.

In another, smaller, photo in place near the back of his desk, his young self stares up at him. Taken the day he was ordained an Anglican minister, he's smiling broadly, his teeth gleaming as white as his brand new clerical collar. It was his parents who had decided that God was calling him to His service. Ernst hadn't uttered a peep of protest. Now he wonders why.

CHAPTER FIFTEEN

ERNST JUMPS UP from his desk. What is he doing daydreaming like this? Important decisions are about to be made concerning the fate of sick Anglicans. He must be in attendance.

He is in such a hurry that he hardly notices what a gorgeous day it is, hot, sunny with only a few clouds in the sky. Laughter bubbles up from the beach but he pays no attention. He heads eastward along the trail that winds past Arthur Jan's storehouse, where the previous night the boys had been caught playing billiards. He notices that the door is open and thinks maybe Arthur is inside. That man makes Ernst nervous, he has such a confident, blasé air about him. But he is a loyal member of St. Bartholomew's congregation – if he's not away on business, he attends services regularly, he'll even read the scripture if asked. Perhaps he can be prevailed upon to join Ernst this afternoon. Arthur is a persuasive man, a man with influence. Surely he can convince those in authority to do the right thing.

Ernst walks up the pathway and peeks through the doorway. It's a dank, cavernous place with boxes scattered everywhere. Arthur and Bibiane Ratt are standing at the rear with their backs towards him. Arthur bends over and, with his left hand, pulls out from one of the containers a round, yellowish object. Laughing aloud, he begins to shake it as though it's a maraca. Bibiane yells out Olay! while his hips sway to a rhumba beat. Ernst stands stock still, mesmerized, until it dawns on him that Arthur's musical instrument is a human skull.

Arthur rummages through a pile of small utensils until he finds a toothbrush. He picks the skull up again and begins brushing the yellow teeth which dangle in the hole that was once a mouth.

"There, you beauty!" he sings. "Now you're ready for your travels. Mr. Ratt here would like to give you a big, fat, farewell kiss." Both men break out in wild laughter.

Ernst has no idea what to make of the scene he's just witnessed, nor does he have a clue what to do about it. Should he say something? Suddenly, Arthur turns his head and from the corner of his eye spots the clergyman. He picks up what looks like an ancient spear and raises it above his head. Ernst thinks 'By God, he's going to throw it. An insect impaled!' Spinning around, he darts out the door and makes for the path. Half walking, half running, he propels himself as quickly as his legs will take him. Finally, he plops down on a tree trunk, trying hard to control his panting. He is so ashamed that he hadn't had the courage to confront Jan and Ratt that tears are welling up. For the umpteenth time, he wonders why a man with so little confidence would be called to service by The Maker. Well, he had no say in the matter, did he? He remembers so clearly the day he learned of his fate.

He was fifteen, and had been taken on one of the rare visits to his father's law firm. Wentworth, Dilly, Cruickshank & Smith occupied an entire floor of the ornate Wentworth Building on King Street. The intense clacking of typewriters and the ant-like industry of his father's employees, mostly men who glanced up not a second longer than it took them to chirp, 'Morning, Mr. Wentworth,' always made Ernst uneasy. As usual he was instructed to pay his respects to the senior partner. Mr. Dilly, with his protruding belly, bald head, thin lips and many, many warts all over his face and head and, Ernst imagined, probably in other obscene places hidden by his clothing, so much resembled *Bufo Woodhousei fowleri* – Fowler's toad – that the boy could hardly keep the necessary straight face.

"What a handsome fellow you've turned out to be, Master Wentworth," cried Mr. Dilly. "So what does the future hold for you? Following brother Will's footsteps into law – can always use another bright light in this office – or brother James into the military?"

Wentworth Senior cut in before his son got a chance to answer. "Neither of these, I'm afraid. We think Ernst would be more successful in a less taxing profession. The Anglican priesthood will suit him just fine."

This was news to Ernst. At first he was indignant that his future had been decided without his opinion being asked even once, but, as he thought about it, not having to endure either the torture of working for his father or death on a foreign battlefield had its appeal.

He was pretty sure that he possessed the correct qualities for a religious calling. He loved the Anglican services; indeed he felt more at home in St. James Cathedral than his own living room. He made a point of assisting anyone he thought was in need, whether, as his father joked, they wanted him to or not. And he was good at the chitchat that the bazaars, tea parties, evening socials – the heart of church life – entailed. Jumble sales were his favourite. Yes, studying for the Anglican priesthood was probably a fine idea.

Ernst enjoyed his four years at Trinity College. The study of Hebrew, Greek and Latin was not so much a chore as a pleasure, and he found his biblical studies stimulating – he received some distinction for a paper entitled "Wisdom in the Book of Job." His professors were often eccentric, but not vicious. And his social life was very agreeable; for the first time he was surrounded by like-minded companions and, to his amazement, he discovered that the opposite sex was attracted to him. One young woman took to calling him "Vicky" because, she said, he had the same wavy hair, plump cheeks and sweet smile as the Broadway actor, Victor Moore. Pretty soon he was Vicky to everyone.

One Sunday afternoon, towards the end of his third year, he was invited by his friend Walter Smith-Rowen to a tea party at the family home. There were a dozen young people there, pleasantly chatting away about nothing of import. During a discussion of the Broadway musical *Wonderland*, Ernst caught sight of a petite brunette with a heart-shaped face who seemed never to stop giggling. She wasn't that much prettier than the other girls but she had a light-heartedness, a sparkle, that he found charming. His thought immediately of *Cupido comyntas*, Eastern Tailed-Blue, with its shades of heavenly purple and little spots of orange. He asked Miss Lucretia Hollingshead to accompany him to a choral concert the next evening. Six months later they were engaged.

Ernst would have been deliriously happy if it were not for one sour note – his future father-in-law turned out to be another tyrant.

Lawrence Hollingshead was a distinguished scholar of medieval literature, the author of the *Dictionary of Old English*, and the prestigious recipient of the Arthur Blodsworth Award for his translation of *Beowulf*. His wife had died of tuberculosis years before, so that he and his daughter lived alone in the ancestral home on Sherbourne Street – a Gothic pile of yellow bricks, all gables and gingerbread trim. Lucretia warned Ernst during his first visit that her father's study was sacrosanct, and under no circumstances must he enter this holiest of places. Even the char hadn't been allowed in for years.

At first, Ernst quite liked Professor Hollingshead. A short, portly fellow, with a head of thick white hair, bushy eyebrows, and a bulbous nose, he had welcomed the young man politely if not with great warmth. What Ernst soon discovered, though, was that the professor was full of disdain, not just for him, but for all of humanity. Except for the few exceptions counted on the fingers of one hand, the entire student body and all his colleagues, every clergymen and politician that ever walked the earth, each shop owner and tradesman within his radius, were all stupid, pig-headed, blathering blunderheads. He never said much to his daughter's suitor, but his small reptilian eyes sent out clear signals – this young man was certainly making a fool of himself.

When he asked for Lucretia's hand in marriage, Ernst expected he'd be dressed down and ordered off the property. But the old man said hardly a word, merely shrugged his shoulders and shuffled into his study. In reality, Lawrence Hollingshead was hugely relieved that the responsibility for his flibbertigibbet daughter was being handed over to someone else.

"Hey, Pop, why are you puffing like that? You look like you've seen a ghost," Izzy calls out.

"I have. I'll tell you about it later," he replies. And, indeed, he will burden his daughter with the macabre spectacle he's witnessed, for she is his valued confidant. If there is one thing in his life that has turned out beyond expectations, it's Izzy. She is everything that he isn't − capable, courageous, intelligent. When he looks at her with that magnificent halo of auburn hair, those green eyes, her slender, shapely body, he thinks of only one thing − *Anartia Amather*, a nymphalid known as the Scarlett Peacock.

He's asked her to act as translator this afternoon, so together they head towards the Nateweyes house. As they climb up a short steep hill, they can hear Bob Taylor and Doc Happy Mac arguing on the other side.

"It is not your job to issue such rash orders," the Indian agent says in a loud, annoyed voice.

The doctor is equally angry. "If I had known that all I was supposed to do was inoculate babies, pull teeth, stitch up cuts, I wouldn't have taken this job. Supposedly I was hired because of my medical training and I tell you this woman needs to be hospitalized."

"You've made similar calls several times during this trip. And I will repeat what I have already said. The expense involved in sending these people to the city is enormous. The Department won't hear of it. If there is the slightest chance of recovery, they must remain where they are."

"And, as I've told you, the woman may well succumb to..." At that point the two men spot the clergyman and his daughter coming towards them and immediately shut up.

"We meet again, Reverend Wentworth. Good afternoon, Izzie,"

Taylor calls out. "The doctor and I have just been discussing Rose Nateweyes' condition, and unhappily, there's little we can do for her. Would you be so kind as to explain this to her husband?"

The four of them have to bend their heads as they pass through the door of the small log cabin. It's Spartan. A half-dozen beds, all covered neatly with frayed blankets, have been placed against three walls – a child of three sits on one of them, his huge round eyes taking in the crowd. A table with two chairs, one of them without a back, is set against the fourth. A wood stove sits in the middle of the room. The place is clean, the dirt floor having been brushed to a dull shine.

After shaking hands with William Nateweyes, the man of the house, the Indian agent and the doctor take up positions near the door as if to secure their escape. Ernst and Izzy peer into the gloom and spot Rose Nateweyes sitting in the corner on a blanket. Izzy immediately goes over, kisses the woman on the cheek, holds her hands. Ernst says, "*Tansi ekwa*, how are you? but then is at a loss for words. The situation is so dreadful.

Rose is thirty-four, and, before tuberculosis lodged in her hip, she was a handsome, lively woman, a regular church-goer and member of the women's guild that keeps the church clean and appropriately decorated. Now she is gaunt – Ernst reckons she's lost at least thirty pounds – and the ferocious pain has etched unhappy lines in her face. She can no longer stand or walk, but crawls about lopsided, on one knee, her arms propelling her forwards or backwards. "And still she manages to cook for me and the children and she keeps the place tidy," says her husband. "But she hurts so much. No medicine man is allowed here anymore, so please, you white men must help her."

After Izzy has translated, Bob Taylor instructs, "Explain to the woman and her husband, that we're very sorry, but nothing can be done for her. We'll give Reverend Wentworth several bottles of Scott's Emulsion to pass onto her, and some extra flour for the family..."

"You will tell them no such thing," Doc Happy Mac cuts in. Izzy and Ernst look at him in surprise – he's usually such a mild-mannered man. "You are condemning this woman to a lifetime as an invalid. Her hip can be replaced – these operations are done all the time – and she would surely walk again. She must be transported to an appropriate facility. If you ignore my advice, Mr. Taylor, I'll report you to the authorities, and I'm sure the Reverend Wentworth will back me up."

Ernst hesitates. He knows how much influence the Indian agent has and how he can make his life difficult, but when he sees Izzy glaring at him, he pipes up. "Of course I will, Doctor."

Bob Taylor doesn't want any more fuss, not in public at any rate, so he mumbles, "I'll take the matter under consideration," although he has no intention of doing so. He then shoulders his way out the door and tramps quickly down the path. Doc Happy Mac marches off in the other direction.

"Wasn't that an amazing scene?" exclaims Izzy.

"I just hope I haven't placed myself in a compromising situation," Ernst replies. He spots the disdain in Izzy's eyes. Oh why am I always such a gutless coward? he reproaches himself. Have been since my service to God began.

CHAPTER SIXTEEN

HE WAS LUCKY TO FIND a position immediately after his ordination, as curate at St. George's On-the-Hill Anglican Church. The Reverend Charles Goldsmith had been vicar there for thirty years. A big, bald-headed man, gone to fat around the middle, he had the longest arms Ernst had ever seen. These were always outstretched as if to embrace not only his flock, but the entire universe. Unfortunately, Ernst was not included. Reverend Goldsmith took an instant dislike to him. "My goodness! Just out of the egg, aren't we?" were his first words to his young assistant.

Ernst did everything he could to win his superior's approval. He took the early Morning Prayer services so the old cleric could lie abed. He volunteered to visit the most querulous of the elderly parishioners. He took over the boys club, arranging butterfly collect-ing excursions for the few who were keen. He presided over the tedious organizing meetings for the jumble sales, teas, whist drives and the Christmas pageant. And he worked hard on the homilies he gave when the vicar was indisposed. Nothing helped. Reverend Goldsmith was never harsh with him, never reprimanded him. And never bothered to give him a word of advice. Not once did he display the warmth that he showed everyone else.

Once Izzy was born, Lucretia complained bitterly that her hus-band was abdicating his duty to his family by leaving the baby and her alone so much. She became so distraught that she packed up her and Izzy's belongings and ran off to her father. "Told you he was a numbskull," Professor Hollingshead had grumbled, although he had done no such thing. Within a week, Lucretia had concluded that her father's misanthropy was even harder to bear than her husband's neglect. She moved back home, but Ernst realized that if his marriage was to survive, his duties would have to ease up a little. When he finally got enough nerve to bring up his complaint, Reverend Goldsmith showed some sympathy – "Not uncommon for young wives to complain, you know" – but Ernst soon realized it had not been sincere. The elderly clergyman hardly acknowledged his existence after that.

One Sunday morning in the spring of 1911, Reverend Goldsmith made an unexpected announcement. He was gravely ill. His retirement would commence at once. Although he wasn't surprised, Ernst was still devastated when he learned that he had not been appointed the old cleric's replacement. It took a while but he finally got up enough nerve to confront the vicar.

"For four years I dedicated my life to this parish. I am being passed over – for what reason?"

"It wasn't my decision to make," the vicar had responded.

Ernst had almost smiled at this prevaricating. He would have liked to say, "The committee listened to every word you said, you old reprobate. You could have recommended Lucifer and they would have done your bidding." But of course he didn't.

The priest mumbled something about church funds that had been imprudently invested. "It was among your duties to see that the financial people were on the right track." Since Ernst had chaired the finance committee only twice while the vicar was on vacation, he decided that the allegation was so ridiculous he brushed it aside.

Ernst was told he could stay on as curate, assistant to the new vicar, and, having no idea what else he could do, he agreed. But it was a hard road to hoe. Thomas Backhouse, the man whose job he should have had, had been a classmate at Trinity, and was regarded then as a light-weight scholar, a man of little substance. "But unlike you," Lucretia had unhelpfully pointed out, "he always went out of his way to be charming to his superiors."

Ernst can't recall how the idea of mission work first came to him. It may have been Reverend Arthur C. Ainger's inspiring hymn, "God is Working His Purpose Out." Even now the words send tingles up his spine. He begins to sing in his sweet tenor voice:

> From utmost East to utmost West
> Where'er man's foot hath trod
> By the mouth of many messengers
> Goes forth the voice of God.
> Give ear to Me, ye continents
> Ye isles, give ear to Me
> That the earth may be filled
> With the glory of God
> As the waters cover the sea.

More likely, the idea jelled during a talk delivered by a distinguished scholar from Christ Church, Oxford. "Of course, the essential work of the missionary," the visiting bishop had said, "is to carry the Gospel to those heathens doomed to damnation without it. But it is far more than that. The missionary is a holy ambassador. To the darkest corner of the world, he spreads, like golden honey, the civilizing influence of the British Empire, and the Anglo-Saxon race."

Now this was something a young clergyman could sink his teeth into.

"Who will go?" the speaker had thundered.

Ernst's heart had leapt. "Here am I, Lord. Choose me! Choose me!"

Once the idea had settled in his brain, he became obsessed with turning it into reality. The first big hurdle was Lucretia. They argued for days. How could she abandon the women's auxiliary she had worked so hard to build up? How could she be expected to compromise her already delicate health? How could a child be raised properly among heathens? What if they were boiled in a pot and eaten as stew? She was astonished at how ferociously Ernst fought back and, realizing he might very well go without her, she reluctantly agreed. "But it must be only for a year or two," she insisted.

Lucretia's father presented the second difficulty. Professor Hollingshead had long ago concluded that missionary work did more harm than good. "Did you ever think the barbarians you are so intent on civilizing might be more civilized than you are? " he asked. "And what about my granddaughter? What are you trying to do, kill her?" Ernst attempted to lay out his ideas on how missionary work was tied to the Enlightenment and British civilization, but his father-in-law let go with a loud guffaw and roared, "Preposterous!" In the end the old man hunkered down in his study, wouldn't even come out to say goodbye.

The third hurdle, and the most serious, was the Missionary Society of the Church of England in Canada. These were the people who would decide whether Ernst Wentworth was made of the right stuff for such gruelling work. He had been warned they were very severe in their judgement so, when he appeared before the selection committee, his mouth was dry and his hands were shaking like a leaf. A woman of an amazingly wide girth began the interrogation.

"I see that both your wife and you have had your physicals and are healthy enough individuals. And we have your references from Reverend Backhouse and a lawyer, Mr. Dilly, who both seem eager to see you in the field. Now what we want to hear from you is why we should send you abroad?"

For fifteen minutes Ernst rhapsodized about missionary work until finally, reaching a crescendo, he promised to devote his life to "setting the heathens free from captivity of darkness through the glorious Gospel of Truth."

The Venerable Reverend Stuart Gilchrist, who looked not a day under ninety, was the next inquisitor. "Well Mr. Wentworth, you're certainly enthusiastic. But it's also essential that you have a solid, and orthodox, understanding of Catholic theology from the Anglican perspective. May I enquire – can you distinguish between Justification and Sanctification? As precisely as possible, please."

Ernst had been warned that a theological question would be asked and had been anxious about it. Relief! At university he had written a paper on this very topic.

"Justification is the work of Christ, Sanctification, the work of the Holy Spirit. Justification is the work of the moment, Sanctification is the work of all time."

The elderly clergyman beamed, "Excellent," and hobbled over to shake Ernst's hand. But the woman of wide girth was not so satisfied. She continued, "Life is hard among the heathens. It's not theological hair-splitting that breeds success so much as whether you can chop wood and shoot lions. We're looking for manly men – strong, gritty, enterprising individuals. Are you in possession of these qualities, Reverend Wentworth?"

Ernst answered with as much manliness as he could muster, but he knew he was on shaky ground. It was therefore a great relief when his letter of acceptance arrived. Later he learned that certain members of the committee had had doubts about his ability to survive in the bush or the jungle or the paddy field, but other factors had weighed in his favour. He obviously had no unorthodox notions, indeed not a single idea he could call his own; he would be "obedient and cheerful" in adhering to the Society's authority. Most important, he had a decent private income, an inheritance from his parents, so his stipend could be set at the lowest level.

At first he was assigned to Frere Town, Zanzibar to establish a mission for the children and grandchildren of liberated slaves. Lucretia hadn't liked the idea of travelling so far. "All those black savages. I can't sleep at night thinking about their naked bodies." So Ernst was relieved when, after negotiations between the Sultan and the British government broke down, he was told he was being sent to northern Saskatchewan to convert infidels "in our own domain."

"I have something I must tell you." Ernst says to his daughter. He then relates what had occurred in Arthur Jan's storehouse. Izzy is troubled by what she hears. "You know, Pop, I've had this sense that something weird is going on around here." At that moment Bibiane Ratt himself comes striding towards them. He smiles his snarly, cynical smile, "Afternoon, Reverend, afternoon, Miss. Any word about Rose Nateweyes? If they decide to take her to the hospital, we'd be glad to transport her there."

"For a large fee, I would presume," says Ernst. If there is one man in Pelican Narrows whom the clergyman cannot abide, it's Ratt. *Myotis lucifugus*. Bibiane has the same tiny eyes, pushed up faced and sharp little teeth as Little Brown Bat.

"I'm shocked that you would think such bad things of me. We half-breeds, baptised in the Christian faith, have been taught to live by the Golden Rule. Still, I admit that for those who are not kind toward us, maybe we would return the favour."

From his belt Bibiane pulls an evil-looking object shaped like a tomahawk. "Reverend, I'm sure, as an educated man, you'll be interested in this. You see, the handle is made from the rib of a moose. A slot has been carved out and the copper blade lodged just so. It might be very old but it's still sharp as any knife of today. Let me show you."

Bibiane grabs Ernst's wrist, twisting his arm upwards, then grazes the blade along the clergyman's skin. Next he makes a sweeping motion from Ernst's forehead to the back of his neck, the knife only inches away from his skull. "It was the custom of our ancestors to scalp their enemies. Once they cut the flesh away, they scraped and scraped until it was clean as a whistle." Bibiane begins to wring the imaginary scalp in his large hands. "They'd work at it until it was soft – a napkin to wipe their mouths." With that the half-breed laughs loudly and walks off into the bush.

There have only been a few occasions that Ernst has been truly frightened, and each time he had been ashamed at how cowardly he acted. Now, once again he stands frozen, petrified, unable to utter a word.

"Are you alright, Pop?" Izzy asks.

He doesn't tell her what an utter fool he feels. When he finally finds his voice, he merely says, "Things have gotten out of hand around here."

Izzy sensibly suggests that they report the incident to the authorities which in this case would be the Indian agent. Ernst knows what an almighty fuss Bob Taylor will make. If he is to keep his parishioners' trust, he must not enlist the help of a man whom everyone despises. There's only one person in all of Pelican Narrows, he can confide in. He says goodbye to his daughter and heads towards the cabin of Chief Cornelius Whitebear.

CHAPTER SEVENTEEN

WHEN ERNST FIRST ARRIVED in Pelican Narrows in the spring of 1912, the Grand Old Man of the Canadian Anglican Church, Canon James Mackay, was on hand to greet him. He was a living legend, for fifty-five years suffering every hardship imaginable "to bring light to the dark hearts of Canada's savages." At age 82 he was grey and stooped, but judging from his handshake, he was stronger than most men two-thirds his age, including, of course, Ernst Wentworth.

"I was expecting a wife and child. Where are they?" the old cleric had demanded.

"We thought it best that they remain in Toronto until I could be sure that the living conditions were adequate," said Ernst, bowing meekly before this luminary.

"What a lot of bother," Canon Mackay snorted. "Why, a rajah would feel right at home here."

Ernst wouldn't have called the rectory luxurious but certainly it was comfortable. A solidly-built wooden structure, it was surprisingly large, with a dining room, parlour, two bedrooms, and a kitchen in a lean-to at the back. Ernst complimented Canon Mackay on both the rectory and the church, which was equally as grand. The old man replied, "I built both these places myself. With very little help from my parishioners, I must say. I wanted Our Lord to be well represented here. You can see the result."

The rectory *was* nicely appointed, much of the furniture having been crafted by Canon Mackay himself. There was a wood-burning stove in the parlour and even though the weather was mild, a fire had been lit. The elderly clergyman settled himself beside it in an overstuffed easy chair, put his moccasined feet up on an ottoman, and motioned for Ernst to park himself beside him. Then he began to talk, and talk, and talk. For three straight days Canon Mackay wound fantastic tales of heroic exploits, all involving himself, until Ernst felt benumbed, bewildered and totally inadequate.

The clergyman did not see his job as merely "preparing souls for admission to the Lord's Table." Indeed, that was the easy part. His mission had thrived because of his expertise – as farmer, carpenter, painter, printer, book binder, wheelwright, wood chopper, fisherman, and hunter par excellence. "We would have been short of food but providentially I went out and shot three deer in one hour."

Over the years he had built up a farm at Sandy Narrows, a three-hour canoe ride from Pelican Narrows, where the only fertile soil for hundreds of miles around was found. His advanced years had not clouded his brain: he could remember the exact harvest yields – on average 200 bushels of potatoes, 60 of turnips, 50 of cabbages, 30 of carrots, 15 of onions. But the main crop was wheat. "And, boy, do we get plenty of that." Not only did he plough the fields himself, but he harrowed and sowed, carted the manure (from the cattle and horses he kept), and harvested the crop. He constructed a grist mill, and, when horse power proved unsatisfactory, he manufactured a huge water wheel, installing it in a nearby stream. He made the stove pipes to heat his house, fashioned harnesses and collars for horses from left-over materials, single-handedly built additions to the barn as his livestock "multiplied mightily." He thought nothing of walking twenty-four hours on snow shoes, "stopping only now and then for a few refreshments."

"I made a push to reach the fishing nets at Lake Athapapuskow that fall but it began to snow heavily, and grew as cold as a devil's tit. So I had to carry the canoe and, boy, was it a walk through hell. Over rough, jagged ice that had been broken up and frozen again – it cut through your moccasins like a hatchet through bear fat. Trudged for miles through fallen timber, the trees and branches creating a thicket right out of Hansel and Gretel. Once, the ice gave way, the canoe tipped over, almost all the supplies landed in the water. I made sure

I fetched them, even though I got soaked. Thank the Lord, I found a trapper's cabin, and there built a fire. It was comfortable enough, except my left foot was frozen. Never mind. Carried on the next day, another thirty miles." He talked on and on and on.

At first Ernst listened eagerly, desperate for advice on the most effective means of bringing the Indian soul to Christ. But although Reverend Mackay was fluent in Cree and had translated a Book of Family Prayer into that language, the only thing he talked about was the machine he had devised to print the little almanacs. He revealed how parishioners, even if they were far away in their winter camp, liked to bring the bodies of their dead in for funeral services at St. Bartholomew's, but instead of some guidance on how to deal with the grieving customs of the Woodland Cree, he described in excruciating detail how he had constructed the coffins. About the only time religion did come up was when he bragged about how he had outfoxed the various "Romanish" he encountered, by which he meant Catholic priests. "I knew the Romanish was at Deschambault, so I went to John Bird's place, with a few beads for his wife, some flour for the family, and helped him build a storage hut. In gratitude he promised to show up at St. Bartholomew's next Sunday. And you know what? He never had anything to do with the devil priest again." At that the old clergyman threw his head back and let loose with a raucous laugh.

Ernst began to feel that he was being smothered with words, that a huge balloon had somehow gotten into the rectory and was slowly suffocating him to death. When he had finally found the nerve to butt into one of the heroic episodes and ask how many Indians had attended the Eucharist service the previous Sunday, the old clergyman jumped up, grabbed his knapsack, clambered into his canoe and paddled away — to where, nobody knew. He did not wish Ernst well in his future pursuits.

It was Cornelius Whitebear who opened Ernst's eyes to the truth. He had been a church warden for years and knew everything about the workings of St. Bartholomew's. Attendance at church service had reached rock bottom because the Reverend Mackay had taken to tongue-lashing his congregation. Cornelius described how, as the old man raged from the pulpit, you could see his spittle spraying the air —"like steam from Nistowiak Falls, and just as loud, too." Jabbing his bony finger at the few parishioners who had shown up, he would storm, "Civilization has brought nothing to you but temptation. You have succumbed to every soul-destroying vice loathed by God — booze, fornication, games of chance. If you do not mend your ways, each and every one of you will suffer eternal flames of hell." For a full hour each and every Sunday.

Ernst also discovered that none of the usual infrastructure had been put in place — no women's auxiliary, no choir, no greeters, no chalice bearers, no altar guild, no Good Food Box program. The Reverend had declared that Sunday school for Indians was a foolish waste of time. And it soon became apparent that Mackay's parishioners loathed his much-admired farm. Ernst was surprised at this because he had read a half dozen stories in *The Living Message* promoting the enterprise as a model for civilizing Canada's Natives. But it turned out that the Reverend dragooned his parishioners into working for him, and the crop was often so poor — almost every September frost pounced leaving the potatoes black and mushy, the wheat wasted — that they received little of the bounty they had been promised for their labours. Yet it wasn't the old clergyman's dereliction of his duties that upset Ernst. It was something else that Cornelius Whitebear made very clear. Sowing the seeds of Divine Truth in the Indian heart had begun years before when the missionaries had arrived in the footsteps of the fur traders, and now, except for a few ancients who remained died-in-the-wool pagans, every resident of Pelican Narrows, and in the country beyond, were Christian, either Anglican or Roman Catholic. Why on earth would a missionary be sent here?

Until this moment Ernst hasn't noticed the black clouds scurrying across the lake. There's another thing about this place that frays his nerves. With hardly a warning, violent storms lash up full of crashing thunder and savage lightening. God booming out his message of wrath, he supposes. He reaches Cornelius' cabin just as the downpour begins.

Ever since he became ill, the old chief has taken to sitting for hours in a wicker chair perched on a rocky ledge overlooking Pelican Lake, protected from insects and weather by a canvas tent raised for him by his sons. So, despite the downpour, Ernst finds him there. A broad-chested man with a head of bristly white hair – he's affectionately called *kakwa*, porcupine, by his grandchildren – and a face that seemed to be made out of putty, every emotion expressed in his enormous liquid black eyes and extravagant mouth. Lately he has lost so much weight that his flesh hangs off of him, especially around the thick bull neck. Although he smiles, his usual joyful face is pale and sad.

"How are you feeling, my friend?" the clergyman asks.

"My time has come – I feel it in my bones. Soon, I'll pass to the other side. Probably by the time the snow falls."

Ernst is genuinely panicked. "Don't even think that! What on earth would I do without you?"

"You'll get by."

His usual straight-talking self, thinks Ernst. His honesty is the main reason that time and again he's been elected chief of the Ballendine Band, despite being an Anglican in a Catholic stronghold. But recently he had to hand the reigns over to Councillor Custer.

Two years ago, out on his spring trap line, he was chopping wood for the evening's fire when he glanced up at a gaggle of swans *kloo, klooing* overhead. In that instant his axe hacked into his leg. He was dying from loss of blood when his two brothers found him an hour later. After staunching the wound, they transported him as fast they could by motor canoe to medical help in The Pas. His life was saved, but his limb had to be amputated just above the knee.

The hospital furnished him with a peg leg, but the device doesn't fit properly, and all he can do is hobble about. A petition was got up, signed by every Pelican Narrow resident, whites and Cree alike, requesting that he be equipped with an artificial limb. The government responded in its usual fashion – too expensive; a precedent would be set. After that Cornelius faded. His wife claims that the thought of never being able to go out on his trap line again broke his heart.

Ernst is eager to tell Cornelius about his run-in with Arthur Jan and Bibiane Ratt, but just as he begins Mrs. Whitebear sticks her head into the tent and tells her husband he must come to the cabin for his dinner. "Nothing like my moose stew to get his strength back," she says. "Come, Reverend, have some tea."

There's a tacit agreement among the three that Ernst will not be invited to partake of the meal. It's a private joke they share.

Cornelius had served as Ernst's guide during the clergyman's very first visit to his parishioners' autumn hunting camps. After paddling for hours in chilly weather, they came across a trapper's cabin. Hospitality was the rule so, although the owner, Jeremiah McCallum, wasn't there, the two men felt free to make themselves comfortable inside. They found nothing to eat, only a little tea. Cornelius surmised that Jeremiah was probably out hunting. Ernst was so exhausted that he had collapsed onto the little bed and fell instantly asleep. He woke the next morning, his nose twitching. Beside him on the floor was a bloody mess of flesh, guts, skin, bones. Jeremiah had returned late in the evening with a moose he had bagged, rudely butchered it, and left the meat where no wild creature could get at it. The stink had been so terrible, the scene so savage that Ernst gagged when a steak was placed before him for breakfast. Ever since, he's had no stomach for moose. At least that's the story. Actually, over the years he has come to quite enjoy it, whether barbecued, roasted, or stewed. But he's never let on to Cornelius. He doesn't want to dampen the joke they shared for so many years.

While Cornelius picks at the food in his bowl, Ernst tells him about his encounters with the fur trader and his sidekick. "Human remains, if you can imagine. What on earth can they be up to? I haven't a clue, but I can guess that the Almighty wouldn't approve."

The old chief sits in silence, his huge face clouding over, tears welling up. He then utters words so despairing the clergyman feels goose bumps crawling up his arm. "It never stops. Our soul is being sucked from us. Our heart snuffed out."

He closes his eyes. "I see my *mosom*. He is hunched over crying, he who had never shed a tear before in his entire life. A white man stands beside him, a man of the Christian God. 'Come now, Whitebear,' he says, 'Remember your promise.' My *mosom* takes the drums from their hiding place under the bed. With shame in his heart, he follows the priest. At the Narrows of Dread he hesitates. The priest says, 'God is watching you.' My *mosom* hurls his precious things into the deep, rushing water. His music, his people's music, gone forever.

"You ask, why did a man as strong and powerful as my *mosom*, a trusted and beloved shaman, let himself be bullied by a scrawny priest? A simple explanation, my friend. Small pox had killed so many. The medicine man could do nothing. We lost faith. The white religious said he would pray for our people's recovery if my *mosom* obeyed. Heathen music was evil, he said, it shored up our superstitious beliefs. St. Peter would never let us through the Pearly Gates with a drum under our arms, a rattle in our hands. Every single piece was rounded up and either axed, burnt or drowned. That ancient beat, the old songs, were heard no more.

"It was only the beginning of our suffering. But I'm too tired right now to talk more."

Ernst is shocked by what he's heard. He always thought Cornelius was such a devout Christian, a loyal Anglican, a soulmate even. He remembers something Canon Mackay said. "For the Indian, Christianity is only skin deep; it never gets into the blood stream." Ernst groans. Another dilemma in a day full of dilemmas. And now he must face a council of war.

CHAPTER EIGHTEEN

ERNST WENDS HIS WAY down the hill towards the lake, passing a dozen log cabins along the way. High in the tree branches ghostly skeletons lurk, stark white against the black green foliage. These are carcasses of bear, moose, beaver that have been hunted, butchered and then strung up. He has always considered this display as a symbol of the paganism still dwelling in the Indian heart, a theory reinforced when Chief Whitebear had explained its significance. "It's so no dogs or other animals can get at the remains. You see, after the animals have been killed, if you show respect, they turn back again. They turn back to life and scatter in the forest again. They are willing to be hunted and we are happy for that." Ernst had reprimanded Cornelius, saying that he hoped he didn't believe such nonsense. Now he wishes he had been more patient in explaining the Lord's Truth to his friend. Confusion and doubt as the end of one's life nears must be a horrible thing.

Ernst's heart is pounding He's terrified of the coming confrontation with Étienne Bonnald. The priest is superior to him in so many ways. He's strikingly handsome – Lucretia says that with his sleek hair, now gray but still thick, his soft brown eyes, and his even features, he looks like a muscular version of the Mexican movie star, Ramon Novarro. Forever calm. Competent at everything he does. Beloved by his parishioners – unlike St. Bartholomew's, his church is filled to the rafters every Sunday. Authority is as much part of him as his shadow. And he gives every sign of loving God passionately. Ernst wouldn't be surprised if when he dies, he is beatified. Saint Étienne of the Woodland Cree has a nice ring.

When Ernst arrives at the rickety shack that serves as Pelican Narrow's post office, he finds Bonnald already there, though there's no sign of the Indian agent. The two clerics greet each other politely enough, although Ernst remains stiff and unsmiling. The priest's tone is soothing, patronizing. "I understand you've complained to the officials that I receive some sort of favourable treatment. I'm very surprised. I had no idea that you felt that way and it's really too bad."

This is what bothers Ernst the most about his Catholic colleague. He's never rude or disdainful; he simply treats the Anglican clergyman as if he was a junior, and rather stupid, member of the ecclesiastical brotherhood.

"I don't think it proper that we discuss the details until the Indian agent is in attendance," insists Ernst. He's promised himself that for once he will show backbone. He will not succumb to the priest's pleasantries.

"I had hoped we could settle this between ourselves and not have to drag in the authorities," replies Father Bonnald.

"That's why Taylor's not here! Once again he's done your bidding. This is exactly what I am talking about."

"Please, I didn't mean to offend. I've simply asked him to give us a half hour alone. We're both reasonable men. Surely we can sort things out between ourselves. The last thing in the world we want is to return to the poisonous past."

Ernst knows about the war waged in Canada's forests by missionaries competing for the Indian soul. You only had to look around; Pelican Narrows has long been a battle ground.

The village is shaped like a deformed lobster. A short claw protrudes a little ways into Pelican Lake and on it sits the Catholic St. Gertrude's. At the end of the longer claw, jutting further out into the water, is situated the Anglican St. Bartholomew's. Running up the lobster's back is a rocky ridge which divides the two religious communities as sharply as the Pyrenees separates France and Spain. The Anglicans build their cabins or pitch their tents on the side closest to their church; Catholics occupy the other side. The antagonism was fuelled years before by two representatives of God who loathed each other – Canon Mackay and Bishop Charlebois, Father Bonnald's predecessor. Winning over an Anglican to the Catholic faith and vice versa became a vicious, all-consuming struggle.

When Father Bonnald arrived at Pelican Narrows, he refused to engage with Canon Mackay, so the tension eased a little. Still the bitterness lingers. Ernst has broken up raging battles, a gang of young Catholics throwing rocks at Anglican kids after the Anglicans had ambushed the Catholics. He's heard of occasions when, on the trap line, a Catholic stole the furs of an Anglican, when an Anglican had turned his back on a Catholic whose canoe had overturned and supplies dumped into the lake. Chief Whitebear said he didn't believe these tales, they're so contrary to Cree tradition. The ridiculous thing is that few of the Indians give a fig for the theological differences between the two Christian denominations; it's simply a matter of which faith you happen to be born into.

While the two clerics make sure their disagreements are not hashed out in public, in reality they detest what each other stands for. Ernst believes that Catholic rituals are garish and hysterical, and, as he often told Lucretia, "Their beliefs are as dogmatic as those held by Brahmins and as superstitious as the Mohameds." Étienne Bonnald considers the Anglican faith as a pale, uninspiring and false version of Catholicism. Lost lambs gone to the devil.

Ernst is relieved when he hears Bob Taylor come rattling through the door – the priest's attempt to mollify him has been thwarted. The three men sit down at a table set up for the summit and the Indian agent pulls out a sheaf of papers from his satchel. "I want you both to know that, although in the past I have attended services at St. Bartholomew's, as a government representative, I'm charged with remaining entirely neutral in such disputes as these. I have here a list of complaints submitted by Reverend Wentworth. I suggest we go over them one by one." The two clergymen nod their heads in agreement.

"First. The Department deposits all emergency supplies with Father Bonnald, food, clothing, medicine, to be distributed to starving, destitute or sickly Indians. He alone dictates who gets them, and Reverend Wentworth feels Catholics benefit far more than Anglicans."

The priest's face flushes, but he maintains his composure. "It's true that I've been performing this duty for years but I adamantly deny that I play favourites. If Reverend Wentworth wants this thankless task, I'm quite willing to hand it over to him."

"Well, we've settled that nicely," smirks the Indian agent. "Let's move on. Father Bonnald has been authorized to judge if an individual has been so severely injured or is critically ill enough to warrant being sent, at government expense, to a hospital in The Pas or Prince Albert. Rev. Wentworth believes that far fewer of his flock than Father Bonnald's have been deemed eligible for such treatment."

"That might be because there are two-thirds more Catholics in this parish than Anglicans," retorts the priest who is struggling to maintain his control. "I'm quite willing to consult with you, Reverend Wentworth. You may discover such decisions are burdens that are hard to bear."

Ernst butts in. "Well, I'd certainly try and help poor Rose Nateweyes, for example. She is in such agony with her tubercular hip. Why, she should have been sent to the hospital for an operation months ago."

Father Bonnard barks his indignation. "I've been trying to do something for poor Rose for many months but…" Bob Taylor's even louder voice overrides the priest's. "Let's move on. We haven't all day." He pauses for a few seconds, knowing what indignation will follow – "Reverend Wentworth maintains that you withhold cash from Indians who have deposited their savings with you for safekeeping."

His face red with fury, the priest explodes. "Are you suggesting I'm stealing from my parishioners? What utter nonsense!"

My God, he's going to hit me, thinks Ernst. He quickly pulls several papers from his satchel. "I have here documents, signed with an X by specific individuals and duly witnessed, accusing you of just that – refusing to give back monies belonging to others."

Furious, the priest grabs the papers. "These are all on Northern Lights Trading Post letterhead, the witness in each case is Arthur Jan. Of course, he wants me to hand over their money so it can be spent in his store.

"I withheld the cash because their wives asked me to. The men get drunk on the brew supplied by Jan and they'd be sure to gamble it all away. If you, Rev. Wentworth, opened your eyes and saw how the Indians actually live instead of secluding yourself in that, that castle of a rectory with that fancy wife of yours..."

"That's enough, gentlemen," Taylor abruptly intervenes. "We are here to resolve these issues in a dignified and rational manner, not get into a brawl. Actually, I'm surprised at your belligerence since you have so much in common."

Both men stare at him.

"What are you talking about?" Father Bonnald shouts.

"Explain yourself," demands Reverend Wentworth.

"Why, Izzy and Joe! I'm surprised you don't know. They've been keeping company. I can hear wedding bells already."

Father Bonnald remains calm enough, but Reverend Wentworth looks as if he's been kicked in the stomach. His beloved little girl, his adored angel, being made love to by a savage! He'd rather be flayed alive.

LUCRETIA WENTWORTH'S SOIRÉE

Friday evening

CHAPTER NINETEEN

LUCRETIA HAS TO ADMIT that everything is under control; preparations for that evening's entertainment are well underway. The place is spotless thanks to Annie Custer's elbow grease. It's amazing. How could a squaw, uneducated, coarse-looking, inscrutable, turn out to be such a fine housekeeper? Lucretia has made it a rule not to tell Annie how well she's doing. Servants perform better when reprimands are delivered more often than compliments – that was a conviction long held by her family.

The finishing touches, though, have been left to the lady of the house. Lucretia places the wild roses and asters which she collected that morning in the only decent vase she has at her disposal. She unwraps her precious crystal sherry glasses and sets them on the rosewood commode. As glossy as burgundy satin, it's the one piece of furniture Ernst allowed her to ship to Pelican Narrows – "because it reminds you of your dear departed mother." Then she sorts through her books, pulling out all those written by Sinclair Lewis. She plans to set them up in a separate display on a side table which she hopes will impress the author mightily.

Thank goodness for her father. If there's any semblance of civilization in this place it's his doing. It's he, or more likely his secretary, who sends her *The Ladies Home Journal* by post every month. The recipe for coconut and chocolate cake, which has been baked especially for this evening's soirée, was found in its pages.

Since the professor never listens to anything but Bach and Beethoven, Lucretia thinks it a wonder that he always picks out the latest hits. She's pleaded with him to use the strongest wrapping possible. He does, but nevertheless half of the records arrive in pieces. But, God bless him, that doesn't stop him, and she has a nice collection from those that remained intact. Tonight will be all jazz and foxtrot.

But it's not Broadway hit tunes that have saved her life in this forsaken place. It's the books that he sends religiously four times a year. Sherwood Anderson, E. M. Forster, Willa Cather, Edith Wharton, D. H. Lawrence, F. Scott Fitzgerald – the moment they arrive she tears into them like a ravenous dog. If truth be told, she prefers Colette and Agatha Christie to Aldous Huxley and James Joyce, but she doesn't tell her father that. He's been trying to improve her mind since the day she was born, and she doesn't want him to think his efforts have been entirely fruitless.

Parcels are sent to Ernst too, mostly radical philosophers – Nietzsche, Marx, and Bakunin – but the covers remain unopened, the pages unturned.

Lucretia realizes that her father has not always been kind to her husband, but still she thinks Ernst should appreciate him more. Although servants drive Professor Hollingshead to distraction with "their ceaseless fussing," he did hire a housekeeper/nanny to look after Izzy so she could live with him and attend a proper school.

It's this arrangement that provided Lucretia with the excuse to travel to her beloved hometown for two months most summers. In June she would make the perilous journey from Pelican Narrows to Toronto to bring the child home for the summer. The first leg was travelled by barge or canoe to Prince Arthur, the next by train for thousands of tedious miles. In the fall the trip was reversed

Izzy was an angel on these long expeditions, Lucretia has to admit that. The little girl spent most of her time drawing – the train, the passengers, the landscape outside, anything that caught her eye. Lucretia would while away the hours making long lists of what she and Izzy would do in Toronto – The Royal Ontario Museum, the Art Gallery, the Canadian National Exhibition. Perhaps they might go and see the imposing King Edward Viaduct that had recently been built across the Don Valley. Why, just to ride a streetcar would be a treat. There would be visits to beauty salons, and manicurists, and the shops. Oh, the shopping! Those hours spent in the Eaton's Ladieswear Department – that was something she dreamed about the entire year.

During her stay, her friends lined up to give dinner parties in her honour. As a dweller in Canada's savage northland, she was regarded as the most exotic, and therefore most desirable, of guests. Of course, she exaggerated her adventures in the wilds. "The redskins, their faces hideous in red war paint, surrounded the rectory. A massacre for sure, but I yelled at them, 'You will roast in Hell for eternity!' and they ran away."

Paradoxically, the only time Lucretia truly feels like a missionary's wife is when she is visiting her hometown. Women's auxiliaries , the Girl Guides, the YWCA, church study groups – there were so many invitations to speak she could hardly accept them all. Naturally, she romanticized the mission work – "Our dear children, their faces glowing, knelt and recited the Lord's Prayer with such fervour that it brought tears to our eyes." But then she could hardly be expected to reveal how dull her daily routine really is.

For some unfathomable reason, Izzy has decided to spend yet another twelve months in Pelican Narrows, so Lucretia will be deprived of her visit to civilization for the second year in a row. She just might go crazy.

She winds up the gramophone, carefully places the needle, and begins to sway her hips – she's on the Palais Royale dance floor in the arms of a handsome man, preferably a sexy film star. In a Bessie Smith voice she croons:

> Bad luck has come to stay
> Trouble never end
> My man has gone away
> With a girl I thought was my friend
> I'm worried down with care
> Lordy, can't you hear my prayer

As she's sashaying past the front window she spots Florence Smith striding towards the rectory. The fat pugs, Artemis and Athena, waddle behind her. "Oh God, the battle axe is upon us," Lucretia groans.

When the Smiths first arrived to take over the Hudson's Bay Company post, Lucretia had high hopes that she and the fur trader's wife would become the best of friends. They would take tea together, gossip about the goings-on in Pelican Narrows, complain about their husbands. But it hadn't turned out that way. The gulf between them is as wide as the Grand Canyon.

The trouble is their personalities are as different as black and white, as dog and cat. For example, Florence is passionate about exercising in the great outdoors. Lucretia shudders just thinking about how that spring, just after the ice was out, she had spotted the big woman high on a rock about to dive into the frigid waters of Pelican Lake. She was wearing her wool jersey tank suit which obscenely hugged her large body. Why, just this morning she heard the children laughing at her, calling Flo a hippopotamus. That's exactly how Lucretia has described her to Ernst. Although he had laughed out loud, he admonished his wife, "But she is so kind and does such good work for the church. You mustn't make fun of her."

Most disappointing, the woman has no sense of style. Today she's dressed in her usual plaid shirt, canvas shoes and corduroy trousers straining over her large rump. She wears not a touch of powder and her grey hair is braided and then wound on top of her head like a coiled snake. Ugly as sin, Lucretia thinks. She, Lucretia, may live in the godforsaken north, but a lady she will always be and a stylish one at that.

In Toronto she always has her hair nicely bobbed, shingled and Marceled. Ernst has complained that it's too short, but she ignores him. Annie, amazingly, is good at cutting hair, and manages to preserve the style until Lucretia can get to a proper beauty parlour.

Even in the hottest weather, she will not do without her stockings, rayon if not silk, and her fashionable leather pumps. She's as slender as she was when she was twenty and her small breasts and narrow hips are fashionably boyish. The Flapper styles look divine on her, even if she does say so herself. This morning, she's wearing a bright yellow sun frock with a pretty white cowl collar and Mary Jane shoes.

Florence pokes her head through the door. "Ready to go?"

"Sit and have a cup of tea. We have time," Lucretia insists.

"Maybe some lemonade. It's so hot out there, I'm sweating like a pig. "

Yes, you are, thinks Lucretia. She calls Annie to bring the drinks and a bowl of water for the dogs who happily lap away.

"So what do you think of our visiting author?" Florence demands in her loud, vigorous voice.

"Very nice, very interesting, very witty," Lucretia merrily replies.

"I think he's a horse's ass. I tell you, something wicked is going on in this place and everybody's attention is diverted by this clown performing stupid tricks."

"What do you mean wicked?"

"To be truthful, I don't exactly know. But I've heard the dogs howling like mad coyotes every night for the last few days. I've seen the Cree elders huddle together, shouting and arguing as if they're in a council of war. When I'm out walking at night, I feel the spirits getting ready to leave this place. We'll be destitute, all of us."

"Maybe we should say a prayer." Lucretia meekly begins, "Lord bless Thy own and bring the heathens to the light of Thy truth..."

Florence butts in, "What a fat lot of good that will do." She bangs out the door, Artemis and Athena scurrying behind her.

By the time Lucretia reaches the fenced compound next to the HBC store, Florence is already busy setting up the tables. She seems to have recovered from her gloomy prophesising and is whistling while she works. Never mind it's hot as hell.

"Just thinking about that knitting machine you brought from Toronto," she calls out to Lucretia. "Damned thing never did work."

Florence always brings this up. For some reason, she thinks Lucretia's attempt to organize a knitting cooperative in Pelican Narrows the biggest folly ever committed by a member of the human race.

"Don't worry, Florence. I've learned my lesson. It's useless trying to do anything progressive here," she spits out.

She never gets the credit she deserves. These bales of clothing, for example. It's she who, on her trips to Toronto, makes the cajoling speeches to the women's auxiliaries, the IODE, the Junior League, the Women's Christian Temperance Union, any group that will listen. It isn't easy to persuade them to organize the drives, collect the donations and ship them to Pelican Narrows. But has she ever heard a word of thanks? No, never.

She had sorted through the donations the previous evening and discovered that this lot is a rich one. A black cloche hat with an art deco design in white was particularly striking as was a cape made of black Manchurian dog fur. There was even a silver compact, seemingly never used, with the initials EMS artfully engraved on the back.

"Whatever could that woman have been thinking of? " Lucretia thought. "Giving away such a precious thing."

She would have liked to have kept the better items for herself, but she knew that, with the housekeepers watching her every move, talk of her greediness would soon spread like an oil slick through Pelican Narrows.

While Florence piles the clothing on the tables, Lucretia tells her she's come up with a new plan. Each person can choose two articles from the children's pile, and these will be free. But there will be a small charge for items selected from the women's and men's stacks, and this money will be donated to the church to carry out good works. "If they have to pay a little they might appreciate what they're getting for once."

"Not a bad idea," Florence replies. "Don't think it'll work though."

Already most of the female population of Pelican Narrows has gathered outside the enclosure. Lucretia calls out, "Everyone, form a line. St. Bartholomew people in front, St. Gertrude's well behind. "

Florence will act as gatekeeper allowing only a few customers in at a time.

At the beginning all goes as planned. The first two women, both Anglicans, carefully poke through the piles, pick out what they want for their children, and then hand over a few coins for a dress and a pair of men's trousers. But just as the third customer walks through the gate, chaos descends. Everyone starts pushing, the Catholics crowding to the front, the Anglicans fighting to maintain their advantage.

Lucretia and Florence flap their arms and yell for order, but they have as much power to halt the bedlam as they would a charge of the Light Brigade. Stockings and jewellery, shirts and hats, corsets and nightgowns fly into the air. Shrieks of laughter spark out like fireworks.

Emile Ballendine pulls a rubber girdle onto her head and struts about imitating a chicken.

Mary Rabbitskin tugs a jersey bathing suit over her calico dress and pretends she's swimming across Pelican Lake.

Young Edith Bear has found a string of fake pearls, wraps them around her neck, and pulls them upwards as if to strangle herself.

Harriet Bird has dug up a pair of T-bar shoes with two inch heels and a rhinestone buckle. She stuffs her big feet into them and then hobbles about like a drunken bear.

They're all jabbering in Cree, so Lucretia doesn't catch a word, but Florence knows what's going on.

"You should be ashamed of yourselves!" she loudly berates them. "Mrs. Wentworth went to a lot of trouble to get these things. And you pay her back by putting on this performance?"

Most of the women look shamefaced, but not Grace Merasty. She has discarded her own clothes and now wears an evening frock made of silk georgette, with a low V neck displaying her ample bosom. The dress is a royal blue colour with a red rose pinned at the hip. She's donned elbow-length gloves, high heels, and a huge pink hat with a drooping brim. Just as Lucretia opens her mouth to compliment her on how nice she looks, Grace begins to mince about, crooning in a husky voice:

> Bad luck has come to stay
> Trouble never end
> My man has gone away...

Lucretia fights back tears. The woman is mocking her and everyone is laughing. She glances at Annie who *does* look guilty. Lucretia knows this isn't the first time she's been made a laughing stock by her housekeeper's gossip. How much mileage Annie will get out of that little dance scene she obviously witnessed an hour before, Lucretia can only imagine.

Oh, how she loathes this place. It's nothing like what it was supposed to be. Before she left for the mission, she had attended a three-day retreat at St. Michael's where wives of retired missionaries gave lectures.

"First thing," one particularly worn-looking woman advised, "set up a Woman's Auxiliary. You'll find the wives are often more responsive to the Christian message than their mates. We can't call them husbands, because most won't have said their vows. Sometimes one man lives with two or three women." At this, the participants had all tittered. "Often these are sisters-in-law or widows who are not able to feed themselves. Nevertheless, as missionary wives your job is to persuade them to get rid of all but one of these spouses. Then, you must insist that their union be sanctified by the church."

Lucretia had been inspired by the retreat, and began planning how she would transform the lives of Pelican Narrows' female population. She would teach them how to crochet, provide helpful hints on modern housekeeping, and form educational groups where she would lecture on such topics as famous women in the bible – she had even packed a copy of Artemisia Gentileschi's painting of Judith chopping off the head of Holofernes to use as an illustration.

But she was quickly disillusioned. She soon realized that the Indians were far more dexterous with a needle than she would ever be. They couldn't imagine owning a "Buck's Sanitary Porcelain Enameled Combination Range," the subject of Lucretia's first talk, illustrated with a rotogravure photo, primarily because they knew it would be years before gas or electricity reached their community. And finally, to her dismay, she discovered they weren't at all fascinated with Judith, or Hannah, or Esther or even Mary, mother of Jesus. Florence, who translated as Lucretia lectured, said, "Perhaps if you had talked about Kiskanakwas, the great medicine woman who converted to Christianity, they would have been more interested." But Lucretia knew nothing about Kiskanakwas, and had no desire to find out.

There was nothing to be done. She must simply be brave and endure this wretched place. In a few years they would return to Toronto, and life could begin again.

CHAPTER TWENTY

LUCRETIA HURRIES BACK to the rectory. She wants a banner painted for tonight's soirée: "PELICIAN NARROWS WELCOMES THE GREATEST AUTHOR IN THE WORLD." Since Izzy possesses the only artistic talent in the family, she was asked to help. The girl mumbled that she would try to find time between the races and the picnic and the translating, but Lucretia knows that she won't show up. Her daughter, it seems, holds her in little esteem. All her affection goes to her father, or to Florence, or to the Indians, Annie and Sally. A bothersome nag is how she views her mother.

It wasn't always like that. As a baby, with that halo of red, curly hair, sky-blue eyes and dimpled fat cheeks, Izzy was everything that Lucretia had dreamed of. The name Isabella seemed perfect. Ernst liked it because in Hebrew it meant God's Promise. And Lucretia thought of all the queens – Isabella of France, Isabella, Queen of Castille, Isabella of Austria. But the little girl was so cute, so affectionate, a diminutive seemed natural – Bella, Spanish and Italian for beautiful, was perfect, her mother thought. But, on the day of her baptism, someone came up with Izzy, and it instantly stuck. Probably a good thing since she's turned into such a daredevil.

As a toddler, she fell out of her crib and suffered a concussion; as a schoolgirl, she tumbled from the roof of a tool shed and fractured her arm; as a teenager, she smashed into a tree while skiing and broke her collar bone. Indeed, games of sport are the only thing she seems to care about.

Certainly fashion is at the bottom of the list. Izzy doesn't know a Chanel from a Patou and, moreover, has said time and again that she doesn't give a damn. How could Lucretia end up with such a daughter? It must be God's punishment for some past sin.

She's told Izzy often enough that she should be grateful for the loving childhood she's enjoyed, so different from Lucretia's own.

On their annual trips to Toronto, Lawrence Hollingshead always sent his big Buick to fetch his daughter and granddaughter from the train station. There were always soft beds with embroidered sheets and feather pillows. Thick towels, scented soap and plenty of hot water made for heavenly baths – a far cry from the tin can that serves as a tub at Pelican Narrows. The dinner table was always set beautifully, with brilliant white linen serviettes, fine china, and heavy sterling silver cutlery. The meals served by the maid were delicious, particularly the desserts – cakes and puddings made especially for Izzy.

Yet within minutes of their arrival, Lucretia would feel the depression descend, smothering her. She'd fight it, not wanting her black mood to spoil their holiday, but it was a terrible struggle. Memories of her loneliness flooded back to haunt her.

That her mother succumbed to tuberculosis when Lucretia was only seven is the tragedy of her life, she realizes that. But what she doesn't know is if her father's coldness, his cynicism and censure were a result of that untimely death. Probably not. Lucretia thinks now that there was something in Leyland's background – her grandparents were dead by the time she was born, so she doesn't know what – that moulded his hatred for most of the human race.

She sighs as she remembers those early years. Day after day she'd race home, eager to describe what happened at school, only to be greeted by silence, her father ensconced in his study, the dour Scottish housekeeper too busy with her washing and cooking to find time for the child.

Her salvation was her school friends, as many as she could cultivate. As Professor Hollingshead was a highly respected academic, their parents opened their homes and their hearts to his motherless daughter. The social whirl was what saved her from falling into the dark abyss. And now, in wretched Pelican Narrows even that has been taken from her.

Well, today will be different. Lucretia opens a carved sandalwood box where she keeps her precious things, and takes out a small perfume bottle. *Cleopatra's Boudoir.* She closes her eyes as she breathes in the heavenly scent. She pats a few drops behind her ears, down her décolletage , between her thighs. She's ready.

From the moment she climbed out of bed that morning she had admonished herself, no, no, no, she would not give in to temptation. She would control herself like the well-brought-up lady she is. But as the hour approached, her resolve melted away like butter left in the sun.

She's lucky today. Everyone is engaged in some silly activity or other so she won't have to take so many precautions to avoid being spotted.

She wends her way up the hill and then turns sharply to the right. The trail here is so overgrown it can barely be made out, there are fallen trees blocking it, and at one point a stream gurgles across it. Lucretia has been here many times before and easily navigates the obstacles. In twenty minutes she arrives at a small, windowless trapper's cabin which, since it's situated deep in a grove of paper birch and jack pine, is barely visible. She navigates through the small door into the gloom. She can't see a thing, but her nose tingles at that intoxicating mix of chewing tobacco and expensive men's cologne. She feels her heart pounding.

He comes up behind her, cups her breasts in his hands, presses his engorgement into her rear – like a battering iron, she thinks. He is wiry, and strong, and hard. He undoes the buttons of her frock, pulls first her dress and then her chemise over her head. There's a routine. She takes her right breast and places it in his mouth. He licks and sucks and bites until, in her rapture, she can bear it no longer. After the left breast has received its punishment, she takes from the corner the switch cut from an elm branch and hands it to him. He motions to her to lean over the rickety table, pulls down her stockings and panties. He whips her bare flesh, lightly at first, then more harshly. Red welts flare up on her buttocks. There is a rule strictly adhered to – he will discipline her until she cries out. She endures it as long as she can. It is so exquisite. Finally, he rams into her from behind. The bliss – savage, fierce – explodes.

He has not uttered a word, but once both are satisfied, and they have caught their breath, he says, "So, my Lady Lucy" – he is the only one she has ever allowed to call her Lucy – "I have a present for you." He takes a necklace from his pocket and is about to put it around her neck. "Let me see," she squeals, and opens the door a little to let some light in. From a leather throng dangles what looks like a human tooth.

"What on earth!" she cries. He grabs it before she can throw it on the ground. "What a reaction to something so precious! My dear, you're looking at our fortune. Soon I'll be wining and dining you in New York City."

He's hinted before that they might run away together. Could it possibly be true? What a scandal if she left Ernst! Far from feeling remorse, she actually enjoys thinking about it. She imagines telling her father, "A powerful, determined man, that's what you've always wanted for me. Meet Arthur Jan, a successful businessman, a lover of fine things, and, you'll be pleased to know, a devout Anglican."

One lovely spring morning Ernst's sermon had been particularly tedious, and Lucretia, looking for something – anything – to occupy her mind, zeroed in on Arthur sitting in the pew across the aisle. With his receding hair line, heavy black eyebrows, and long pointed nose, he could hardly be called handsome. Nonetheless, there was something rakish about him which on that particular boring morning was tremendously appealing.

"That jersey chemise suits you," Arthur told her at the lunch afterwards. "The soft gray plays up the azure of your eyes perfectly." She was astounded. That a fur trader would even notice what she wore never mind intelligently comment on it was miraculous.

Not long afterwards she had been out soliciting donations to buy wool for the knitting group. Since Arthur Jan was one of the church's major benefactors, she knocked on his door. He was delighted to see her.

"Come on in, have some tea," he said. "I'd be happy to give you a tour of my little abode." She couldn't believe her eyes – a virtual palace of treasures! The china, the oil paintings, the bronzes, the porcelain. From then on, whenever they met, they talked about nothing but his latest acquisitions – on one occasion, a Vincennes milk pot, on another, a porcelain cockerel from the Edo period in Japan. Lucretia came to believe that he was the most knowledgeable, the most intriguing man she had ever met.

One afternoon they met by chance on the trail leading up the hill behind the HBC post. He took her by the elbow, and, without saying a word, led her, not to his home – with the housekeeper in attendance that would have been too dangerous – but to a trapper's cabin.

Lucretia knows that depravity has entered deep into her soul. Everything that defines her worth – her family, her moral authority as a clergyman's wife, her God – are being darkly besmirched by her affair with Arthur. She should be devastated by her guilt, but all she feels is excitement, elation. The terrible tediousness of life in Pelican Narrows has vanished. She's intoxicated with the clandestine world that has miraculously fallen into place.

She believes that her sinfulness is as much Ernst's fault as her own. Caspar Milquetoast in the flesh. His whole life has been one caving in after another, the worst example being the fiasco at St. George's On-the-Hill. That wretched vicar, Charles Goldsmith, had the gall to blame Ernst for the financial scandal that *he* had spawned. And what did Ernst do? Turn his cheek and whimper into his pillow. That's how they had ended up in this dreary place, pretending to be missionaries.

Of all the many men who had courted her, why on earth had she chosen Ernst Wentworth? He was kind, that was a big attraction, and sweet, and good-looking in his round-faced, boyish way. Everyone called him Vicky, and there was something appealing in that. But, in reality, it had more to do with her father. Of all her suitors, Ernst was the one he disapproved of the least. Lucretia still has no idea why.

The first few years of their marriage had been happy enough although they had quarrelled. Because of his duties as curate at St. George's On-the-Hill, he was away more often than he was at home, and that made her angry, but it was nothing that a kiss and kind words couldn't patch up.

And she had relished her role as a clergyman's wife, performing her duties well, so *she* thought. It was a charming joke, the odd items she rounded up each year for the church bazaar's white elephant booth – a stuffed beaver, a likeness of Alexander the Great, a set of ivory toothpicks once owned by the Earl of Derby. She was thought to be witty and refreshingly outspoken, at least by those in the congregation who mattered.

Ernst had been overjoyed when Izzy was born and, no question, he's been a good father. But after his humiliation by Canon Goldsmith, any romance left in their marriage had drifted away like chimney smoke. And with the arrival of offspring, Ernst had decided that his conjugal duties had been discharged; passion in the marriage bed was now as rare as hyacinths in the Pelican Narrows' spring. Her husband's butterflies meant more to him than any human, with the exception of Izzy. Lucretia is sure of that.

CHAPTER TWENTY-ONE

IT'S ALREADY FIVE P.M. Lucretia hurries along the path to the rectory and, on the way, meets her daughter coming from the opposite direction. She hopes she doesn't look too dishevelled. After Arthur left, she'd combed her hair, powdered, put on lipstick. Still, a certain tale-tale odour might linger. But all Izzy says is, "Mother, you're all aglow. You must be excited about your party tonight."

Annie is busy laying out the good silverware and china for the buffet. By now the housekeeper is exhausted from all the work she's had to do for this stupid dinner. For days Lucretia talked about the menu but, of course, it was up to her, Annie, to perform miracles.

She's emptied the larder of all the delicacies in fancy bottles and cans that Lucretia brought back from Toronto and stored for a special occasion. The guests are to start with a *macédoine de fruits* – canned fruit cooked with syrup and then cooled in a big kettle set in the lake. Next will be served the main course – creamed chicken with bread croustades. Annie talked Angus Highway into giving up one of his precious hens; Florence has been prevailed upon to bake the crusty buns. There's a dish called Perfection Salad which has been nothing but a headache. Annie kept peering in the ice box, praying that the damn thing would jell, and somehow miraculously there it is, jiggling away. And then, finally, there's the coconut and chocolate layer cake. Lucretia takes credit for finding it in the magazine, but it was Annie who had to actually create it.

Lucretia chooses her best dress, a rippling, deep-violet, satin, flapper-style with a drop waist, the bodice covered in lilac sequins. To Annie it looks like a sack, albeit a tarted-up one. She thinks Izzy is much prettier in a slim-fitted, belted frock of flower-print cotton with a bow at the neck.

Lucretia, however, is outraged. "For goodness sake," she cries. "For once couldn't you dress with just a little style? You remind me of a farmer's wife."

"Annie thinks I look nice, and so does Father, so maybe you're the one who is wrong," was Izzy's impudent answer.

Once again her daughter has gone out of her way to annoy her.

It's a little cooler this evening, there's a breeze but it's still a blast furnace inside. Lucretia is about to tell Izzy to open the door when she realizes the screen has a hole in it and the mosquitoes will descend like an avenging army. Oh, the torment of this place, she thinks.

Izzy counts on her fingers the number of invited guests. "There are not enough chairs. We're at least two short. Sure hope someone doesn't show up," she says to her father who has just walked into the room.

"I'm sure Father Bonnald won't come. We had a major disagreement this afternoon."

Lucretia has been wondering what was bothering her husband – he's even more taciturn and irritable than usual. And, since Izzy has rushed outside on some pretence, she is obviously avoiding him for some reason. Well, Lucretia hasn't the energy or patience to deal with it now.

The first guest, Doc Happy Mac waltzes in arm and arm with Izzy. "Please excuse if I'm early," he beams. "I'm desperate for a taste of something that's not from a can."

"We're delighted you're here," Ernst says, and offers him some sherry. "We keep it for medicinal purposes, of course."

The doctor plunks himself down on the sofa, but he's obviously excited about something. "I suppose you've heard the news?"

Izzy, Lucinda and Ernst shake their heads no.

"The Famous Author is abandoning us. Apparently he's fed up

with roughing it in the bush. Sunday morning he leaves for The Pas and will catch a train there for Winnipeg and then New York. Mr. Jan's arranging everything. In fact, he's travelling with him."

Lucretia heart leaps. How will she bear Arthur's absence? And yet, what he told her this afternoon, it must be true. "Big metropolises, wonderful city, here I come," she sings to herself.

A loud bang at the door announces the next guests. Bob Taylor, Claude Lewis and Joe Sewap all try to get through the door at once.

"Hi folks," the Indian agent calls out. "I've just been telling Doctor Lewis here about our trip in the hydroplane this afternoon. Joe and I went up, and I can tell you it was a thrill."

"I was there when it arrived," butts in Claude. "We were in Arthur. Jan's store when somebody yelled, 'A flying boat is coming.' We ran out and joined the Indians heading for the beach. The big bird swooped down – you couldn't believe the size of it. I'll bet you it was twenty feet long. It landed in an amazing cascade of water and taxied right up to the dock. The fellow standing beside me said, 'I wouldn't have bet two nickels that that sucker could fly.' It's the first aeroplane the Indians in this place have seen."

Bob Taylor explains that the pilots were taking aerial photographs of the Churchill River and Reindeer Lake so that the surveyors could be more accurate in their work.

"They said they were finished for the day, but I asked them if they couldn't do one more short run. The photographer and mechanic didn't feel like going, but the pilots said okay, seeing I was an employee of Indian Affairs. Joe was standing next to me, I grabbed him, and away we went. It was wonderful, I can tell you, feeling the wind rushing around you like that."

"That machine was a beauty," adds Joe. "All mahogany finish inside. Plenty of room for the crew and all their supplies. They told me it used to belong to the Royal Flying Corps, left over from the war. Boy, would I do anything to fly one of those."

Abruptly he remembers why he is there. "By the way, Father

Bonnald has asked me to apologize, but he can't make it tonight. His brother's not feeling well, and he thought he'd better keep an eye on him."

Ernst feels a lurch in his stomach. "Oh Lord, I've made a lifelong enemy out of that priest. What will he do to me?"

Izzy says to herself, God Bless Father Bonnald for sending Joe in person to deliver his regrets. "Hey, Joe," she shouts, "why don't you join us? Plenty of good food and conversation." He nods and she beams.

At that moment Russell and Florence Smith arrive. They too had witnessed the marvel that afternoon.

"Do you know," says Russell, "at this very moment two American army float planes are hopscotching round the world. They reckon they'll cover 27,520 miles. Unbelievable!"

"That's all very interesting," interjects Florence, "but what I want to know is why the heck those surveyors docked at Arthur Jan's post rather than our place."

"Because that's where the gasoline was stored," Bob Taylor says sarcastically. "Maybe the old HBC should jump a little quicker."

The talk then turns to how weird the times are. Every day, someone is performing some crazy feat or other. "Did you hear about that stunt actor, Alvin Shipwreck Kelly?" Doc Happy Mac asks. "The chap sat atop a flagpole on the roof of an L.A. hotel for thirteen hours and thirteen minutes. All for the publicity. What an idiot!"

"And what about that couple in Cleveland?" Izzy adds. "They dragged themselves around the dance floor for a full ninety hours until they finally collapsed. At least they got a pretty good cash prize." To herself she says, I wouldn't mind doing the tango with Joe for the next thousand years.

"Even royalty is getting into the act," hollers Florence. "Did you hear about the Prince of Wales? He's on a tour in America and wanted to be taken to a dance hall. Once there, he pushed the drummer aside and banged away all night. It's a wonder that he's not deaf."

The conversation continues as lively and as interesting as Lucretia had hoped, but she is worried. Time is flying and her guest of honour has not arrived. She's heard rumours that Arthur's been supplying The Famous Writer with copious amounts of liquor. She hopes that he hasn't passed out, although she understands that an affinity for alcohol is certainly what one might expect of a great artist. She's relieved when the door opens and Arthur and Sinclair walk in.

Glancing around, the Famous Author booms, "You are to be congratulated, Mrs. Wentworth. You've turned this rectory into a palace fit for a king."

Lucretia cheeks redden. "Welcome, welcome," she gushes. "I can't tell you what an honour and a privilege it is to have a writer of such greatness and renown visit our humble abode."

Ernst gives his wife a look of pleading – please, Lucretia, don't make a fool of yourself. As he shakes hands with the two men and directs them towards chairs, he notices that his wife says not a word to Arthur Jan, indeed hardly glances at him. "Wonder what sin he's committed," he thinks.

Sinclair Lewis plunks himself in a chair, pulls out his cigarettes. Lucretia notices that, without even looking at Arthur, he automatically passes the package to him. "They've become great friends," she thinks. How wonderful. Soon she'll be sipping cocktails in the Algonquin Hotel's Oak Room, The Great Writer having introduced her to all manner of famous people

Once the new arrivals are settled, Bob Taylor continues, "We were just marvelling at all the bizarre fads that have taken hold in our modern society – crossword puzzles, Mah-Jong, fox-trotting, you name it."

"It's madness what people do. There were lineups for blocks and blocks in New York just to hear Howard Carter give a lecture at the natural history museum," says Claude Lewis. "He's that English chap that discovered King Tut's tomb last year. They say anyone who fools with the little Pharaoh's grave is cursed. I didn't believe a word of it until Lord Carnarvon, the man who put up the money for the expedition and was there when they opened the sarcophagus, was bitten on his cheek by an insect and died a few months later. Well, we'll see what happens to Carter himself."

"It's true, people can't get enough of Tut," adds Russell Smith. "But it's not only Egyptian antiquities they're nuts about. Last year that New York millionaire George Heye bought some tatty old blankets from Peru. I think he paid over $6,000, if you can imagine that. Apparently he'd do anything to get his hands on the relics of even our long-dead Indians. You've had dealings with Heye, haven't you, Arthur?"

The trader is taken aback at this. He waves his right hand across his face as though brushing aside the question. "I've heard of him, but never met the chap. Can't think of why I would."

Lucretia is desperate to steer the conversation towards The Distinguished Author and his opinion on current literature. "Mr. Lewis," she begins, "have you found anything here at Pelican Narrows that tickles your writer's imagination?"

"There might just be a novel stirring in this addled brain of mine. Arthur Jan here would make an interesting character."

"Villain or hero?" Izzy calls out.

"Both, of course." Everyone laughs.

"I've read all your books, Mr. Lewis," Lucretia pipes up again. "Some of them, three or four times. I loved *Main Street* even more than *Babbitt*. I know how lonely Carol Kennicott must have been when she arrived in Gopher Prairie. And believe you me, I could understand how she suffered when her efforts to improve the town were just laughed at."

To everyone's astonishment, Lucretia stands up, straightens her back, and begins reciting from memory a passage from *Main Street*. "'Oozing out from every drab wall, she felt a forbidding spirit which she could never conquer.' That's exactly what I felt when I first walked around Pelican Narrows. Carol complained about Prairie

Gopher, but at least there was a Main Street, and a drug store, and a meat market, and a clothing shop, and a hardware store, and a home furnishing emporium, and a Ford garage, and a shoe store – so who cares if only Oxfords were displayed in the window? – and two banks, and Ye Art Shoppe, and a motion picture theatre, even if it was small and showed only old movies. What is there here? A bunch of log shacks, two churches and two trading posts which carry only merchandise that appeals to Indian taste and you know how awful that can be.

"Carol had the opportunity to join a bridge club; they met once a month for dinner. Here the only people who play cards are Indians and half-breeds and..." – she glances at Arthur – "the odd fur trader."

Suddenly aware of the faces gaping at her, she attempts a joke, "And somehow I can't imagine myself part of that crowd."

"Certainly not playing strip poker," Russell Smith guffaws.

Lucretia ignores him. "Carol's set looked down on the immigrants, called them socialists or anarchists, but at least ideas were discussed. Here, the only thing anybody talks about is when the next mail is arriving. Sure, there's a class structure in Prairie Gopher, the town's upper crust were snobs, but, when they met on Main Street, the people at least talked to each other. Here there are the Indians and the whites, and never the twain shall meet.

"Carol thought she'd be the town's sunbeam and I did too when I first arrived at Pelican, but she, like me, found only 'misery and dead hope.'"

Everyone gawks in amazement as Lucretia's tirade grows louder and more passionate.

Ernst is stricken – could his wife really hate this place that much?

Izzy is embarrassed. How could her mother put on such a performance? Has she no idea of the beauty that is here?

Only Arthur Jan smiles. He looks like a fox that's captured a wounded rabbit.

To the relief of everybody, Annie announces that dinner is served.

Lucretia lies awake savouring how well the party went. Everyone raved about the food, the music, the conversation. As he was leaving, Arthur gave her arm a little pinch and whispered, "See you soon, my Lady Lucy."

It's the happiest she's been in a long time, but, of course, it has to be spoiled. Ernst, for some reason, begins to paw at her.

"Too tired tonight," she says as she pushes his hand away. Then feels a twinge of guilt. After all she does have a wifely duty. But Ernst rolls over and soon begins snoring, obviously relieved that his overture has been thwarted.

Lucretia hears the door close softly. Izzy is off on one of her night prowls. Any other place and she'd be worried about her attractive daughter, but there's no chance she could get into trouble here. There's not a suitable young man within two thousand miles. She's probably out star gazing again, her usual idiotic passtime. Lucretia falls fast asleep.

Izzy spots Joe in what lately has become their meeting place, a grove of white birches that tonight shimmer silver in the moonlight. He is leaning nonchalantly against one of the trees, smoking a cigarette.

"Want a puff?" he asks her.

Izzy has never smoked, not once. It was forbidden at school, of course, and she was not one of the nervy girls who snuck out the back door, lighting up butts they had found in some laneway. "Sure," she says, and casually inhales. He laughs out loud when she begins to cough. When she recovers, their eyes meet, and like two magnets, they draw together hungry for their first ever kiss. Except at that moment the militia shows up.

It's a straggly regiment, a mixture of Merastys, Birds, Ballendines, Cranes, Custers, Bears. Izzy spots three of Chief Whitebear's sons who are in their twenties, but eighty-year-old Isaiah Dorin is marching along as well. A few wear parts of World War I uniforms;

all carry weapons – rifles, hatchets, knives. At the head of this parade marches Florence Smith dressed in leather-kneed jodhpurs and an army coat. "Buck up, men. Hup, one two, one two," she commands.

Izzy and Joe remain hidden, but once the army has tramped passed, Joe bursts out laughing. "What the heck was that?"

"If you think it's a joke," says Izzy, "you don't know Florence very well. Whoever she's waging war against, you can be sure they'll come to grief."

FATHER BONNALD'S TEA PARTY

Saturday

CHAPTER TWENTY-TWO

ETIENNE BONNALD HAS ARRIVED at the unhappy conclusion that God enjoys playing tricks on humans. His elder brother had been a man of such sharp intelligence, clever wit, and joyful piety – their mother claimed that angels sang to him in his cradle – that Étienne had spent his young years worshipping him. Indeed, his very reason for existence, his religious vocation, had come to fruition under Ovide's guidance. And now Ovide is driving him mad.

Buzz, buzz, buzz, all day long, wrapped in his silly apron, a cigarette between his lips – he takes short puffs, blowing the smoke in front of him with exquisite pleasure which irritates Étienne to no end. Incessantly humming 'It's a Long Way to Tipperary,' he never stops shuffling about, dusting the furniture, peeling the potatoes, feeding the stupid rabbits which Étienne had not wanted and now hates, chopping wood, weeding his garden.

This morning Ovide is positively frantic. He leapt out of bed in a panic. His voice rang out, "The tea! It's today. We must begin the preparations at once."

Straight away, the two brothers quarrelled. Ovide was determined to serve cold tongue with a French mustard sauce. Étienne was against it. "Why go to so much trouble to entertain a writer of English, an American, who is probably an infidel, and certainly a blasphemer?"

"It was you who thought up the idea of an afternoon tea," Ovide shot back. "Why, I don't know, since you have no intention of being civil."

Étienne doesn't know either except that Joe had wanted it. "Mr.

Lewis and me, we became quite good friends on the Treaty trip. He gave me that fantastic knife. Would really appreciate it, Father, if you would return the kindness." And Ovid had put in his two cents – Everyone else is entertaining the famous author, how could the priest hold his head up in Pelican Narrows if he didn't do likewise. Étienne finally acquiesced. "Yes, all right. But it will be simple fare."

Slices of bread and butter served with Ovide's Saskatoon berry preserve was what he had in mind. But his brother insists on a much more elaborate affair. Besides the boiled moose tongue, there is to be on offer pemmican larded with blue berries – Ovide calls it *paté myrtille* – and pineapple sponge shortcake, since a can of the fruit was found in the pantry.

And, of course, every crevice of the rectory must be scrubbed.

Ovide begins his tasks by waving a duster in his brother's face. And this is a man, thinks Étienne, who once could recite Thomas Aquinas by heart. Fortunately, he has a legitimate excuse to escape the mayhem. The new chief of Ballendine Band is to be chosen this morning – the government allows such elections only when the Indian agent makes his annual visit – and as a pillar of the white community he must attend.

It's a lovely, breezy day. Peaked waves on the lake sparkle in the sun. Wild asters, pink-purple in colour, boasting bright yellow faces, bloom along the path leading from the rectory. They remind Étienne of young missionaries, so sprightly and eager to do the Lord's work, and yet so vulnerable in the hostile boreal forest.

As he walks by, he peeks into a tent that has been set up on a meadow just above the lake front. This is Doc Happy Mac's makeshift clinic. Cree kids, supposedly standing in a straight line, squirm about, making faces, laughing, jabbing at each other, as they wait to be inoculated against a variety of diseases. Harold Linklater, his face swollen like a Puffball, sits patiently hoping the good doctor will yank his abscessed tooth. And Mary Sewap wants her newborn examined – he has a bad rash.

Étienne waves at them and walks on. Soon he reaches the Hudson's Bay Company post, behind which a bald patch of ground has been fenced off. It is here that each year the Ballendine Band officially meets the Canadian Government. And, since Chief Whitebear's illness has forced him to step down, a by-election will be held.

Most of the Cree trappers have already arrived and are laughing at each other's jokes. Their wives and children, dressed in their best frocks of bright calico print, are milling about outside the barricade, although half a dozen women, mostly widows, have joined the male heads of households. Étienne thinks this is a good sign – the women are often wiser than the men – and he hopes Bob Taylor won't object. There's probably some government regulation against it.

The priest waves and smiles at various Merastys, Birds, Ballendines, Cranes, Custers, Bears, McCallums, Dorins, Linklaters, Sewaps, Morins, Highways. All nod back at him with enthusiasm.

"*Tansi ketishahen?* How's your health?" they call out.

"*Mithosin taskoch kitsha*, As good as yours," he volleys back, and they laugh.

Étienne spots Bibiane Ratt deep in conversation with Pierre Bird. The priest despises that shifty-eyed puppet of Arthur Jan's. Although Bibiane is a full-fledged member of the Peter Ballendine Band, his Cree father having provided his entree, in the past he has taken no interest in its affairs. So what's he doing here?

Traditionally, the Indians crouched in a circle on the ground, standing only when they had something to say. Last year, Chief Whitebear complained that they were being treated like dogs, so it has been agreed that this time they may bring something to sit on. Today, scattered about, are rickety willow-branch chairs, bear-skin blankets, old satchels, shipping crates, canvas sleeping bags, goose-feather pillows. A junk heap. The priest smiles when he thinks of how this will offend the Indian agent with his ridiculous obsession for orderliness and decorum.

Bob Taylor arrives, and, after shaking hands with Étienne, he parks himself in a chair set out along the south side of the building, facing away from the lake. There they will be shaded from the sun, growing hotter by the moment. The only Indian invited to join them is Chief Whitebear. He was determined to show up for what he suspects will be his last gathering of the tribe. But he is so pale and emaciated that those who haven't seen him for a while are shocked.

Ernst Wentworth comes prancing in, smiling and bowing – like an organ grinder's monkey, thinks Étienne. The priest is still rattled from the previous evening's confrontation. Imagine being accused of stealing from your parishioners! With Arthur Jan, no less, as accomplice! Doesn't Wentworth know what kind of man this is? The fur trader doesn't just cheat the Indians, he mauls them like a wolf devouring rabbits.

The Anglican should have been witness to what Étienne had seen on a fact-finding mission to the Churchill River two weeks ago, where a hydro dam is being constructed. There had been bitter complaints about the living conditions there, and the priest quickly discovered why. The Cree, who did the hard labour, were paid 30 cents an hour – not in cash but in groceries. The little company store was pretty well stocked – anything Crosse & Blackwell could stuff in a tin could be found there, including olives to be served in martinis. Of course, only for the white population, those with the important, albeit temporary, jobs. Indians were not allowed to even set foot in the store. Their meagre groceries were shoved at them through a little window at the back.

Arthur Jan had been contracted to bring in food supplies with the understanding that he would be as economical as possible, and he came up with a brilliant idea. Pay the Indians with the half-eaten ham sandwiches the white bosses enjoyed at lunch and the left-over roast beef from their Sunday dinners. "There was a bone, but it only had a little bit of meat on it," Ronald Ballendine had complained. And Arthur Jan had been handed a nice bonus for this ingenious cost-cutting. When Étienne heard about it, he confronted him.

"At least it wasn't baloney," the fur trader sneered. If Étienne hadn't been wearing his clerical collar, he would have punched the man in the mouth. He hopes that today Jan will at last get his comeuppance.

Agent Taylor is about to begin the proceedings when Dr. Lewis, followed by his brother, The Famous Writer, comes strolling into the compound. Two stools are quickly rounded up for them. Étienne feels that what goes on here is no business of theirs, but he decides that for once he will be civil and not cause a fuss. Not long ago he wouldn't have given a damn what anyone thought, he would have objected in no uncertain terms. "I've become complacent in my old age," he sighs to himself.

Joe Sewap steps forward. He is to act as translator. In the past, Étienne had been obliged to perform this task, so he feels enormous relief, and pride, that his protégé has become so capable.

Taylor begins by welcoming everyone. He then asks one of the elders, Charley Linklater, to step up. Charley's speech is simple. Turning towards the beloved old man, he says, "Chief Whitebear, all of us, we give thanks to you. You have given your life for us. We will always remember and love you." Everyone claps and hoots their respect.

The old man struggles to stand, gives a little bow, then collapses back into the chair.

The Indian agent then reminds the crowd that this is their opportunity for the Department of Indian Affairs to hear their grievances and requests. Once Joe finishes rendering the English into Cree, Noah Ballendine, who is dressed to the nines because he's running for the chief's job, jumps to his feet.

"Same complaint," he says. "White trappers come into the country in the winter and set out poison in the bait. Beaver are all but wiped out. Other creatures eat the carcasses, including our dogs. Fourteen died last year. Agonizing deaths, vomit everywhere. You tell us we have to leave the white trappers alone, that you will handle it, but nothing ever happens."

He certainly has a point, thinks Étienne. There is a law against lacing the bait with strychnine. Why don't the police search the gear of these white trappers on their way in? Why aren't druggists prohibited from selling the stuff? He knows what Joe would say — because the government doesn't give a rat's ass about the Indian.

Noah pushes his fancy sunglasses back on his nose, and continues. "The same thing goes for white fishermen. They leave the guts lying on the ice. In the spring the rivers and lakes get poisoned, the newly-spawned fish die. We see them floating on the surface. And we're supposed to drink this crappy water."

The crowd claps enthusiastically. "It's true what he's saying," several yell out.

All the Indian agent can do is nod his head up and down like one of those plastic birds that decorate highball glasses. Every year he sends a list of complaints to the Department but nothing ever changes. With a stern face, he promises, "I'll notify the authorities of these issues. They'll be dealt with as quickly as possible."

"And wild roses will bloom in January," Étienne says to himself.

Then comes the usual requests for provisions — nails, fishing twine, window glass, carpentry tools, ammunition, a light plough and harrow, a bobsleigh. There is particular dissatisfaction with the flour that was part of last year's rations. Emanuel Bear yells out, "It was so poor my wife couldn't even make bannock out of it. It's old and mouldy, probably been sitting in the HBC warehouse for years."

The Indian agent industriously notes everything down, although even he understands that this is a futile exercise. The government is niggardly to the point of foolishness, even cruelty. Étienne still becomes infuriated whenever he thinks of the cavalier and demeaning manner bureaucrats dismissed a proposal that Joe and two friends had put together the previous year.

When the lakes are free of ice, the young men of the Peter

Ballendine Band are hired by the trading companies to transport supplies by canoe to the various posts. The money is good – $25 for a
round trip to Sturgeon Landing, $35 to South Reindeer Lake and
back. Why not carry on the business in the winter? All that was
needed was a team of horses, harnesses, and sleighs, and they would
be set to haul on the winter ice roads.

Joe knew it wouldn't be easy, breaking trails through snow drifts
and slush ice, suffering the bitter cold and stabbing wind, shivering
through the night in open camps. But it would be worth it – for a
sixteen-day trip, a freighter could make as much as $65.

Étienne was amazed at how well the inexperienced young man
put together the business plan. He'd figured out exactly how much
it'd cost to keep the horses and how much profit could be made.
Even Bob Taylor was impressed, and said he would champion it with
his superiors. To this day Étienne's face grows red with anger when
he remembers the reply. An official wrote – the priest could imagine
the supercilious grin on the man's face – "This is surely a joke. In
two weeks we'd hear that one of the animals had died of neglect; the
other will have broken its leg. The last thing we should do is purchase
expensive items such as horses and sleighs for irresponsible Indians."

Étienne invested some start-up money of his own, and the business is doing okay, but the stupidity of Ottawa's bureaucracy
continues to enrage him.

Once the band's concerns have been heard, Taylor announces that
the election is under way. The chief's position is much sought after,
not only for the prestige, which is considerable, but for the $25 cash
and the spiffy new suit of clothing handed out every year.

Taylor hushes the crowd, and then announces that each of the
three candidates will be allowed to speak once. Since similar occasions
have gone on for three or four hours, Étienne is not unhappy that a
time limit of fifteen minutes will be strictly enforced.

First up is Alphonse Custer. He is a thin, shaggy-headed man of
thirty-eight, the bread-winner of a large family consisting of his six

children – three of them Izzy's students – his wife, his mother, his wife's mother, his wife's sister whose husband had died three years ago of tuberculosis, her brood of four kids, and his wife's crippled cousin.

"Good thing he's such a good hunter," Étienne thinks to himself.

Alphonse begins his speech by thanking the Indian agent, the doctor and the two special guests from America for attending. He then commences to harangue his fellow Cree. "You are all over-trapping. The truly valuable furs, red fox, cross fox, ermine, mink, are disappearing. The beaver is all but extinct. Even muskrats are small in number. This is foolishness."

A voice from the crowd yells out, "It's the white trappers' fault. They come into our country and take everything they can get their hands on without a thought to the coming years."

"This may be so," replies Alphonse. "But we too are careless, taking too many, especially the young, trapping the same territory year after year."

The speech will not sit well with the voters, Étienne predicts, but it doesn't matter. Alphonse is an Anglican. He doesn't have a hope in hell of being elected amongst all these Catholics. He's simply using the campaign as a soapbox to trumpet his favourite cause. Good for him, the priest thinks.

Next up is Angus Highway. This is the candidate whom Étienne and the rest of the white establishment whole-heartedly endorse. He is a heavy-set, bulky-featured man with a large head of brown-black surprisingly curly hair – how this happened, nobody knows – and handle-bar moustache trimmed regularly by his aunt, who cuts the hair of all the pretty boys on the reserve, including Joe Sewap's. Angus wears a dazzlingly white shirt and a maroon tie with pink polka dots. Where on earth did he get that? Étienne wonders. Probably an Anglican handout. Angus is a devout Catholic but his wife has decided, for some strange reason, that the Church of England suits her best. This didn't please Étienne, of course, but today it might be fortuitous. The Anglicans might be prepared to vote for the most suitable candidate.

Years before, Angus built a cabin at Sandy Narrows, about twenty miles across the lake from Pelican. The earth there is remarkably fertile, and his garden, full of cabbage, carrots, potatoes, beans, is a wonder. He also grows hay, which allows him to keep three horses and one cow. And he has chickens, the eggs so greatly prized by Pelican Narrows' citizenry that they will undertake the three-hour canoe trip to fetch them.

Étienne thinks Angus's speech is well prepared, although he has an annoying habit of dropping English jargon. "Holy Mackinaw" is his favourite, as in "Holy Mackinaw, *mackachisitino ana* he's trouble," or "Holy Mackinaw, *wicikisiwak kinosiwak*, the fish stink."

Angus begins by laying out his vision of a rosy future. A road will be constructed connecting Pelican Narrows with the outside world. Tourists will flock from all over to rejuvenate themselves in the unspoiled wilderness by fishing, hunting, trapping, trying out basket-making, birch-bark chewing, hide stretching. Tepees and sweat lodges will be built for all those thousands of white tourists who, Angus is sure, dream of becoming Red Skins, at least for a few days.

Fish processing plants and fur marketing organizations will be established. Schools and hospitals will spring up like mushrooms in September. Electricity and radios and hydroplanes – all are part of his dream.

"There'll be a grocery store to compete with the HBC and Arthur Jan's. Bring prices down," Angus promises.

"And a marina where you could get your outboard fixed," Joe interjects.

"That too."

The crowd, which has sat in silence, some half dozing in the hot sun, seem entranced by the speech. Then Angus's tone of voice abruptly changes.

"All this will come to nothing," the candidate suddenly bellows, "if our young people continue to give in to the devil's temptations."

Everyone knows what he is talking about. Some of the boatmen – Please, not Joe, Étienne had prayed – had recently returned from a trip to The Pas with liquor in their packs. There followed a raucous party during which a fight broke out. One boy was stabbed – thankfully the wound wasn't too deep – and one girl was later found to be pregnant, although whether it had happened during the debaucheries was hard to ascertain.

"I will put an end to this," Angus shouts, "if I have to patrol the beaches and bush myself. The Lord is sure to punish those who offend Him."

Étienne wonders if this harangue might not irritate the electors. But it's the truth after all. And he knows many Cree elders feel the same way. "Good going," he mouths at Angus.

The third candidate is the jaunty Noah Ballendine. His government-issue gabardine suit, allotted during his term as councillor, has been altered by his wife so that it nicely sets off his slim frame. His silver-white hair curls under a fashionable fedora. His small goatee is heart-shaped, his silky grey moustache and splendid sideburns well-trimmed. He sports large, wire-rimmed sunglasses, and carries a cane made of driftwood, the head of which has been carved into a bear's claw. A rake, thinks Étienne, but admittedly an intriguing one.

Noah speaks with absolute conviction. All the ills that afflict the Cree, the poverty, the sickness, the spiritual malaise can be laid at the feet of the white man.

"We signed the treaties in good faith and every promise made has been broken. Time and time again.

"Where is our medicine? Under lock and key at the priest's house." Étienne blushes at this. "Where are the provisions that were guaranteed us? We're lucky to get a piece of fishing line. Our land has been stolen, and now they are threatening to kidnap our sons and daughters, lock them up in a white man's school. We were once proud warriors of the forest, now we're nothing but slaves and toadies to our white masters."

Étienne, along with everyone else, is shocked. The passion, eloquence, militancy – nothing like this has been heard at Pelican Narrows for a long time. It's certainly irresponsible to fan the flames of discontent among the natives, but in his heart the priest can't help agreeing with at least some of what Noah has said.

Bob Taylor's face is screwed up in irritation, but he manages to spit out, "Thank you, Mr. Ballendine. I now declare that the election for chief of the Peter Ballendine Band is underway."

The three contenders stand in a line about three feet apart facing the Indian agent.

"The vote is called," Taylor bellows.

Everyone bustles about, lining up behind the candidate of their choice. When the dust settles, Noah Ballendine's row is obviously longer than anyone else's. Taylor, looking very displeased, reads the final tally – fifty-five for Noah, forty-eight for Alphonse Custer. The favourite of the white establishment, Angus Highway, has managed only ten votes.

Étienne feels irritation growing in his belly – this is not the first time his flock has ignored his advice. His one compensation, if you can call it that, is that Indian Affairs will certainly nullify the election and name Angus Highway in Noah's place. But that is hardly something to take satisfaction from.

CHAPTER TWENTY-THREE

THE PRIEST DOESN'T FEEL like socializing – there's such a racket going on with the crazy American writer waving his arms and bawling out war whoops while the real Indians roar with laughter – so he quietly extricates himself, and makes his way to his sanctuary hidden in an enclave of spruce and white birch on a plateau overlooking Pelican Lake.

One day years ago, wandering along a path that runs into the bush, he had come across a granite protrusion covered with emerald-green broom moss and silver lichen. He'd painstakingly dug up rocks and stacked them in a semi-circle in front of the outcrop. Slowly a grotto emerged. It has been his refuge ever since.

The insects are as ravenous as usual. After all the years of being attacked by mosquitoes, black flies, deer flies, and God knows what else, you'd think there'd be some immunity, some respite, but Étienne is as tormented as ever. He sighs with relief when he reaches the top of the hill – here there is breeze enough to keep at least some of the wretches away. He sits down heavily on the rock he uses as a prayer bench.

It's such a relief to escape the pandemonium below, if only for a half hour. Pelican Narrows is usually a quiet place, nothing much happening day by day. Except for once a year, when the Treaty Party sets up camp. In only a few days every important decision affecting the lives of every single individual must be made. All under the command of the Indian agent, a tin pot dictator who gives not a fig for the welfare of the Cree, or anybody else for that matter. And this year, the inclusion of The Famous Writer has resulted in a whirl of social events, including St. Gertrude's tea this afternoon. Étienne will have to endure the madness, but he can hardly wait until the whole kit and caboodle take off. In the meantime, he savours these few moments of calm.

On a ledge of quartz, protected from the elements, sits his most precious possession – a rough but lovely statue of the Madonna and Infant, carved from a piece of driftwood years before by a Métis parishioner. As if to salute the Mother of God, prickly roses, fireweed, and yellow aven had taken root at the base of the shrine.

His supplications to the Mother of Missionaries, as he thinks of her, come easily, his old rosary, with him since his days at Collège de l'Assomption, sliding effortlessly between his fingers. "Mary, Mother of God, have compassion on me." He asks once again that she intervene with the Sacred Heart to forgive his many trespasses, most of them to do with his impatience with Ovide. His mortal sin, the slayer of his soul, he refuses to discuss with her. But he will not, here in this his private place, pray directly to the Almighty. Étienne believes Him to be a cruel, unjust and vengeful God. He doesn't deny His existence. He just despises Him.

The priest's disillusionment began to incubate shortly after his arrival at Cumberland House, his first posting as a missionary. Word came one day that a Diphtheria epidemic had broken out. He rushed to his parishioners' hunting camp about ten miles away. Hell on earth was what he thought as the stench from the first log hut accosted him. A dozen people, rolled up in soiled, tattered blankets were stretched out on the ground – he had to watch that he didn`t tread on an arm or leg, they lay so close together. Two of the bundles turned out to be corpses, the others hovered near death. Having long ago vomited everything in their stomachs, several of the ill were retching painfully. A high-pitched keening – like a fatally injured dog – was the most unsettling sound of all. When Étienne was finally able to pry the baby from the grieving mother`s arms, he found that the infant had departed this life some hours before.

The priest ran around administering last rites, although few of the victims seemed to have any idea what he was doing. He tried to help, cleaning up the putrid throw-up, washing faces and bodies, trickling water down throats. But he knew that in this, his first test as a missionary, he was an utter failure. No one was comforted by his words because he spoke no Cree. Right then, he pledged that either their way of life would become his or he would give up his vocation.

His study of Indian languages – he is now fluent in several of them – was the easiest part. Far more difficult was overcoming the scepticism that took hold in his mind, like bindweed choking a rose bush. What kind of God would inflict torture on such guileless people? If he had had time to ponder the question, he might have given in to despair, but all his energy went to surviving the brutal country.

His first posting, St. Joseph Mission at Cumberland House, had consisted of a single log shack, twenty-two feet square, with the interior partitioned by a blanket into a small room for the priest's bed and his few personal effects, and a larger space for the chapel. There were no pews. Worshippers stood, jammed together during services, one body resting on another. Not that Étienne celebrated mass for his flock that often. The only time his congregants came to Cumberland was during the summer months and, in the heat, nobody felt like being packed like sardines into what was jokingly called God's House.

His congregation consisted of twenty families of Swampy Cree living in the vicinity of Cumberland, fifteen families at Le Pas forty-five miles to the east by winter road, 100 miles by canoe, and another twenty located at Grand Rapids, another 145 miles to the southeast. It was Étienne's duty to visit them in their various camps, so that, during the twelve long years he served at St. Joseph's, he journeyed thousands of miles through the dense boreal forest. He always travelled by himself.

Since most of the neighbouring Indians were Protestants, Étienne did not enjoy the respect that Oblates working in predominately

Catholic dioceses usually did. He was required to pay for every little service – even his own parishioners held their hands out. And since St. Joseph was a poor mission to begin with, he ended up doing everything himself. Chopping wood, fetching water, hunting geese for his dinner, these tasks were no problem – his childhood on a farm hewn from the forests of Quebec had hardened him for such labour. Travelling was tougher, but in no time he taught himself to manipulate a canoe, even over rough rapids, and to handle a dogsled, mushing behind the team of big Huskies for miles in the coldest weather, his bedding, his trunk full of religious paraphernalia, his grub box, lashed onto the birch toboggan. The physical exertion, he felt, was good for his body, good for his soul. What almost broke him was the solitude.

He had been ordered by his superiors to have nothing to do with the Hudson's Bay Company employees. It was thought that the Indians had become debauched through alcohol handed out by fur traders, and, as well, HBC employees were almost to a man Protestant. Étienne followed this rule until he realized how ridiculous it was. It meant years of being cut off from the friendship he yearned for, from those who could have helped him improve his English, an important consideration since most Indians where he served weren't the least interested in learning French.

It was also drummed into him that to form personal attachments with his parishioners, *les sauvages*, was unseemly and inappropriate, and for some time he obeyed this order. But it had crippled him. To this day, bouts of *ennui* descend, so severe his mind topples into a black hole. He can't pray, he can't think, his body seizes up. The smallest thing brings it on – aspen whispering like conspirators in the autumn breeze, dogwood bushes turning yellow in late summer signalling the unbearable cold that would soon come, whooping cranes high overhead, garbling that they, at least, were escaping to the south.

Étienne hears twigs crackling. Someone puffing. He jumps up. The Indians, both his parishioners and the Anglicans, understand that his sanctuary is out of bounds so the intruder must be some dolt from the white community.

"So sorry to intrude," Florence Smith calls out. "I didn't realize you were at prayer."

"Actually, I'm not. Just thinking." Étienne is glad to see Florence. He likes this homely, warm woman so much. It's not that she's jolly, which she is, but that she is the only nonnative he knows that truly appreciates the Cree way of life. He pats the spot beside him and she plops herself down.

"So what are you doing up here, Mrs. Smith?" he asks.

"For heavens sakes, I've told you a hundred times, call me Flo like everyone else. I'm just bumbling about trying to get the lay of the land."

"Surely you know this territory inside out by now?"

"These days I feel like I don't know Pelican Narrows at all. Something weird is going on, Father. Something untoward. Last night the wolves were howling and there wasn't even a full moon. And that mysterious, anguished chanting that went on all night. You must have heard that."

Étienne shakes his head no. "I've become so hard of hearing, soon I'll be as deaf as a post. But please tell me what you think it's all about."

Florence is tempted to tell the priest what she witnessed that night – Arthur Jan and Bibiane Ratt ogling Indian relics they had dug up in the graveyard. But no. She's going to handle that nasty business herself. She gets up to leave. "Well, Father, something is going on that you and I can't fathom. If you do happen to discover what precisely is tormenting the elders of this village, please let me know."

Étienne has no idea what Florence Smith is talking about. But he has no doubt there's something to what she says. She has a deeper understanding of Cree culture than he does, or any white person he knows. And he hears the confessions of his Indian parishioners every week. Not for the first time he feels hopelessly inadequate and so utterly, utterly alone. He's felt this way for so many years.

His brother had been his one comfort. Ovide, too, had taken his vows as an Oblate of Mary Immaculate and was serving at St. Peter's Mission on South Reindeer Lake, a posting even more remote than Cumberland House. The two brothers spent hours writing to each other, giving advice, offering comfort. Sometimes as many as twenty of Ovide's letters would come in the same packet, arriving either by dog sled or canoe depending on the season. Étienne lived for those days.

They had so much in common, their family in Quebec, daily activities at their missions, the state of their own health, and the strength of their faith. But in the eighth year of their correspondence, Étienne noticed a change in his brother. Was it in tone, or temper, or sentiment? He's still not sure, but he remembers the first letter that worried him. It was a response to one that Étienne had sent to Ovide earlier.

"I cried a great deal over your letter, brother dear," Ovide wrote. "You will find my tears in the Sacred Heart where I have carefully deposited them. The Sacred Heart renders my tears sweet and delicious. To weep for Jesus is the greatest earthly happiness."

In a note written a month later, Étienne offhandedly joked that his parishioners sometimes got on his nerves. The return letter from Ovide was startling. "To be a missionary among these ingrate Indians is death to refinement, death to sensitivity, death to one's soul."

Such outspoken, and, to Étienne, distasteful sentiments continued to pour from Ovide's pen. One particularly distressful missive arrived in the spring that followed the ferocious winter of 1905.

I want to become a martyr. Brother, you'll say that's no small ambition and you'll ask me, 'Who will be my executioners?' This is very simple: they will be the mosquitoes and black flies; they will be the heavy packs I must carry on my back when I travel; they will be the children of my catechism class who do not listen; they will be

143

*their parents who fall asleep at each and every mass. And they will
also be my faults, my temptations, my pains, my privations.*

*I do not seek a little martyrdom lasting just a few hours, but a
life-long martyrdom. Surely God will be as pleased with this as he
would the short-lived suffering of the saints. I now realize I am
being burned at the stake, a slow fire that allows me to live perpetually in agony.*

Not long after, Ovide was celebrating mass for a dozen faithful
when he suddenly cried, "Oh my Lord, why have you forsaken me?"
Grabbing a metal poker sitting atop the wood stove, he swung it
wildly, almost hitting the head of an eight-year-old boy, the most
troublesome student in his catechism class. The slender priest was
easily subdued by a burly Chipewyan so that none of the parishioners
were hurt. Ovide's hands were singed, but only slightly. His mind,
however, was reduced to ashes.

He was shipped, comatose, to the Oblates' St. Christopher mission house. It took years for him to regain his speech and take hold
of any sense of reality. When Étienne visited him, he was saddened
to see that his brother's life had become entirely circumscribed. The
outside world didn't exist for him, people were of no interest. What
engaged him were the minutiae of daily existence – whether the
tomatoes were ripening, whether the sacramental wine decanter
was filled to the correct level, whether the laundry should be hung
pending a snow storm. He now saw his life's mission as insuring
that everything, and everyone, was well scrubbed and in their
proper places.

A year ago, the St. Christopher Mission underwent a 'reorgani-
zation', and, as a cost-cutting measure, Ovide was handed over to
the care of his brother. Étienne often feels that now it is *he* who is
being martyred.

The priest stands to stretch. These days his legs are often stiff and
sore, probably the joints wearing out. To the northeast, he can just

make out a bustle of activity. Men are running from Arthur Jan's store to canoes at the water's edge. He tries to spot Joe. The boy has been hired to help build the wooden containers that will be shipped as part of the expedition accompanying the American writer.

"The funny thing is," Joe had told Étienne the previous evening. "I didn't see any piles of pelts or rock samples waiting to be packed, so I don't know what's being carted."

Whatever it is, the priest thinks, Arthur's pockets will soon bulge with dollar bills.

CHAPTER TWENTY–FOUR

ÉTIENNE BEGINS HIS TREK down the hill. It's growing hotter by the minute and under his heavy cassock sweat is building between his shoulder blades. Many of the younger missionaries are rebelling against this type of apparel, at least when they're in the bush, insisting the clerical collar is sign enough of their service to God, but Guillaume Charlebois, the bishop of the diocese, is as old-fashioned and pig-headed as they come – Étienne can't abide the man – and he insists that full religious garb be worn at all times. Étienne doesn't really mind. He's been encased in this armour for so many years he wouldn't be comfortable wearing anything else.

The priest heads towards the low-slung log cabin shared by Joe and his mother, Sally. It's the neatest place in the neighbourhood, with a picket fence and patches of wild roses – Étienne has seen to that. He knocks quietly and, without waiting for an answer, walks in.

He loves this cozy place, today brightly lit by sunshine pouring through three glass windows. The wood-burning stove stands in the middle of the room, its chimney stack running at an awkward angle up to the ceiling. Étienne smiles. Joe's laundry, hung up to dry, dangles from it.

In one corner is an iron cooking range/oven on which sits a kettle and various pots. Étienne lifts a lid and sees that a cauldron of veg-etable soup is simmering. Probably either Annie, the Wentworths' housekeeper, or kind Florence Smith brought it. He's glad of that. It will go down easily, and Sally eats hardly anything since she took sick.

Against the walls are arranged a table covered with yellow oil-cloth, and a couple of wooden chairs. How many congenial cups of tea has he enjoyed here? Too many to count, that's for sure.

There's a cupboard in which tin plates and pretty porcelain cups are stored, and a long, low commode on which water buckets, cooking utensils and a glass oil lamp have been placed. A bearskin rug is spread on the floor. It's here that Sally used to sit cross-legged for hours, sewing, preparing vegetables, weaving exquisite birch bark baskets. Several are displayed on the shelves of a carved wooden hatch, by far the most elaborate piece of furniture in the place. Étienne had it shipped from Quebec and presented it to Sally in tribute to her twenty-five years of service as his housekeeper.

Above the door hangs the bronze crucifix which he presented to Joe at the time of his first communion. The boy's bed is on one side of the room. It's quite elaborate, the frame made of fancily-wrought iron – discarded by an HBC manager moving on. Sally's small sofa is on the other side. She lays there, tightly wrapped in blankets despite the heat.

"Sally, my dear," Étienne whispers, "how are you today?"

He doesn't expect an answer, and there is none. A month after Ovide arrived she fell into this bed and has been comatose ever since. Nobody has been able to diagnose what's wrong, not Cree specialists in herbal medicines nor Dr. Happy Mac after he examined her yesterday. Étienne has visited her twice every day since she fell ill.

He sits on the chair beside her bed, and tries to pray. Words soon fail him and his devotions peter out. He can do nothing but whisper to her, and hold her hand.

She was only fourteen when she came to him. Her family was part of a heathen tribe that lived in the hills above Cumberland House. He had made it his special project to convert them, with little success. Perhaps in gratitude for his efforts, although there were likely other more plausible reasons of which he hadn't an inkling, her uncle had shown up at the mission one day with the girl in tow. No man should live alone, he had blurted out. He was willing to give his niece to the priest. Étienne attempted to explain the reason Catholic clergy practised celibacy. The man had looked at him blankly and said he was leaving her there anyway.

As it happened, a new church and rectory had just been built and Étienne had been thinking about finding a housekeeper to clean and cook. So he agreed to take the girl on for a trial period. He thought that she probably would have no useful skills, but she was so willing, and, he had to admit it, so beautiful. Her thick lustrous hair was braided and parted in the centre which emphasized her prominent cheek bones. Her huge, almond-shaped eyes, black as a bear's, stared curiously at him. Her nose was small and perfectly shaped, and while she seldom smiled, her lips were always parted as though she was about to say something intriguing.

Since she'd likely never met a white person before, never mind a tall, stern-looking man dressed in an ugly black gown, he thought she'd be frightened, but she appeared simply curious.

"Happy to be your keeper of house," she said in Cree.

Étienne was surprised at how quick she was. Show her how to gently dust the inside of the tabernacle and thereafter she would perform the task perfectly. She cooked Indian style, of course, but quickly adapted to his tastes – no prairie turnip in the rabbit stew. Physically strong, she could chop wood like a man. She seldom began a conversation, but she would sit and listen to him rattle on all evening, although he knew that she understood only half of what he was saying. Just being close to her, all his fears and disappointments evaporated .

He undertook her religious education, drumming catechism into her head whenever he had a spare moment. "Who made you?" he would ask.

"God made me," she'd reply in heavily accented English.

"What else did God make?"

"He made all things."

Why did God make you and all things?

"For his own glory."

If he had been truthful with himself, he would have admitted she wasn't really keen about these lessons – she seemed to be in another space – but eventually he decided that it was time she was received into the Catholic faith. He baptized her himself while the congregation prayed for her salvation. Her parents had called her *Otipeyimisow*, Cree for "Independent," but if she was to become a Christian, her name must be changed. Étienne suggested Sally – he thought it as pretty as she was – and she had agreed.

In mid-January, six months after Sally's arrival, Étienne came down with a cold that grew more troublesome by the hour. A raging fever gripped him, a cough rattled his lungs. None of the medicine that he had brought from Quebec helped. On the third night, an excruciating pain pressing against his chest, he felt his heart beating out of control. There would be no Last Rites for him here in this isolated place. He prayed that, nonetheless, he would be welcomed by the Heavenly Host.

That night Sally's uncle and two other male relatives – he never did find out who they were – barged into the rectory, wrapped him in a blanket, and bundled him out the door. Étienne tried to resist – he wanted nothing to do with heathens at the moment of being accepted into the arms of Jesus Christ – but he was too weak to put up any kind of fight. They laid him on a sled pulled by dogs, and after a fifteen-minute journey, they arrived at a small conical-shaped wigwam. Several men were waiting for them outside. In his delirium, he thought the face of one was smeared with bright red paint.

They rolled him off the sled on to his belly, shoved him through the small slit that was the doorway and onto a bed of sweet-smelling balsam boughs. The blackness was so complete, he thought, surely I've arrived in hell, yet at the same time, he was curiously elated. A strange voice, high pitched like an injured hare or weasel, intoned what sounded like a prayer, although Étienne could not make out the exact words. Other voices, soft and low, began echoing from the walls. In a way he never understood, this bizarre chorus soothed him; he felt his panic begin to loosen its grip.

The singing suddenly ceased. A shape barely discernible in the dark waddled towards a heap of rocks in the middle of the tent, raised the bucket sitting nearby, and carefully poured water on top of the pile. A sharp sizzle sliced the silence. Soon Étienne was enveloped in hot steam.

He gasped for breath. The vapour seared his throat. He was sure the sweat pouring off his body would begin to boil. "Oh God, how long before I perish?" he pleaded, but the torture continued. More red-hot rocks were brought in, the water poured time and again. Then came a loud, otherworldly intonation which filled the wigwam, "*Onde, Onde.*" Voices echoing from hell.

Just as Étienne felt he could not endure one more second, the door was flipped up. The searing cold rushed in, hitting him in the face, pummelling his body. Gasping, he crawled outside and fell face first into the snow.

He had no idea of how he got back to the rectory or how long he lay unconscious. He was shaken awake by Sally, who was holding a spoon of greenish-yellow syrup. She told him, "This is made from roots of squashberry, water smartweed, calamus, and many other plants which I can't reveal. Our medicine man mixed this for you because he thinks you're a good person." Too exhausted to resist, he allowed her to pour the concoction into his mouth. He was expecting bitterness and so was surprised at how sweet the syrup tasted. Soon he fell into a deep, untroubled sleep.

Étienne never figured out whether it was the sweat lodge or the medicine, but three days later he was fully recovered. It was an epiphany for the priest, the point at which he began to understand that the Christian God of his schooling lived in a narrow, constricted world. In this foreboding place, the supernatural existed in every crevice, in every tree, a guiding light, certainly not a vindictive punisher of sins.

Étienne spots one of the larger birch bark boxes that Sally had crafted long ago. It has been placed near her on a bedside stool. Good news! Perhaps she is at last recovering. The box is very special – a bright red cross has been beaded on the lid, the first indication that she had fully embraced Christianity. She had never learned to read, but Étienne hopes that the drawings he had painstakingly sketched for her depicting the life of Christ will still be stored there. Maybe they've become an inspiration for her. He lifts the lid, looks insides and sees a mound of scrap paper. The drawings have been shredded into tiny pieces. Sally's true feelings revealed. He is bereft.

CHAPTER TWENTY–FIVE

AS TIME PASSED Étienne grew fonder of Sally. She was so sweet, so compliant. Then one day, three years after her arrival, she announced that she was going home. She missed her family, she said. He was so disappointed – she was such a comfort to him. Even his fits of terrible depression had eased. Nonetheless he had no choice but to agree.

"Your job will be here if only you'll come back to me," he told her.

Not long after, he was reassigned to St. Gertrude's Mission at Pelican Narrows, over 300 miles north. She'd never find him now, he was sure. Then one night, a year later, he was surprised to find her standing at the rectory door. In her arms she held a baby boy.

He likes to tell himself that it was entirely her fault. Mid-January, a frigid minus forty degrees. She had said, "What if neither of us wakes up in time to feed the fire? Lying close to each other, we won't freeze to death." But he knows that that is mere delusion. The truth is more sordid. He had just returned from visiting his parishioners' camp near Frog Portage. As he nattered about his journey through the bitter night, she had rubbed his near frostbitten feet. She asked if he'd like more tea. He said no thank you, then stood up, gathered that lovely, young body in his arms, and carried her to his bed. He could no more have stopped himself than she could have resisted. And she didn't resist, he's sure of that.

When she disappeared, he had had no idea that she was expecting a child. She told him later she wasn't sure what would be best for the boy, to have him grow up among strangers or to remain with her family. Her father had argued fiercely that his grandson was to be brought up a strong, independent warrior of the forest. But her eldest brother had convinced her otherwise. The Cree way of life was changing, he said, and not for the good. Better the boy should know something of the white man's modern world. Despite her father's opposition – she wasn't called Otipeyimisow for nothing – she had found out where the priest lived and returned to him.

Étienne made her understand that, no matter what, their secret must be kept – both their lives would be ruined if the true nature of their relationship was revealed. She bowed her head and accepted his edict.

The timing was fortunate. Sally had left Cumberland House before her pregnancy showed, and, as far as Étienne knew, nobody at Pelican Narrows was aware of their previous connection. As for the child's appearance, although his complexion is a little lighter than most Cree, his hair is straight and jet black, the cheek bones denoting a Mongolian ancestor. The only thing that concerns the priest is those strange eyes. He often wonders if anybody has noticed that his brother Ovide's are the same brown/yellow colour.

An Indian father had to be concocted; Sally had insisted on it for the child's sake. Whenever Étienne overheard her weaving elaborate stories about the imaginary George Sewap, a hunter and trapper extraordinaire, an important medicine man who had been killed when lightning had zapped his canoe, he became irritable. The priest knows how ridiculous his jealousy is, how irrational, but nonetheless he's determined that, sometime before his death, he will tell his son the truth. Joe is the son of a Roman Catholic priest; his roots lie as deeply in Quebec farm country as they do in the Saskatchewan forest.

After Sally's return, their lives took on a semblance of normalcy. The mother and son settled into the little cabin Étienne built for them beside the rectory, Sally continued with her housekeeping duties, the priest carried on his mission work. The nights however were dark and troubled. He tried hard to fight it, but often the out-rageous craving grabbed hold of him. He would scurry like a besotted rat to the log cabin and slip into her little bed, hoping that the boy wouldn't wake. First ecstasy transported the priest, but then sour, degrading guilt assaulted him. And, to this day, it has not ceased.

Living in mortal sin as he does, he accepts that he is no longer God's representative on earth. And he no longer asks for His compassion. How could he? Each time he says mass, he partakes of the Body of Christ, and, since he will not make a confession, this is the most deadly transgression of all.

Dreams of his childhood haunt him, his mother weeping for her debauched son, his father railing at his weakness, his siblings, including Ovide, upbraiding him. He relives the rigid routine of his early years – the Way of the Cross, the rosary recited three times a day, hymns sung morning and evening, prayers before and after meals, signs of the cross over every loaf of bread ever eaten, devout readings by his mother, fasting, the blessing of the children, attendance at mass at least five times a week. Creation, original sin, the Incarnation, the Redemption, the Ten Commandments – he has been so steeped in the religion of his ancestors, he wonders how he can so easily shun their God. But he has.

During his annual retreats at St Christopher Mission, he will not allow himself the comfort of confession. That would mean the termination of his bodily bliss, yes, but also the end of his terrible mental suffering. Yet he has never seriously considered it. As the years go by, his love for Sally and the boy has grown – even to save his soul from eternal damnation, he will not abandon them.

Étienne lets go of Sally's hand, stands up, stretches. He walks across the room to where the laundry is hung and fondly strokes one of Joe's socks. Beside his bed is a bookcase and the priest glances at the titles on the top shelf. The Bible, of course, but also Jean-Jacques Rousseau's novel *Emile*, Zola's *l'Assommoir,* and in English, Hardy's *Far from the Madding Crowd.* Étienne smiles. His son, unacknowledged by the world as he is, has turned out as well as he had hoped. Étienne's love for this boy is sometimes unbearable.

He's had to walk a fine line with Joe. He can't lavish as much attention on him as he would like lest the truth be revealed. Teaching the son of his housekeeper to read and write was reasonable, but instructions in Latin, French and English literature, mathematics, natural science, history would be suspect. It had to be done surreptitiously. Étienne said, "First we finish our daily work and then we study." Long into the dark night, they laboured. Joe was clever, malleable and eager to please, reward enough for Étienne, although the teacher was a little disappointed when the student obviously enjoyed the novels of the English Dickens more than those of the French Flaubert.

Joe's religious education has not been neglected. Étienne himself might be damned, but he wanted the child to love the Son of God. By the time he was ten, he had memorized the four principle parts of the Catechism. Sally assented to this religious training, indeed to everything Étienne wanted, so he was surprised that she rebelled, forcefully, even obnoxiously.

He had made the necessary arrangements through an old friend, the principal of his alma mater, the Collège de l'Assomption near Montreal. It helped that no sponsor was necessary as Étienne had money enough to support the student. But Sally had shrieked with pain when he announced his plan. "Enough of this mean, spoiled white world. He must learn Indian ways," she had cried.

Étienne would have brushed aside her concerns, but, much to his amazement and sorrow, she had looked him in the eye and spat out, "I will tell the world your ugly secret if you dare send my child away." There was nothing he could do but acquiesce.

For three years Joe lived with his mother's family, mastering the art of survival deep in the bush. Then tragedy struck, the sadness descended, and Joe had come home to weep at his mother's knee.

Étienne brushes Sally's hair from her face and kisses her on the cheek. "It's time to go, my darling." Time to attend to a most unpleasant business.

CHAPTER TWENTY-SIX

AS HE WALKS ALONG the dirt path, he watches the brown, glistening bodies of the Cree children frolicking along the beach like energetic sandpipers. He remembers he and Ovide, also naked, also joyful, diving off a cliff into a deep, cold quarry. Their sister had spotted them there in that prohibited place and had told their father. They were made to kneel and say their rosaries while he beat them with a willow switch until their bare backsides glowed red. Mary, Mother of God, why does it hurt so? Étienne can still feel the bite of the lash, feel the humiliation at the tears. Yes, he thinks, it was their eagerness to escape their harsh father as much as their devotion to God that had spurred them on to become missionaries. He hates despots, which is why he has lodged the complaint against Arthur Jan. Outside of God, he is the biggest bully of them all. The hearing is to take place this afternoon.

Étienne has arranged to meet his star witness for a last-minute pep talk. He smiles just thinking about his first encounter with this delightful man. A couple of parishioners had warned him, "When you meet him whatever you do, don't call him Weasel. Otherwise he gets upset." So when Étienne shook his hand, he said, "Hilliard Morin, isn't it?"

"Just call me Weasel," had been the response. And, with his little moustache, sharp nose and beady eyes, he looks just like the creature he's named after. His personality, though, is very different. Étienne has never met a milder, kinder man.

Weasel uses a warehouse owned by St. Gertrude's as a base for his carpentry business. He's very skilled and much in demand. He's also a trapper *par excellence*.

Étienne spots Weasel through the door. He walks in, and the usual sour feeling washes over him. The dog halters, whips, and dried up pelts hanging on the wall are all that's left of what was once a thriving enterprise.

A month before Étienne arrived at St. Gertrude's Mission some twenty years ago, a forest fire had savaged the territory. While the village of Pelican Narrows was saved, the surrounding woodland was devastated. The priest had never seen anything so ugly. Mangled black trees lay across one another – he thought of Christian martyrs burned at the stake. Not only had the fur-bearing animals disappeared, but so had woodland caribou, moose, bear, grouse, ptarmigan, hare, woodchucks, porcupines, even rabbits. By January, the Cree were barely surviving on the few fish that could be jerked through the ice.

The manager of the Hudson's Bay Company Post at that time was a particularly obnoxious individual, haughty, opinionated and, as Étienne realized after one conversation with him, full of ambition. The way to get ahead, the man had concluded, was to be as stingy as possible with his native customers.

With the arrival of trading posts on the east side of Hudson Bay, a tradition of gift-giving had evolved over centuries. The Indians presented the white traders with their most valuable furs – an unusual pelt, a silver fox for instance, was especially prized – and the Whites handed over exotic European goods – lace, embroidery, silk, gartering. By the turn of the twentieth century, this exchange was pretty well one-sided. The HBC donations of canned foods, tea, oatmeal, often kept the Indians alive during those times when hunger threatened. But just when the need was greatest, the company abruptly eliminated these handouts, claiming it could no longer afford them. Étienne arrived at St. Gertrude Mission to find his parishioners near starvation.

Day after day, all through that long winter, he trekked out to the winter camps, to comfort his flock and to distribute flour, lard, bacon, bought with donations from charitable Catholics in Quebec.

In the spring the forest bloomed again. When beaver and muskrat appeared in the lakes, rivers and muskegs, the trappers set aside a small portion of their catch in appreciation of what the "good Father" had done for them. When Étienne returned to Pelican Narrows with these furs, he discovered that there were plenty of middlemen eager to buy them.

The business grew like wild fire. A trapper would bring Étienne his catch, the priest would sell the furs to buyers in Prince Albert, and turn the profit over to the trapper, thereby eliminating the mark-up imposed by the HBC. Étienne had a head for business and the enterprise expanded.

The HBC manager was, of course, furious at this assault on his trade. He decided to confront the priest face to face. Étienne had smiled pleasantly while he sipped his tea, but promised nothing, and the next day he sent over one pelt, ragged and dried up with age. It was meant as a joke, but it resulted in the gauntlet being thrown down. Over the next year a fur war had raged between the HBC and the Bonnald enterprise.

It was the Cree trappers who benefited. To squelch the business flowing to the priest, the Company had to restore gift-giving, hand over substantial advances, and pay decent prices for furs. Eventually, an equilibrium of sorts settled in – the HBC and St. Gertrude's each got about half the business. Then, one day, Arthur Jan showed up with Bibiane Ratt in tow, and the battle resumed with new ferocity.

Among Étienne's trippers – those hired to travel to the Cree camps and transport their catch back – Antoine McAuley was the most skilled, always arriving with the most valuable furs. One passion ruled his life – his sled dogs. Ciderboy, the leader with his bright blue eyes and orange coat, sharp-nosed Rainbow, Tina, sleek and jet black, snow-white Bud, smart-as-a-fox Reggie, burly Busker, and the joker of the bunch, Mickey. They were champions, having won the famous long-distance race at Nome, Alaska. Antoine's wife claimed he loved these animals more than his children.

One evening Antoine was calmly smoking his pipe beside his cabin's stove when he heard a strange growling sound. He rushed outside to find the dogs vomiting up black blood. After a half hour of agony, all six lay dead.

Word spread that Bibiane Ratt had mixed a poison with their food. Although never proven, it was warning enough for the devastated Antoine. He cut off all ties with Étienne, even stopped attending services at St. Gertrude's.

About the same time, Étienne received a letter from Bishop Charlebois pointing out that there was a long-standing, written agreement in place – Oblates could set up missions in the HBC-dominated territories as long as they didn't engage in the fur trade. Someone with inside information had sent a letter outlining the priest's operation in such detail that the church authorities had no alternative but to act. Étienne was ordered to stop trading or he would be transferred to another mission. The last thing he wanted was to be separated from Sally, Joe and his parishioners whom he had come to love so deeply, so he acquiesced.

One last grand sale took place in Prince Albert – six lots of furs which brought in the princely sum of $6,200. The entire Pelican Narrows population partied for three days on the proceeds.

In fact, Étienne was relieved that the business was closed down. His parishioners were beginning to see the church more as a market place than a House of God. And his conscience was acting up. He had taken fees for bookkeeping and other services, money he had banked for Joe's education and certain luxuries he hungered after – an expensive first edition of Walt Whitman's *Leaves of Grass* for example. But it bothers him still when now and then he hears Jan bragging about his great victory – "The priest's job is to save souls, not poke his nose into business he knows nothing about." Étienne thinks that everything that is corrupt and abusive about the fur trade is personified in this man.

The same scenario is played out over and over again. A trapper arrives with his season's catch. Arthur pokes at each pelt with disdain. "Look here, this one's torn and too greasy. That one's too dark a colour on the skin side, no gloss or thickness, dried up. Obviously caught summers ago. This bunch is almost worthless but, because I like you, I'll give you seventy-cents for each of these pathetic specimens."

The trapper squeals in pain. Haggling follows, and a final price of ninety cents is agreed upon, a good fifty cents below the going rate.

Russell Smith at the Hudson's Bay Post is a far fairer man, and many trappers do business with him, but many others, mostly those working area far away from Pelican Narrows, have become entangled in Arthur Jan's net. His bait is so enticing.

Since the fur business began, the traders had allowed the Indians to stock up on provisions which they then paid for with the next season's catch. It led to abuses. Some trappers got so far in over their heads they could never in their lifetime pay back what they owed. The HBC finally decided that credit would no longer be given.

Étienne has watched with dismay the repercussions of this stupid, short-sighted decision. Arthur Jan hands out advances like St. Nicholas does candies. He stocks the most modern goods, anything customers want but don't need – toothpaste, hard candies, canned meat, umbrellas, and the much loved HP sauce. And there's an added attraction in doing business with Arthur which the priest finds despicable. Every now and then Bibiane Ratt cooks up a batch of liquor so potent it could render a person blind if he drank too much, and this is sold for exorbitant amounts of money. Despite Étienne's warnings, many Cree have fallen for Jan's trap. They are so deeply in his debt that the fur trader can toy with them as he likes.

Emile McCallum for example. Last January Bibiane Ratt and two accomplices walked unannounced into Emile's cabin. They tied him and his wife to a chair, stuffing their mouths with rags. The three men carried in buckets of water which they used to put out the fire, the stack was removed and the handsome new stove carried off to

Arthur Jan's warehouse. Never mind it was 50 below and Emile's large family almost froze to death. No use asking the Mounties for help – the nearest depot was at Prince Albert, 300 miles away – so Emile pleaded with Étienne to intervene. When the priest did so, Arthur just laughed at him.

"That McCallum half-breed's a piker, a lazy no-good. But you can tell him the stove cancelled out his debt. My door is open to him again. He can pick out a fancy hat for his wife any time he likes."

Étienne realized that not only was there was nothing to be done about the man's predicament, but soon Mrs. McCallum would show up at St. Gertrude's decked out like a harlot, having picked out a new outfit at Arthur Jan's store. More debt for poor Emile.

The situation was untenable. The priest began methodically collecting evidence against the trader. Last winter he sent a barrage of letters and telegrams to members of parliament, to cabinet ministers, and finally to the prime minister. The effort paid off – an inquiry has been ordered by the government into Arthur Jan's dealings. Étienne is gratified; a reputation built up from his forty years acting as God's emissary finally counts for something.

CHAPTER TWENTY-SEVEN

BY THE TIME THE PRIEST ARRIVES, the little post office connected to the Hudson's Bay Company is packed. It is stifling hot, and the stink wafting from arm pits is breathtakingly sharp. He nods assurances at the Cree milling about. He's had a hard time persuading them to come forward with their stories and none of them look happy – Arthur Jan is such a vindictive man.

Normally, the justice of the peace would have presided over such a hearing, but in this case that individual is the accused himself. The Indian agent will take his place, although, to the relief of everyone, he is not to act as a judge but merely to preside over the inquiry, and then send the details on to Ottawa.

Bob Taylor, who sits behind a desk at the front of the small room, announces that the proceedings will begin, but "Only an hour will be allotted. I have not a minute more to spare."

Étienne groans. How is he to get the story out of these slow-talking, long-winded Cree in such short a time? He wondered how the Indian agent would undermine the investigation. Now he knows.

Hilliard Morin is called as the first witness. He swears on a bible that he will tell the truth.

"Mr. Morin," the priest begins, "would you please tell us what happened three years ago last April."

"I was out tending my trap line – a good season that, lots of beaver, muskrats. Weather was good so I travelled quite a ways – new territory, eighty miles east of Pelican.

"I sort of stumbled across it. It had rained, but that afternoon the sun was shining brightly and I spotted this white rock. It dazzled my eye. I looked closer and there was a gold vein running through. There'd been a lot of rock hounds around Pelican that year so I had an idea it might be worth something. I chipped a bunch of pieces off and put them in my sack."

"What did you do with them then?"

"I'd heard that Mr. Jan knew something about minerals so when I got to Pelican I showed it to him."

"What happened after you handed over the sample?"

"Nothing much. Mr. Jan told me he'd send the pieces I'd brought in to Ottawa, see what they were made of. Heard nothing, so kind of forgot about it. Then a few months ago, Mr. Jan told me there was a mine going to be built right where I'd found them rocks. And he wanted to thank me."

"And how did he do that?"

"He gave me some tea, a bag of flour, a little lard, sugar, a blanket, and five dollars."

"Thank you, Mr. Morin. You did well."

"And I thank you, Father Bonnald. You are always a friend to us Indians."

The priest then tells the Indian agent that he wants two documents to be included as an addendum to the complaint.

"I don't believe that's permissible," says Taylor. "We're supposed to be taking down witness statements only."

Étienne eyeballs the man. "If you refuse," he says in the sternest voice he can muster, "I will inform not only Mr. Krail, Director of Indian Affairs, but also the Prime Minister, Mr. William Lyon Mackenzie King, that you have obstructed these proceedings."

Bob Taylor's face reddens. The priest has always been a nuisance but never such an outright troublemaker. "Very well, but please, Father Bonnald, don't waste time."

"The first is the official registration of mineral rights issued at The Pas, on November 24, 1921 for 80 acres, longitude 101°, latitude 55°, the very place from which Mr. Morin says he took his samples and gave them to Arthur Jan. You see that those listed as claimants are Mr. Jan, Mr. Thomas Whitewood of Vancouver and you, yourself, Mr. Taylor."

The Indian agent looks as though he's swallowed a chicken bone. Without hesitating, the priest continues, "You will notice that Mr. Morin's name is nowhere to be found.

"This is the second document I would like included." He holds up a newspaper. "This is the front page of the Prince Albert Herald dated January 15, 1923." Étienne points to the headline: 'HUGE NEW MINE AND SMELTER TO OPEN SOON.'

He continues reading the paragraphs underneath. "The Dominion government announced today that it would invest $10,000 to develop a zinc and copper mine at a site 120 miles north of Le Pas. The Hudson Bay Mining and Smelting Company expects the operation to be underway as soon as next year. The company has paid the consortium that staked the original claim over $200,000. The deposit of copper, zinc and gold is said to be the richest in Canada."

The priest stands directly in front of Taylor. "Now, I will ask you, Mr. Indian Agent, since you are so heavily involved. How will lying, cheating and bullying our native people persuade them to become part of Canadian society? Isn't it your job to take care of their needs, not to join ranks with the most unscrupulous predator that I've ever had the misfortune to come across?"

Taylor, who sits stiff and ashen-faced, doesn't answer the priest, doesn't even glance at him. He says, "Now we'll hear the other side of the story. I'm sure it will be presented in a more civil and respectful manner."

Arthur Jan and Bibiane Ratt have been leaning nonchalantly against the far wall. The two men have set their faces in deadpan although red spots, like two heated pennies, appear on Arthur's cheeks. He strolls to the front of the room.

"I'm sure all of you feel gratified that Father Bonnald has taken up your cause. Here he is, wearing his long gown with his silver crucifix around his neck. A man of God. Who wouldn't believe his every word? But I tell you he is anything but an impartial observer. For years he and I have been competitors. He is out to destroy me and will use any trick to bring that about."

Ah, the fur-trading business. Étienne thought Arthur might use it as a weapon. Well, let him. It has nothing to do with cheating Weasel out of his share of the mine.

The small post office is now unbearably stuffy. Everyone is praying the proceedings will soon end, but Arthur's high-pitched defence of himself yelps on. "Like a coyote in heat," Weasel whispers to Étienne.

Suddenly two large women, one in her forties and one in her sixties, charge into the room. What are the Weasel's wife and mother-in-law doing here? The younger one carries the bucket, but it is the elder who heaves it. Just so. The stinking, yellow liquid soaks both Arthur Jan and Bibiane Ratt.

Étienne is astonished – How could anyone manage to collect that much piss from just one horse?

The crowd bursts out of the post office, many holding their noses.

Indian agent Taylor notes that the proceedings have taken a half hour less than the allotted time.

CHAPTER TWENTY-EIGHT

WHEN ÉTIENNE ARRIVES HOME, he's surprised to find everything is in order. The one good tablecloth has been retrieved from the cedar chest and the china and cutlery – the rectory has only one set for both daily use and entertaining – are nicely laid out. The scones turned out beautifully, a jar of excellent mustard was found in the pantry and sits in a pretty dish beside the tongue, the pineapple sponge shortcake looks a triumph. And, wonder of wonders, Ovide is calm, almost cheerful.

"What a beautiful job you've done, my brother," Étienne exclaims.

"With good help, you can accomplish anything," Ovide replies.

At that moment Izzy Wentworth strides out of the kitchen. She's carrying a tray on which sit three jars of preserves. Judging from the way Ovide smiles at her, she has charmed and soothed him. Joe had asked her to help out and Étienne is discovering that he likes this exuberant girl with her lovely, fresh face, always in a smile, that amazing red hair trying so hard to escape its bun. Could it really be that she's fallen for his Joe? If anything comes of it, no question, for the sake of their children, she will have to convert to Catholicism. What will The Reverend Ernst Wentworth think about that?

"We're all set, Father Bonnald," Izzy beams.

"Wonderful! We all have to thank you, Izzy."

Joe, who is busy squeezing lemons for the lemonade, beams.

At that instant the guests arrive, all in a crowd. "What an incredible story! Piss! Drenched in piss!" The Distinguished Writer roars as he walks in the door. "I thought squaws were supposed to be docile creatures, lambs, not avenging raptors."

Étienne glares him. "Certainly, it was an unfortunate incident, Mr. Lewis. I hope Mr. Jan is treating it as the joke it was meant to be."

Given the donnybrook that afternoon, the priest is surprised that Bob Taylor has shown up, but the man has more cheek than anyone Étienne has ever known. "Arthur's as mad as hell, and who could blame him?" Taylor says . "I have it in mind to charge these women with assault."

"Oh, come on, Bob," says Russell Smith. "Arthur deserves it and you know it. In fact, it's lucky he didn't get a bullet in the head." While nothing is said, the expression on Russell's face signals that he thinks the Indian agent is as guilty as the fur trader.

"Tea is served," Izzy announces sweetly as she pours the brew into rose patterned cups. They all stand up and head for the table – it's as though they haven't eaten in days. Étienne is thankful now that Ovide had insisted they serve more than bread and jam.

"My, what a sumptuous *repas*, Father Bonnald," Florence Smith smiles. "I didn't know you had it in you."

"It's mostly the doing of my brother. Who, by the way, offers his excuses. He feels a cold coming on." Actually, Ovide has fled to the chicken coop and will not be coaxed out. "And, of course, Izzy Wentworth was a great help."

Ernst has declined the priest's invitation – after yesterday's confrontation what else could be expected from such a timid man? – but Lucretia could not pass up another encounter with The Famous Writer. The priest sits down beside her. "That girl of yours is a gem," he says.

Lucretia replies with amazing haste. "I'm sure we'll all miss her when she leaves. Which will be very, very soon."

Étienne feels a stab at his heart when he sees that Joe has overheard this and flinched as though he's been slapped.

The Lewis brothers are sitting side by side on a small velvet settee. This is the one piece of furniture that has a hint of luxury about it – Étienne had it shipped from the family home in Quebec – and he hopes it doesn't buckle under their weight.

Claude smiles at Étienne. "Father, I've been told you Catholics here are doing a superb job of civilizing your aboriginals. Educate them and the whole idea of Indian will disappear – isn't that your philosophy?"

Bob Taylor butts in. "You wouldn't believe the magnificent school Bishop Charlebois has managed to get built. It's truly a palace." He turns to look at The Famous Writer. "Sinclair, you'll have a chance to see it when you get to Sturgeon Landing tomorrow."

The Famous Writer smiles wanly: "That'll be nice. I can hardly wait." There's a sarcastic edge to his voice but the Indian agent takes no notice and barrels on. "Next September, one hundred and fifty Indian children from Pelican Narrows and surrounds will be introduced to the modern world. Classrooms, dormitories, kitchens, laundry and sewing rooms. Vegetable gardens. Barns and stables. Horses and cows. These kids will be real Canadian farmers by the time they graduate. Father Bonnald, you must be so proud."

Étienne is speechless – what on earth should he say? The nightmare still haunts him day and night. The previous spring he had been invited to preview the new residential school at Sturgeon Landing. He wanted company on the trip and several volunteers had come forward, but the Linklater boys, Angus age eleven and Gordon twelve, were so keen, that, despite their parents apprehension, he had chosen them. The journey was unbelievably difficult. One hundred and forty miles by canoe, via rivers strewn with rapids, over long or steep or swampy portages, across lakes where the wind howled and the furious waves held them on shore for days. They were stormed by mosquitoes, drenched by heavy rain, sweating by day, freezing by night. Angus came down with a cold that turned into pneumonia and, shortly after they arrived at Sturgeon Landing, he died. The senior Linklaters haven't forgiven Étienne. For very good reason, he thinks. And next September all the children will have to undergo this horrendous trip; the parents will rarely visit because of it.

His first impression was of a dismal, menacing fortress. The schools sits on a plain above the Sturgeon River, far from human habitation. Even in spring, when he had visited, a cold north wind blasted down. He was even more appalled by what was going on inside.

Although construction had not yet been completed, the first batch of students had been sent for a test run before the full complement of kids were to arrive come September. Étienne was shocked that the nuns who ran the place, Sisters of Saint Joseph of Saint Hyacinthe, seemed to be entirely out of their depth. They had certainly not prepared properly – no beds had arrived so the children slept on the floor, the clothing they wore during the day serving as blankets; since no dishes had been acquired, they ate their meals from cans; the toilets hadn't been installed, so they had to walk fifteen minutes to a makeshift latrine. The garments they arrived in were burned in a huge bonfire and replaced by beige-coloured sack-cloth gowns, but sweaters and jackets had not been ordered, so the kids shivered all the time. Étienne was dismayed to find that many were running high fevers. And night and day they cried – each and every one.

At first they were afraid to say anything because the nuns had already whipped them for speaking Cree, and they knew no English. Étienne finally convinced them to confide in him and he was aghast at the stories.

One boy told him the photographs of his parents and grandparents, decked out in their best suits, had been taken from him and burned. "My ancestors, they're bad, bad people, already in Hell, or they're on their way there. That's what Sister Marie told me," he sobbed.

Another talked about how frightened she was of the white women floating around in black gowns who screwed up their faces in disgust as they swabbed the children's bodies with a lotion that stung, whispering "filthy, filthy" under their breath.

The students' long black hair, so precious to them, had been hacked off to well above their ears. "I'm so ugly," one of the girls confided in the priest. "How can I face my family when I get out of here? I'd be better off dead."

All of them complained that they couldn't eat the food. Étienne was outraged to discover that the meals consisted mostly of macaroni soup, white bread, and diluted milk. When he confronted the Mother Superior, she pointed out that they did get bologna at least once a month. "How do you expect us to feed them anything else on five cents a day. That's the magnificent amount the government hands over," she told him.

The priest had returned to Pelican Narrows utterly demoralized. He hasn't been able to forget for one moment the misery of those children. He is sure Joe would have perished in a place like that.

"You have no idea what the government and the church, my church, is inflicting on those children," he bursts out. The supercilious white people gathered in his parlour collectively frown at him. "I'd like to know how you'd feel if some authority figure decked out in a uniform showed up on your doorstep demanding that you hand over your children," he went on. "And carrying the legal warrant to do so. Imprison them in a place where they will learn to hate everything about you and your culture, to be taught that everything their grandfathers and grandmother believed in was wrong, depraved even. All this because you had the misfortune of being born an Indian."

He is about to continue his tirade when suddenly the fraught, high-pitched voice of Ovide wafts through the open windows. "Off this property, you son of a gun, you mongrel whore. No devils permitted here."

Étienne rushes outside to find his brother pressing a spade to Bibiane Ratt's chest.

"I'm not coming to your fucking tea party," Bibiane yells at Étienne. "I've come to collect Joe. We have to finish loading up for tomorrow's departure."

The guests disperse quickly after Ovide's embarrassing performance. Anyway, they're happy to not have to hear more slander about residential schools. "We'll discuss this later," the Indian agent hisses on his way out the door. "Father Bonnald, you are dead wrong. These schools are the perfect solution to the Indian problem."

Étienne simply looks at him with sadness in his eyes.

It'll be four hours before Joe returns home and hopefully lets Étienne in on what's going on. Instead of preparing his sermon for the next day's mass, as he should do, the priest walks over to Sally's house. He sits beside her bed and tells her about the extraordinary events of the day, just as he would if she was her old, bright self. But he doesn't take her hand – he feels himself growing impatient. All those years of caring for her, of loving her, of giving up his very soul for her, and she has fallen into a dark hole of her own making. Everyone assumes it has something to do with the arrival of his brother Ovide, but Étienne knows better. It's him she's spurning. Curling into herself, snail-like, as though he's too monstrous to confront. And, really, he has no idea why.

He's relieved when Joe walks in the door. "How'd you make out?" he calls out.

"I think Mr. Jan has forgotten that I can read. He didn't try to hide the labels from me. All these boxes are going to New York City, to a Mr. George Heye."

"Son of a bitch," the priest shrieks.

THE DANCE

Saturday evening

CHAPTER TWENTY-NINE

JOE PRAYS THAT THE FAMOUS WRITER won't make an ass of himself. During their three weeks of travels they'd become friends of sorts – Joe laughed at Sinclair's jokes; Sinclair never stopped talking about what a great fisherman Joe was – so Joe feels protective of him. But how to prevent the man from becoming the laughing stock of Pelican Narrows when he's as drunk as a skunk? Divert his attention maybe. Joe heads in his direction, but just at that moment Pelican Narrows' finest musicians, the fiddlers, accordionist, and spoon players, strike up a lively rendition of 'Rig-A-Jig-Jig.'

Sinclair Lewis staggers to the centre of the dance floor. His long, grasshopper legs wobble a pathetic version of the rise and grind, while his arms flail about in six/eight time making him look like a duck about to take off. The music's so fast, The Distinguished Author can endure only about forty seconds before he stumbles to the sidelines just as the raucous laughter – directed at him – begins to swell.

Arthur Jan hushes the crowd. "We're only moments away from announcing the winners. Patience everyone." Since it's Arthur's warehouse that has been transformed into a dance hall and he has put up the prize money, everyone shuts up, at least for a few seconds.

Joe's pretty sure he did well. His footwork, he feels, was rapid and intricate, and he'd included several steps he'd devised in the hope of adding spice to that old turkey, *The Red River Jig*. Still, he knows he has no chance of winning – the competition was too stiff.

The first prize is announced and he's proven correct. Raven Jared is the champion, and everybody agrees he should be. He's Métis so rightly comes by his jigging talent. Moreover, he's famous. He once danced one hour and fifty-two minutes without resting for an instant, sixty-seven different steps included in his repertoire. Although he was baptized Pierre-Luc, he's always called Raven because he reminds everybody of the famous trickster. Since Joe likes this skinny bird of a man, he's not unhappy at the decision.

He's less sanguine when his bête noir places second. Joe was sure he had danced rings around Moses Rabbitskin. Then he hears his own name being called. He climbs on to the little stage and graciously smiles as he accepts third prize. Two bucks is nothing to sneeze at, especially when his boat motor needs an overhaul. And there is Izzy Wentworth beaming at him. That certainly makes it all worthwhile.

Now the musicians can begin warming up for the evening's main event. There are two callers, Solomon McCallum and Florence Smith, which is fortunate since the square dance will go on for hours, probably until sunrise. Solomon can't carry on a conversation in English, yet somehow he has acquired a complete square dance vocabulary. Everybody agrees that, although his is a more powerful voice and he certainly knows his stuff, Florence is better. She's full of surprises, and there's great fun in that.

"Grab your partners," yells Henry Highway, the accordionist.

Like everyone else Izzy and Joe dance fast and furious as Florence calls out, "Bow to the partner, bow to the corner, join hands, circle to the left. Hey now, don't step on her foot!" Never mind the noise, the heat, the bodies rushing past, their eyes remain locked. They exist only one for the other.

Finally a break is called. All rush to the side tables where heavily buttered slabs of raisin bannock are piled high, and tea, loaded with milk and sugar, is poured.

"Isn't Florence Smith terrific?" sings out Harriet Bird as she nudges closer to Joe. For months she's been trying to catch his attention, but he's been as responsive as a dead walleye. This was understandable given his great tragedy. But if he's come back to life, she wants a chance to snare him. So does Marguerite Linklater,

Madeline Ballendine, Flora Michel, Helen Bear and Juliette Bird. Suddenly a crowd of sweating females is pressing in on this prize. Izzy decides she'll go for a walk. Her reckless pursuit of Joe week after week has resulted in a resolution she intends to keep. She's jealous, yes, but she will not be humiliated further.

She stands outside, staring at the shimmering moon, until ten minutes later Joe shows up. "Thank goodness I escaped that bunch," he says. She breathes a sigh of relief. He is hers after all – she feels it in her heart. A warmth floods over her.

They find a copse of white birch, well hidden from the path; the trunk of a fallen tree provides a bench of sorts. They sit shoulder to shoulder holding hands. They are silent as though the moment was too precious to be disturbed by words. Finally he turns to her, looks directly into her eyes, says in a low, flat voice, "My head's clear now and I've come to a decision. I have to tell you the truth even if it means you'll hate me."

"Never!" Izzy pipes up.

Joe takes a breath and then, almost in a whisper, begins what is a long confession.

"I once loved someone so much my heart still aches at the thought of her. I lost her, and I haven't been able to get over it. I've been crippled, actually. Wanting to be alone, barely able to talk to anyone. But since you've come into my life, I've felt a stirring of something, a glimmer of hope maybe. But I don't know. Am I too broken to be of use to anyone? After I've told you what happened, you'll have to decide."

"I've already decided. Nothing you could have done, nothing that could have happened to you, will ever change my opinion of you."

"Wait, please. I have hidden a very dark secret. You will be the only one I tell it to. If it ever comes out, it would destroy my family, my people."

He looks up at the sky, pinpricked with brilliant stars. Is silent for a minute – he seems almost to be praying. Then he begins his story.

JOE'S CONFESSION

CHAPTER THIRTY

I'D STUDIED SO HARD for so many years with Father Bonnald that I was shocked and angry when Mother unexpectedly stepped in and forbade me from attending college in Quebec. No matter how hard I pleaded, nothing would change her mind. I was to learn the Cree way of life and that was that. I had met my relatives only once or twice and then only in passing, yet I was expected to spend three whole winters with them. I'd be miserable, I knew that.

"Your grandfather is old-fashioned, it's true," Mother told me. "He believes the Indian way is the best. And he may seem stern. But he loves you and wants the best for you."

I wasn't convinced, but I caved when she added, "I know that your father – that wise and brave warrior, George Sewap – would have wanted it too."

In August of 1918, just after I turned seventeen, Mother arranged that her family, the Blackfish and Charboyers, travelling from Cumberland House, 300 miles to the south, would stop in Pelican Narrows to fetch me. Together we would continue on our way, hunting and trapping, eventually, after a few months, setting up winter camp. Since Grandfather considered our town to be a white man's cesspool, he wanted his time here to be as short as possible. I had better be ready.

Since I was a small boy, Father Bonnald had taken me hunting, so I was used to handling a rifle. In fact, I was considered something of a crack shot. No, I didn't need to worry about that. It was everything else.

Right away I found out how clueless I was. On the morning we were to leave, I was told to help dismantle camp. I stacked the poles that formed the skeleton of the wigwams in a neat pile and was about to load them in a canoe, one of six that made up our party, when Uncle Raymond came striding over.

"Why would we bring those damn things? We have a whole forest full where we're going. Leave them right where they are. Someone else will make use of them."

I had carefully selected a half dozen books I wanted to bring along, but when I showed up at the dock, everyone laughed at my bundle. Their baggage was so light – a few clothes, a packet of sewing supplies, a few caribou skins for blankets, a small box of store-bought provisions, tea in particular, a pouch of medicinal herbs, a papoose, rifles, ammunition, fishing rods, that was about it. I felt ridiculous, and got rid of my load, all except for the *Daily Book of Psalms* which Father Bonnald had given me and, a favourite of mine, Henry Thoreau's *Walden*. Later, that would seem a stupid choice.

I was assigned to Grandfather Blackfish's wigwam, my designated home for the entire journey. Our group included my grandmother, my cousin Lucy whose husband had died months before of tuberculosis, her boy and girl, ages six and eight, and my great grandfather, Isaiah Blackfish. Another wigwam was occupied by my uncle Raymond Blackfish, his second wife Charlotte, their two sons, Leon and Cornelius, Charlotte's elderly mother, Maria Morin, and a friend, of sorts, Charlie Laliberté. The Charboyers, who were related by marriage to the Blackfishes, made up the third group. This family included my aunt Louisa, her husband, Harold, my cousin, Harold Junior, his wife, Rita, a baby, and an orphan girl called Marguerite Settee. Years before, her parents had drowned when their canoe overturned in a violent storm on Lac La Ronge. She had been brought up by the Charboyers who now regarded her as their own daughter.

The women were kind, poking at my ribs, laughing that they'd have to fatten me up for the winter. But the men were cool; out of the corner of my eye I'd catch them looking at me scornfully. I came to realize that, because I had grown up in a world they considered was debauched, I had to be soft and spoiled. Yet I had power and influence simply because I had lived in white society. And it didn't help that I was so sullen. I was still angry about not going to college, felt bitter and resentful, and didn't mind showing how unhappy I was. My bad temper, of course, irritated the adults.

The first day of travel, nine hours of paddling, utterly exhausted me. As soon as we set up camp, I flopped down in the wigwam and fell into a deep sleep. The next thing I knew Grandfather was poking me with his toe. "Wake up, *kakepatis*, stupid," he roared. It turned out that I had committed a terrible crime. I had fallen asleep on the wrong side of the wigwam.

"Can't you see that the cooking and food supplies are stored on this side so the women can easily get at them? The hunting and trapping equipment are on the men's side. That's where you belong even if you're hardly what I'd call a man. You've been assigned a particular spot at the rear where you must remain, no matter if you are sleeping, eating or mending fishing nets."

As a final humiliation, he spat out, "And make sure that you don't curl up like a dog. You sleep with your head against the rear wall, your feet towards the fire."

I felt totally confused. And utterly embarrassed. "What a lot of bullshit," I said to myself. There was not a note of affection or warmth in my grandfather's voice. He despised me, I was sure of that.

Fortunately, I did make one friend right away, my paddle mate, Charlie Laliberté. He was short and skinny with the biggest nose I'd ever seen on an Indian. Unlike the others who were perpetually glum, he was always cracking jokes and laughing at them himself since nobody else did. He liked to hum Cree lullabies as well as belt out Christian hymns, and once, when the camp fires were lit in the evening, I spotted him performing a wild jig to music he apparently heard in his head. He was generous and sympathetic and always tried not to cause offense. While they couldn't help liking him, the other men considered him a lightweight. This was to be expected. He was not a Rock Cree like us, but an unreliable Swampy from the south. I never did figure out how Charlie ended up with my relatives.

My young cousins, probably because they didn't know that I had been corrupted by the white man, attached themselves to me. The eldest, Leon, at fifteen two years younger than me, was a tall good-looking kid, but so quiet that I thought he might be a little slow. Eleven-year-old Cornelius, on the other hand, was as outgoing as his brother was shy. He never stopped chattering, asking questions, dissecting the world around him. He drove his parents to distraction, but I liked him a lot.

The first weeks of travel were hectic. Rain or shine we would wake before sunrise, gobble down a little tea and bannock, dismantle the wigwams, pack the canoes, and set off. It was rutting season, the perfect time to hunt moose and woodland caribou. If we could slaughter enough game now, we'd be sure to survive the winter. Of course, big animals weren't found every day, so we also went after beaver, fisher, otter, ptarmigan. Once I shot a half dozen ducks in short order and I thought maybe the men were looking at me with new respect. We fished like crazy – whitefish, trout, walleye, pike, and, when we got further north, sturgeon which were not only delicious but the source of the oil used by the women in cooking, heating and many other things.

One day I spotted a big black bear crashing through the wood. I was excited, and shouted at Grandfather that I'd better go for my rifle. Another mistake. With disgust in his voice, he scolded me. "We never kill bears. Why? Because they are so much like us humans. They are sacred." In my experience bears were shot all the time. People in Pelican Narrows loved bear steak. How was I supposed to know that this bunch considered it a sin?

My relatives had been baptised into the Catholic faith two decades before, so I assumed that their beliefs would be much like my own. Before every meal, Uncle Harold Charboyer mumbled the same prayer as Father Bonnald: "Bless us, O Lord and these Thy gifts, which we are about to receive from Thy bounty, through Christ our Lord. Amen." But gradually it became clear to me that their Christianity was paper thin. What controlled their lives was a parallel, shadowy universe, inhabited by strange spirits and ruled by weird ceremonies. And in this world I was at a total loss.

One afternoon, as we were travelling on Lake Deschambault, we heard a moose call echoing through the bush. Not far was a place where the animals often came to drink and nibble on lily pads and skunk cabbages and, since there'd been a forest fire a few years before, forage on new grass and berry bushes. There we camped for the night.

After the evening meal, rattles and drums suddenly appeared, from where I had no idea. While I stood watching, trying not to laugh out loud, the men sang together in gruff voices. "This is the land which is the home of the moose. I am going to live with the moose. This is the land where the caribou dwell. I will accompany the caribou home."

Everybody said Uncle Raymond was the best moose caller in the entire world. He'd cup his hands over his mouth and let go with loud grunt which sounded like a cross between a burp and the hoot of a tuba. "That oughtta get the attention of Mr. Bull, if he's anywhere around," he insisted. Then we all went to sleep.

The next morning during breakfast a container of moose piss — where he got this was his secret, and he refused to tell a soul — was passed round and each of us dabbed a few drops over our hat or scarf. "Those young ones, they go crazy for this smell," said Uncle Raymond. Then he let go with another series of what sounded like loud farts. "To wake these beauties from their beds."

We hunters were divided into three teams. Each would follow a different path through the bush. To my dismay I was assigned to Grandfather's group.

"Those animals, they can smell your dirty socks a mile away, so remember, wind in the face, sun at the back. And these moose, when they finish eating, they turn back. To rest, I guess. So when their trail ends, you can be pretty sure they're about somewhere," Grandfather explained.

I was told to beat the willows with a club, to lure the animals from the bush. This was to imitate the sound of the moose thrashing with their antlers to let their rivals know they were around. During the rut, the bulls, old and young, are always ready for a fight. I could feel my heart beating – now *this* was exciting.

After about a half hour, a shot rang out. The first moose of the season was down! It was a big bull, a two-year-old, so that the meat would be especially tender. I was glad it was Charlie who had executed the kill, neatly with one bullet between the eyes, and not one of the bad-tempered Blackfishes.

Immediately, a complicated, mystifying set of rules came into play. These were entirely foreign to me, and I prayed that in my ignorance I wouldn't do something too stupid.

While all of us hunters helped with the butchering, it was Charlie's privilege to cut the head off. He did so with several blows of his axe, the blood squirting upwards in a great gush like one of the grand fountains of Rome. I laughed out loud until I saw Grandfather staring at me with daggers in his eyes.

After the quarry was quartered and skinned, the meat and carcass were hidden in the bush and covered with spruce bows. Leon and Cornelius were left behind to fend off scavengers, while the rest of us returned to the camp, bringing along mementos of our success – the heart, the lower intestine, and two kinds of fat. These were handed over to the women who laid them out on a cloth on the ground so lovingly the organs could have been newborn babes. Everyone crowded around to admire them. I was about to yell out, "Charlie, the magnificent hunter!" when, thank the Lord, I became aware of the silence around me. No one was saying a word, no one was excited. Even the children were quiet. Only Charlie was allowed to speak. Slowly and calmly, with not a hint of bragging, he described how the moose had been hunted down.

"We give thanks to this animal for giving his life that our stomachs may be full," he prayed.

The next day, all the men helped transport the butchered parts back to camp. As the bloody remains were piled at the back of Charlie's wigwam, Grandfather explained that the animal's head must face the door, "so he can see out into the world." Then everyone crowded in to admire the rewards of the hunt. Old lady Morin, Charlotte Charboyer's mother, whistled at me and, taking her by the arm, I helped her hobble over. She stroked a little hair that had been left on the moose's left leg.

When the chunks of meat were finally distributed, I was amazed at how precisely they were divided; each family received exactly the same portion.

When Grandfather announced that a feast would be held to celebrate the first kill of the season, the children went wild with excitement. For me it meant more mysterious, maddening rituals. And it was made clear that if I didn't precisely follow the rules, the consequences would be dire, not just for me, but the entire group. Sickness, quarrels, starvation would threaten us all winter.

The first step was to set up the special tent in the bush some distance from the main camp. As usual, I found myself in a dilemma – how could I lend a hand without breaking the rules? Perhaps I should collect the balsam bows that would cover the ground. "No," said Grandfather, "that's not your job; it's the little children who do that." He assigned me to make the fire pit in the centre. "It's usually women's work, but it'll give you something to do."

Grandmother inspected me carefully. Had I washed properly? Did I stink? Were my clothes clean and mended? After she was satisfied that I wouldn't cause her embarrassment, she gave me a cup and a plate carefully covered by a clean cloth and I was allowed to follow the others, all carrying the same thing, to the sacred tent.

Our seating position was determined by our age, sex, and hunting ability. I was placed between my two teenage cousins, which meant

I was still considered a youngster. Well, I didn't give a damn what they thought. I plunked myself down, a scowl on my face.

The moose head, now boiled and ready to carve, sat in the centre of the circle. Around it were placed little birch bark bowls of fat and the animal's intestines, as well as plugs of tobacco. Every now and then, someone would throw bits of this material into the fire. "In honour of the spirits who will help our hunters this winter," Cornelius whispered to me.

More food was carried in, steaming heaps of roasted, grilled and boiled beaver, goose and fish that were to accompany the most important dish – the moose meat. Because it was a special occasion, the men had prepared the main course – the entire day was spent at this – but the women also contributed with puddings, pies and doughnuts, cooked in a makeshift oven over a fire.

My mother had always made native dishes, but in a way that pleased Father Bonnald –walleye baked with the green onions from his garden, bannock served with maple syrup shipped from Quebec, roast grouse made with dried prunes. Despite this, or maybe because of it, I've always been a finicky eater. This infuriated Mother and was one of the reasons she had decided I needed to be toughened up in the bush. Whenever he saw me picking at my food, Grandfather would scowl, "Eat what's put before you, you spoiled, ungrateful white trash." Now I was to be truly tested.

While the first course – cold moose soup, a broth in which the head had been boiled – was passed around, he eyed me like a hawk. I have to do this, I said to myself. Trying hard to stop my hand from shaking, I picked up the birchbark bowl and poured the entire greasy lot down my throat. I sat there not saying a word, not moving, until grandfather turned to chat with someone nearby. I got up, and, as calmly as I could, walked out the tent opening. Over a nearby wild rose bush, I barfed up the entire mess.

After the so-called feast was over, we were allowed to return to our tents. I tried to sleep but my stomach was still roiling. I badly needed fresh air. As I walked along the path towards the lake, I spotted a large bonfire. As I approached it, I could see five men, Uncle Raymond, Uncle Harold, cousin Harold Junior, Charlie Laliberté and Grandfather sitting in a circle, smoking pipes. I didn't want to be seen so I hid in the bush, but this made it difficult to hear what was being said. I could see that Grandfather was very agitated, shouting, waving his pipe about, jumping up, and then sitting down again. Uncle Harold finally interjected, saying something that obviously infuriated the old man. He began shouting, and I caught a phrase or two. "What are we, pathetic flunkeys, forever offering our arses to the white man? We must avenge the souls of our ancestors, or we die."

Grandfather moved as though to walk away from the circle. Afraid he'd get to the wigwam before me, I scurried back as fast as I could. I would ask Charlie what it was all about in the morning.

CHAPTER THIRTY-ONE

SOMEONE IS THRASHING ABOUT in the bushes nearby. Joe grumbles, "I knew I'd be interrupted. No way a person can find peace around here."

Then comes a familiar whine, plaintive and irritating – Izzy thinks of an angry crow. "Oh darn," she sighs.

"Izzy, where are you? I know you're around somewhere. Come here at once! Isabelle, I must speak to you!"

Izzy puts a finger to her lips. "Shush!"

Joe is amazed. Hiding like that – he'd never dare do such a thing to his mother or any other elder for that matter.

"Not now," she whispers. "I'll see to him later."

They sit in silence, holding their breath, until Reverend Wentworth is heard charging in another direction.

"Sorry about that, Joe," Izzy murmurs, and cuddles a little closer. "I know what he wants. Can't deal with it now. So did you find out what the gathering was all about? I'm dying to know more."

"I did eventually. But you have to let me tell the story in order so I don't miss anything."

By November snow had fallen and the small lakes and bays were frozen over so travel by canoe was no longer possible. Anyway, by this time we had arrived at our winter camp located north of Lake Deschambault. It was ideal – a river nearby would provide fresh water, rabbits and other small game were plentiful, and there was plenty of dry, dead wood around. The women were particularly busy readying the wigwams for the freeze-up, the birch bark outer covering replaced with caribou hides and chinked with moss.

The men's first, and most important, task was to set up the camp's holy place, and I was assigned to help my uncles in this.

First off, my cousins and I were sent to fetch a large canvas bag that had been stored in a crevice a mile away. When this was tipped over dozens of skulls – beaver, otter, rabbit – clattered to the ground. We couldn't help giggle, but when we saw Grandfather frowning at us – he had the thickest, most threatening eyebrows I've ever seen – we immediately shut up. We strung the animal parts onto ropes and tied them to the branches of a tall jack pine. "You must make sure the bones are facing in the direction of sunrise," Grandfather instructed. "Otherwise the spirits will not be pleased."

While this was going on, Marguerite, the orphan girl, was painting the antlers of Charlie's moose a bright purple, using a dye she had made from crushed plants. On the horns, she tied red ribbons. I helped her place this creation in the crotch of a white birch tree. We both stood back and laughed. To me the place looked more like a dance hall than a sacred shrine. But sacred it was. Several times I spotted my grandfather or one of my uncles sitting there, very still, very quiet, as though they were praying. But to whom or what I hadn't a clue.

Gradually, thanks to Charlie who had taken on the job as my tutor, these strange rituals began to make more sense. He explained, "You gotta love the animals. You gotta be grateful that they are giving up their life for us. That's why you shoot 'em real quick so they don't suffer. Why you don't leave their bones out for the dogs to get. You put their remains up in the tree like that, and they say, 'Yes, we see you respect us. We will come back.' And next year your belly is full again."

"Why would any creature agree to self-sacrifice?" I asked.

His voice full of impatience, he answered, "Because they know they're going to be reborn."

This did nothing to clear up my confusion.

I had become good friends with Charlie so one day I got up enough nerve to ask him about the discussion that had gone on around the bonfire. Why was Grandfather so upset? He brushed aside my question, but I guess I pestered him so much, he finally gave in. "I'm telling you this bit, but you must not ask me any more questions. Your grandfather would skin me alive. Do you know about the massacre that happened a long time ago at Pelican Narrows?"

"I've been told something about it," I replied.

"I guess it's not talked about much any more, never mind that hundreds of our elders, women and children were butchered like so many moose. The Sioux did it. Our people hunted them down, tortured and killed them, and still the tragedy festers. Your grandfather, for example. He thinks of little else. And, you see, he lays the blame entirely on the white man."

"Why? What did they have to do with it?"

"Moses Blackfish knows a lot more about history than you might think. The Sioux were in the pocket of the French fur traders who paid them very well to get rid of anyone doing business with their enemy – the British. The Cree sold their furs to the Hudson's Bay Company, which meant they were allies of the English. So, according to your grandfather, those poor women and children were doomed. And the fault lies not with Indians, but with the white man."

"That's ridiculous! From what Father Bonnald told me, the Sioux were blood–thirsty, savages."

"That's not your grandfather's interpretation. And he's out to get revenge."

"What kind of revenge?" I yelled.

"I won't say a word more. If he wants to tell you, he will. Now let's get going with our wood chopping before we're in trouble."

Since the hunting was so good, large stores of meat, fresh, frozen, by being buried in the ground, and smoked, placed on racks over a smouldering fire, had been cached. No worry about hunger this year. Our camp relaxed, although there was still plenty of activity. The women made pemmican from moose, deer and occasionally elk and got ready to cure the caribou and moose hides. And, except on the coldest days when the temperature dropped to minus forty or even fifty, the men tramped into the bush to tend their traps.

I was told I could trap beaver for clothing or food – beaver stew was one of the favourites – but I was not allowed to sell the skins at the trading posts, because, according to Grandfather, this was how Indians had been ruined by white men. As chief of the Cumberland House Band he had forbidden this trade. Charlie told me a rebellion had broken out, and he had been ignored. The old man, however, didn't hesitate to impose his will on his close relatives, especially me.

I knew something fishy was going on, though, and then I discovered that my uncles were secretly storing pelts which they would later cash in. This infuriated me. I'd hoped to get my hands on some hard cash that winter – it was the only thing about being exiled that had appealed to me. A new Evinrude motor might be worth it all. But Grandfather strictly forbade me from trapping for trade and, of course, his eagle eye never wandered far.

"I want you to find out what it was like to be an Indian before the white man arrived in our land, corrupting the likes of you with his foul ways." The old man's expression was so grave I thought his face might crack. I bit my tongue and said nothing, but I felt even more resentful.

There was one thing I did enjoy about that winter – being cocooned in the wigwam during the frigid evenings. Wrapped in a caribou skin, my feet to the fire, it felt so cosy with the lazy smoke curling upwards past the rack filled with smoking meat and drying clothes. Fresh balsam boughs covered the floor and the smell was so intoxicating, I dream of it to this day.

My young cousin Cornelius always made sure he sat beside me and, as the evening progressed, would snuggle closer. Half asleep, we'd listen to the drone of voices, for always, without end, there was storytelling.

Everyone took their turn although Charlie was the most enthusiastic. The Battle of the Trickster and the Water Lynxes, The Origins of the Beaver, The Tale of the Traveller and the Wolf Spirit – these stories would wind on and on. Some of them were interesting, but often I'd become bored, and I'd pick up a book, either the *Daily Book of Psalms* that Father Bonnald had given me or *Walden*, although the author's ideas seemed pretty useless, even ridiculous, here. If Thoreau thought self sufficiency was so wonderful he should try a winter in the Canadian bush. Of course my reading annoyed Grandfather. "Pay attention," he hissed at me. "These are your ancestors' stories, the history that made you."

One evening while Charlie was rambling on, I caught sight, in the golden light, of a silhouette playing on the side of the wigwam. Marguerite Settee, the orphan girl, was stretching moose hide for a garment she would later embroider. Instantly, I knew that the she would one day be my lover and my wife.

Joe pauses to light a cigarette. In the glow of the match, he notices that Izzy looks startled – and dismayed. "I'm not sure I want to know anything more about her," she cries.

"I promised myself that I would tell this story only once in my life. All of it, every detail, even the risqué parts. You came along and seemed to me so full of sympathy and understanding, so I grabbed my chance. But I'll shut up now, if you want."

"No, no. Go on, please. I'll just have to bear it when you speak of loving someone else. Or even the sexy bits. "

"You are brave," Joe said.

What was it that appealed to me so? I still ask myself that question. She had a lovely round face, but what sixteen-year-old Cree girl doesn't? She was sweet and good-natured, and that was certainly nice. She was curious about everything – bats, butterflies, honking swans, anything that crossed her path – and this I found endearing. But more than the beauty she saw was the beauty she made. Her bead work on moccasins, vests, birch bark boxes, was amazing. The snowshoes she webbed and then painted in an intricate design were considered by us all as a prize. Even the way she cut hair made the men more handsome. At least I thought so. I was happy and content in her company, a relief after feeling anxious all the time. But that first winter we were both young and shy, nothing more than friends.

One day in mid-March, Charlie announced that he had dreamt that night that Skeleton was angry. "I've been neglectful of *pawachi-kan*, forgetting his sacrifices," he said. "If I don't hurry and do so, he'll come here rattling his bones like a bunch of dried beans, and crying in that frightening loud way he has – 'Hey! Hey!' I have to think of the safety of our little ones."

I was disappointed that the offering turned out to be nothing more than a bowl of grease and some tobacco left on a rock one evening.

"So what does Skeleton look like?" I asked. My sarcasm must have been obvious, but Charlie ignored it. "First of all he's skinny, nothing but skin and bone, having died either of consumption or starvation. He's as bald as a blown up bladder. He's usually a green colour, although sometimes he's black. And he has a giant, boney prick which clears the bush as he walks."

I burst out laughing. "Now that is a guy I'd like to meet!" I chortled. Then I noticed my grandfather glaring at me. A day of reckoning would follow, I was sure of that. It came, with a vengeance, in the second week in May.

All during the winter, the adults had argued about whether Cornelius, at age eleven, was old enough to undertake a vision quest. The women said no, it was too dangerous for so young a boy. The men insisted that he was strong and alert and therefore ready and, in the end, they prevailed. Cornelius was to undertake his vision quest that spring.

Father Bonnald had told me about it. "It's a kind of rite of passage. The Indians acquire a guardian spirit which they keep for life. They call it a *pawachi-kan*." It infuriated him that Christian missionaries had regarded this ceremony as superstition and had made giving it up a condition of baptism. "The vision quest, that's exactly what these young bucks need to keep them in line," he insisted. So I was fascinated to find out what would happen to my young cousin.

For months, Cornelius talked of nothing else. "My *pawachi-kan*, who will it be? Who will come to me in my dreams? A wolverine would be good, or an eagle or a duck. But what I really hope for" – and here he stretched his arms wide – "is a gigantic sturgeon."

After the ice had melted in the bays of Lake Deschambault, the walleye and pike were practically jumping into the boat, so I was surprised when, one morning, my grandfather, a fanatical fisherman, laid his rod aside. I was more astonished when, after he lit his pipe, he began peppering me with embarrassing questions.

"So my grandson are you *pēhkisi*, chaste? Or have you polluted yourself?"

I was mystified. What was he talking about?

"What I'm saying is, have you lain with a woman in the last while?"

Of all the stupid questions! First, I had been under Grandfather's watchful eye for the last nine months. Did he really think I could have snuck into the bush for a quick snatch with some female who suddenly appeared out of nowhere? Second, as a devout Roman Catholic, I was, of course, a virgin. But I was so intimidated by the old man all I could do was whisper, "*pēhkisi*."

"Well, that's good news 'cause you've got to be in a pure state to dream the dreams. I've thought about it since you joined us, considered one side then the other. You have to believe with your entire soul for the spirits to come to you, and since you are so much a doubter, you could easily fail. On the other side, never will you be a true Indian unless you find your own *pawachi-kan*. He will stay with you your whole life. Show you how to see into the future. Help you heal the sick. Give you the power to deal with evil spirits. And, if you are in trouble, he'll come, even if it's a big trouble for him. But I cannot force you to go on a vision quest. This you must decide yourself."

I surprised myself at how quickly I responded. "I'm ready."

I had been feeling a little guilty that I'd been so surly and pig-headed with my relatives. I knew I'd have to try harder if I didn't want my mother angry at me — being told off by her was not something to look forward to. But really it was the challenge that appealed to me. Three days completely alone in the bush, exposed to all kinds of weather, without a sip of water or bite of food — that would prove that I was as Indian as any of them.

The first sunny, warm morning in May, we men travelled up a wide and fast-flowing river that ran into the west arm of Lake Deschambault until we reached Beaver Portage. Cornelius and I were not allowed to paddle; our strength must be preserved for what lay ahead of us.

Since he felt partial to aquatic creatures — otters, leeches and, of course, the mighty sturgeon — Cornelius's quest was to take place on water. The men made a raft from birch and elm branches and moored it to the shore by ropes.

"So here the spirits from both underwater and underground might visit you," Grandfather explained.

Since he was so young, my cousin was allowed to drink from a container full of water and to wear his clothes for warmth. Scrambling onto his raft, the boy put on a good face, but I could tell that he was frightened. As we paddled away, I cupped my mouth, silently yelling that everything would be okay.

I hadn't been able to think of a particular kind of *pawachi-kan* that appealed to me until one day I casually mentioned that the idea of a bird was interesting. If this was so, Grandfather said, than he knew exactly the place for my vigil. "It was built long ago. Both your aunt and uncle met their guardians there."

Located about a half mile upstream from Cornelius' raft, it was perched on a cliff over-looking the river. I was amazed at how high the rickety structure was — at least twelve feet above the ground. It consisted of two levels, the first had been used as a scaffolding to construct the second. The higher structure consisted of a platform made from horizontal poles tied to nearby trees, with branches trimmed of leaves criss-crossing vertically. Brush had been attached to two sides, grasses strewn about on the floor. "The higher you go the more powerful will be the spirits who visit you," said Uncle Raymond. "That first stage, only deer or moose, not much. Higher up, sky creatures of all sorts."

"A gigantic bird's nest," I shouted. "I shall fly like an eagle."

After I stripped naked, the men bundled up my clothes and took them away. Grandfather then blackened my entire body with soot. "You are leaving us here on earth for the world of dreams. It's a sort of death, yes, but if you let them, the spirits will embrace you and you will come back again."

I had eaten a fortifying breakfast – deer steak, bannock, berry preserves, tea. Still, by evening my stomach was rumbling. More uncomfortable, though, was not having anything to read. I always went to bed with a book. How would I manage without one, especially since the sun didn't set until an hour before midnight? But I hadn't realized how exhausted I was. I quickly fell into a deep sleep.

In the morning the sun shone brilliantly, but still I was chilled, my throat parched. I felt sick to my stomach – from lack of food, I guess. Once I'd peed over the side, I curled into my nest. How I would bear the boredom of time passing so slowly I had no idea. But soon my thoughts floated away. I was enjoying a picnic on Pelican Lake, such fun, fishing and then cooking the catch over a fire, high on a rock, Mother, Father Bonnald and me. There I was with my friend William laughing as we picked off spruce grouse so stupid they didn't know enough to fly away even with a rifle pointing at their heads. The trip to Trois-Rivières that I had taken with Father, oh, what an interesting time that was. The priest's brothers and sisters and all their kids, hugging me, wishing me well. Finally I drifted off to sleep. At that moment the phantom arrived.

It wore a bright red dress with a glittering, diamond necklace and pretty silk shoes. It was the thing perched on its scrawny neck that was so horrifying. A moose's head, sort of. Dangling from elaborate antlers were ribbons and brightly coloured feathers like a peacock's. Its two beady eyes were scornful – I felt I had somehow offended it. "Who am I? Who am I? Can you guess?" it bellowed. When I answered that I didn't have a clue, it sneered, "You soon will, my boy." The creature's ears suddenly turned into wings. It flapped away, snorting out mocking laughter.

When I awoke the next morning, the horror of the bird/moose's visit was still with me, but I was so hungry that all my attention focused on my crabby, nagging stomach. As I lay curled up in my nest, I tried to keep my spirits up by remembering the orphan, Marguerite Settee. What would Mother and Father Bonnald think of her? What kind of lover would she be? I imagined my hands caressing her smooth, brown limbs, her silky nether bush. My prick stood up straight, but only for a few seconds. Then it collapsed like a fallen soldier. So much for fasting, I thought to myself.

That night the spirit appeared again, but in an entirely different shape. It had the body of a snake dressed in a shiny blue suit with a green bow tie, but this time its head was human. Although it seemed to be male, its pinched, thin face reminded me of Mrs. Wentworth, and its long grey hair braided on top of its head was like Mrs. Smith's. It hissed the same words in the same voice as the previous night's visitor had. "Who am I? Have you seen me before? Can you guess?"

Again I said I had no idea, and it slithered away.

By the third day, I was so hungry that I was tempted to eat pieces of my grass blanket, but Grandfather had warned that would only make me more thirsty, and thirst was worse than hunger – you could become unconscious or even go crazy.

"Only a day to go. You have to hang on," I lectured myself.

I tried to recite my prayers, say a few Hail Marys. Blank, all blank. My mind, perhaps it was my soul, floated upward again. More memories of my childhood came, but these were darker than before.

Children's faces screwed up in mockery, taunting me over and over, "Poop eyes! Shit eyes!" My mother flinging a pot on the floor, raging, "That priest is never satisfied, always complaining, always whining!" Father Bonnald screaming at me in a fury when one day I barged into his bedroom and asked who the person was so tightly wrapped in blankets beside him. It was almost a relief when the vision arrived.

A white, scrawny seagull this time. It said nothing, but tipped its wing, indicating that I was to follow. I had no choice but to obey. High above the trees we flew until we arrived at a green and flowered mountain, on top of which sat a huge white nest. Inside, coloured feathers, jewels and glossy fur glinted in the sun.

The seagull pointed his wing at a stump. I was to wait there. After what seemed like an eternity, I heard a loud whoosh of wings, and from the nest flew a magnificent, albeit weird, bird. It had a large, bright-red bill which overhung a downward curving mouth outlined in black. Sky-blue circles accented its beady eyes, so ferocious, that I thought they would spark lightning. A curled topnotch of red, blue, black sat straight up on its enormous head. Its wide wings were out-stretched.

"Now do you recognize me? Do you know who I am?" it exclaimed.

"Yes, I know. You're Thunderbird."

"Of course I am. Who else would I be? I'm a powerful *pawachikan*, the most powerful, so count yourself lucky that I've decided that you're worthy of my guardianship. Now let's get down to business. Here's how to contact me."

Thunderbird then chirped a few complicated notes; I whistled along trying to follow the tune. "When you sing this song, I'll fly to you, but it had better be serious. If you summon me for something frivolous, you'll pay for it."

She then recited a long list of what was expected of me – an annual ceremony with singing and dancing, regular gifts of tobacco and food. "I'm particularly fond of the liver and intestines of caribou and would want to be served these as often as possible. And remember, I'm as thin-skinned and jealous as any human lover. Don't neglect me, don't thwart me. Now we'll begin our instructions in the use of medicinal plants..."

Suddenly the creature let loose with a terrified squawk. Her wings turned into propellers she flapped so hard to get away. I woke to a bolt of lightning so bright I thought a meteorite had fallen from heaven. There followed a terrible crash of thunder that shook the platform. The rain came pummelling down in a hellish torrent. Then I remembered Cornelius. Surely he'd be drowned!

I shimmied down from my perch and, stumbling through the bushes in the downpour, I made my way to Beaver Portage. I looked everywhere, frantically trying to find Cornelius's raft, but it was pouring so hard, I could hardly see a thing. Finally, I heard a faint noise, a moaning sound, and there was the boy, pinned under a tree branch that had fallen in the storm. He was unconscious, blood leaking from his mouth, his left arm twisted in a frightful angle, but – and I thanked God for this – he was alive.

I tried to lift the branch, at least enough to pull Cornelius free, but it was far too heavy. I realized that I had to seek help. I ran back to my canoe – Uncle Raymond had insisted it be left in in case of emergencies – and picked up a sheet of oilcloth, stored for stormy weather. With this I covered the injured boy and, even though I knew he couldn't hear me, I whispered, "Hang in there, *niwecewakanis*, little chum. I'll be back as soon as I can."

The rain thinned and then stopped, and, since it was the time of the year when sunset almost meets sunrise, I was able to paddle fairly quickly. Naked, shivering, exhausted, I fell into the arms of Grandmother Blackfish.

She didn't want me to go, but I insisted. I pulled on a dry shirt and trousers, and joined the rescue crew. It took the four of us men to lift the log, but we finally pried Cornelius free. We carefully laid him in the canoe, and hurried back to camp. He was badly injured but, thank the Maker, whether Christian or Cree, he would recover.

I must have risen several notches in Grandfather's esteem, for the next day he told me we were to have an important discussion. "You must have heard of the tragedy that befell our people," he began and then described in gory detail the bloody massacre that had been inflicted by the Sioux on Pelican Narrows Cree two hundred years before. And Charlie was right. Grandfather blamed it all on the intrigues carried out by the French and English. The Sioux were not bad people, not at all. They had simply been led astray. And now, it was time for revenge.

I was afraid to ask how, but he calmly continued. "We have made a plan. And you're part of it. That's the reason we agreed that you could join us."

Not because I'm his grandson and he loves me dearly, I sneered – but only to myself.

"You've probably heard that the white trappers are using strychnine to poison the fur-bearing animals. Because the bastards are too lazy to trap them. I have managed to get my hands on this stuff. Enough to kill each and every white son-of-a-bitch living in Pelican Narrows."

He said this without raising his voice, as though he was discussing next year's moose hunt. I was so shocked that I could feel the blood draining from my face. He either didn't notice or chose to ignore my growing panic for he pressed on as calmly and resolutely as before. "Now, this is what we want you to do this summer after you've returned to Pelican. You must make a drawing of each place where a white person lives. Show where they store their food, where they make it, where they eat it. Write down at what hour they eat – morning, noon and night. Who they eat with – we don't want to poison any of our own people."

Particularly his daughter, my mother, I thought.

"Now that you have found her, be guided by your *pawachi-kan*. You're a real Indian now so act like one."

CHAPTER THIRTY-TWO

THE FIDDLERS HAVE TAKEN a break, and everyone is lolling about out-side, catching their breath. Laughter echoes through the trees. Joe stands up, stretches. "I'm yakking too much, you must be bored out of your bean," he says.

"Are you crazy? It's mesmerizing!" replies Izzy. "So what hap-pened?"

"Actually, that summer, not much. Let me go on with my story. I have to get this off my chest now because I know for sure that I'll never talk about it again."

On the way to their summer camping grounds at Cumberland House, the Blackfishes and Charboyers stopped at Pelican Narrows for a day. They were delivering me home, but Grandmother also wanted Florence Smith to look at Cornelius's injury; he had broken his arm. She was shocked when she examined the boy. "Look at how crooked it is," she scolded. "He's never going to have the full use of it. You women should be ashamed of yourself."

This criticism made Grandfather angry. A white woman was insulting the sacred knowledge of the ancestors! "You see what I mean?" he demanded, after cornering me. "These people show no respect. To them we are nothing but pissing babes."

I didn't know what to think. I too was annoyed at the superior way Mrs. Smith had talked to my female relatives. I also knew she was right. Cornelius's arm had not been set properly.

I would spend the entire summer anxious, confused – and torn. I now felt a strong connection, a passion really, for the Indian part of me. Yet I knew deep down that, given my up-bringing, I could never entirely be part of that world. And what Grandfather had asked me to do — scrutinize my neighbours in order to murder them — that, I knew, was ridiculous. I tried not to think about it too much.

I was kept busy that summer, weeding the gardens, catching and storing whitefish for the sled dogs, chopping and piling firewood. Too bad if I was tired at the end of the day — Father Bonnald insisted I study during the evenings. "The fortitude you will develop during your three years in the bush will serve you well when you finally attend Collège de Montréal," he said. "But you must continue to hone your intellect."

The lives of the great western philosophers was the assignment, but it was hard slogging. I got through Plato and Aristotle but with St. Thomas Aquinas, I could taste dust in my mouth. One evening we were dissecting one of his many weighty pronouncements: "All that is true, by whomsoever it has been said, has its origin in the spirit" when it occurred to me that this might be the right moment to raise a question that had been nagging at me. The spiritual beliefs of my Indian relatives, have they any value? Is there any truth in them? I had been sure that Father Bonnald would insist that it was nothing but ridiculous superstition, so I was amazed by his response.

"Do the Cree have a supreme being?" he asked.

"Sure. He's called *Kisēmanitow*, the Great Spirit. As far as I can make out, he's the boss of all that's good in the world. May I recite a little prayer, or maybe it's more like a lecture that I heard many times in camp?"

Father nodded his head, yes, and I began in a loud, gruff voice imitating Grandfather Blackfish: "You people, destroy nothing. Take good care of everything, and do not waste anything, because it is *Kisēmanitow* who is the master. Do not insult the wind, *Kisēmanitow* has made it. Do not foul the water, *Kisēmanitow* created it. Accept rain or snow without complaining, *Kisēmanitow* sends them to us. Do not abuse the trees, the plants, the fish, or the animals because

Kisēmanitow has provided **these** things for our use."

I noticed that Father Bonnald was smiling. "Do these people practise a form of prayer?"

I thought for a bit. "Yes, if you consider sitting on a rock contemplating the sunset praying."

"Who do they call upon when they're in difficulty? Anyone or anything that's equivalent to our saints?"

"That's easy. Their *pawachi-kan*, their guardian spirits. Just like angels, they can fly. They help you if you call them." I was tempted to tell Father Bonnald about my Thunderbird visitation, but I wasn't sure the priest would understand. He might start asking questions. And, to be honest, I didn't want him prying into what I thought of as the Indian part of my soul.

"And what about the devil? Is there such a concept?" Father Bonnald continued.

"Why the *Witigo*, of course. The eater of human flesh. Nothing could be as frightening as he, or sometimes she."

"Is there anyone in the Cree religion who is similar to our Saviour?"

I pondered this for a good few minutes. "No, not a son of a god who gives up his life for the good of mankind. But there is the idea of sacrifice – the animal offers itself up to the hunter so his people won't go hungry. It's a strange belief which I have trouble understanding. The deer you encounter in the forest is a kind of spirit or shadow of what is the essence of deer. Rather like Socrates' ideas, I guess, the shadow against the wall. So, you're not really killing an individual creature but a representative of that thing which has offered itself to you. If you honour this prey, it will do so time and again. And if you don't pay the proper respects, the spirits will be really pissed off."

Father Bonnald grinned. "Maybe all those years of study have been worthwhile, eh, Joe? What would you say was the Cree's primary philosophy when dealing with each other?"

I was amazed at what popped into my mind. "Why, the Golden Rule, of course. 'Do onto others as you would have them do onto you.'"

"So now I'll ask *you* the really important question. In comparing Christianity and Cree religion, is there perhaps more of a sameness than a difference?"

The fiddlers are back at it; everyone has returned to the dance floor.

"I'm sorry to be talking your ear off," whispers Joe as he nuzzles his nose into Izzy's neck.

"My goodness, Joe, it's so interesting. How extraordinary that a Catholic priest could have so much respect for what is usually considered primitive superstition. If only my father could see things his way."

"Yeah maybe, but what a hypocrite I was! Prattling on about essential goodness of Cree philosophy when Grandfather was planning mass murder. I couldn't say a word. I couldn't. My connection with my Indian self – whatever that is – was too new, too strong. And maybe I was hoping that nothing would come of it. But let me get on with it.

Overnight, on the last day of August, the temperature plunged twenty degrees. Summer was over, time to rejoin my Indian relatives. I was now more comfortable with the idea of travelling with them – the Cree way of doing things was more familiar, and, of course, there was Marguerite.

Every day, I imagined her walking in the woods or sitting with her beadwork or looking after the kids as she so liked to do. I never stopped worrying that she had forgotten me. The camp where she spent the summer would be full of young guys as attracted to her as I was. I was sure of that. But when we met at the end of summer, she presented me with a pair of moccasins so exquisitely beaded that they were obviously a token of love.

"But I have nothing for you," I cried, ashamed that I hadn`t thought of bringing her a gift.

"I know something you could give me, but it'll be so much trouble, I'm afraid to ask."

I looked at her in surprise. "But I'll do anything for you."

"You can teach me how to speak English and how to read and write."

I was taken aback and hesitated, but it was only a minute before I chirped, "I'd be honoured."

I managed to hide some pencils and papers in my travel pack, and we worked whenever we could snatch a few moments together. At first it was hard going. She could easily copy the alphabet, beautifully print words, but pronouncing the sounds, remembering the vocabulary was difficult for her. Then it occurred to me that the subject of our study should come from her own experience.

"Sit," I would say, "S-I-T"

She would carefully write it down.

"And what does it mean?"

"The dirt dogs and humans make."

She punched my arm as I laughed my head off.

All summer I had worried about the assignment Grandfather had imposed on me. I had made a few rough sketches of places around Pelican Narrows – the houses of the Smiths and Arthur Jan, the Wentworths' vicarage and the interior of Father Bonnald's rectory. Also, I assembled a list of what time they ate their meals. But really it was nothing, and I was terrified that Grandfather would be furious with me. I needn't have worried. By the end of summer the plan of revenge by strychnine poisoning had been discarded. A new method of mass destruction had gained favour.

Grandfather may have loathed white society but he loved the battery-operated, short-wave radio a fur trader at Cumberland House had sold him. He has just enough English to catch the gist of what was being said. All summer long, his ears were glued to news of the

European war, now at last coming to its dismal end. There were many discussions broadcast about what to do with surplus materiel, in particular hand grenades. That was it as far as Grandfather was concerned. He would somehow get hold of a supply of these wonderful weapons and simply blow Pelican Narrows up.

"But what about the Indians that live there?" I yelled. "My mother, who happens to be your daughter, for example. Are they to be blown to smithereens too?"

"Of course not," he replied with disgust in his voice. "That will be your job. Evacuating our people before we attack."

I groaned, but said not another word. I fervently hoped that grenades would go the same way as strychnine poisoning.

The hunting that Fall was poor. Uncle Raymond managed to bag one old bull in early October. Charlie and I each shot a deer. But after that an eerie silence descended on the forest. It had been wickedly hot and dry that summer, fires had sprung up all over. Not only had many animals died in the inferno, but, because of the charred forests, they were not following their usual travel routes. As the weeks went by without anything more than a few ducks or rabbits being shot, the mood in our camp grew gloomy.

In the third week of October, just before freeze up, a fierce debate broke out, unsettling since I had never heard the adults argue in public before.

"No animals anywhere. We gotta do it. We gotta ask him," pleaded Uncle Harold.

"He's so old, so frail. Maybe he hasn't got the strength," Grandmother said. "He could easily pass to the other side, maybe..."

Grandfather interrupted, "That father of mine, he knows his duty. He can't say no."

Actually Great Grandfather wasn't in the least interested in cooperating. "I can do it, I've never failed, but I'm an old man on his last legs. Why should I put myself in danger? The spirits are angry at you, not me. Maybe you neglected them, or maybe they don't like that bathtub booze you bunch get into every night. Or probably it's that white punk you have traipsing around with us."

"He's a born Cree, as Indian as you are," Auntie Rita replied.

"Maybe he looks a little like an Indian, but his head's full of white garbage."

Although he slept in the same wigwam, I had paid little attention to my great grandfather. The old man sat chewing tobacco and spitting it into a tin can with a disgusting gurgle of the throat, saying not a word to anyone, so I hadn't known that he disliked me so much. Thank goodness I had Marguerite or I would have taken off right then, never mind I probably would never had made it out of the dense bush.

Grandmother tried to soothe my anger. "Your great grandfather was a famous medicine man once. But when the white man's sickness came, he could do nothing. Most of his relatives and friends died. His wife too. And four of his children. He cried and beat his breast, and then not a word came out of his mouth. For years now. Still, we know he has great powers to conjure up the spirits. He could save us if he wanted to."

By November the situation was desperate. No sign of big game anywhere. Beaver and otter had vanished. Even the fishing was poor. This time Grandfather decided to confront the old man alone. For a half day they sat smoking their pipes, not uttering a word, until finally Grandfather said, "Please, my good and powerful father, you must help us."

"If I die with the effort, it'll be on your head." The ancient man had finally spoken.

There was to be no audience, Great Grandfather insisted on being alone, but Cornelius had found a hole in the wigwam wall and invited me to watch with him.

From his bag, Great Grandfather took out his sacred nostrums – roots, herbs and rocks – and laid them on the ground. After sucking on his pipe for a good long time, he began beating the drum and shaking rattles. I put my ear to the hole and could hear him singing, "Come my intimates, visit me. Tell me what I want to hear." Then silence. Cornelius finally got bored and wandered away and I soon did the same.

The old conjurer slept until noon the next day. When he finally emerged, he looked grey and drawn. Even more ancient than usual, if that could be possible.

"Listen carefully to what I have to say. All the powerful spirits came – bear, north wind, lynx – all came to me. They say, travel west up the river past two trees that have been struck down by wind and, on a hill, on the second plateau, you'll find a young cow that has been downed."

With that he sat down, sucked once on his pipe, and fell back to sleep.

My uncles Raymond and Harold set out immediately, and sure enough, in exactly the spot Great Grandfather had described, they found a small female moose recently dead. Unfortunately it had been attacked by wolves, so only a little flesh was left, hardly enough for one decent meal.

"Did any of the other guardians talk to you?" Grandfather asked when the old man awoke.

"My *pawachi-kan* warns, 'The animals have gone. Beware the *witigo*.'" Then he fell silent again.

A few days later, Lionel Bird, a cousin of Grandmother's, arrived. He explained that everyone was so worried about the lack of game that they had sent messengers to Big River to ask the famous shaman, Jimmi Benaouni, to conduct a shaking tent ceremony. The Blackfishes and Charboyers were welcomed to participate.

"Now, you'll experience something you'll never forget," Charlie told me.

The ice had set so we travelled by dogsled, arriving at the Bird camp in a day and a half. Six family groups were already gathered there, as well as Shaman Benaouni. He was busy over-seeing the construction of the shaking tent. "Nah, not good enough. We need a tree that will please the spirits," he said time and again, as his three assistants, Charlie among them, followed him through the bush. Finally he decided that a particular white birch, which to me looked the same as every other white birch, was perfect.

They chopped it down, and whittled half a dozen poles out of it. These were pounded into the ground in a circle – the shaman had heard an owl calling so he knew exactly the right spot. The sides of the sacred wigwam were then covered with moose hide. A small hole was left in the top. "So the guardians, they can come and go freely," explained Cornelius who had experienced a similar event when he was younger.

The ceremony took place at dusk the following day. Moosehide robes were placed on the ground outside the tent for us to sit on, and blankets provided. Fortunately, clouds were thick overhead, and there was little wind, so it wasn't too cold.

Once everyone was assembled, Shaman Benaouni emerged from the bush. He was a big impressive man, dressed in an exquisitely embroidered deer skin jacket and moccasins. On his head sat a huge hat – I thought it looked like a lady's bonnet, the kind you could buy at Arthur Jan's store, except it was made of crow feathers. With a slow deliberate pace, he circled the tent clockwise once. His assistants then bound his arms tightly behind him and tied his feet together with a thick rope. Once that was completed, they pushed him through the flap of the small door into the tent.

We all sat in silence for what seemed to me to be an eternity until, suddenly, from the opening in the top, the ropes which had bound Benaouni came flying out, landing in Charlie's lap.

"My God!" I cried out, but the others took it all in their stride, their faces pure granite.

We could hear the shaman still inside the tent. "Come, my dearly beloved *Mihkināhkw*, come to us." Then he merrily shook his rattle. In a high pitched voice he sang, "Come my turtle, come to us."

After about ten minutes, there was a loud flapping noise and the tent shook. Then a cheery, squeaky voice was heard. "*Mihkināhkw* here! Master of Ceremonies and translator par excellence, at your service. It's a pleasure to see everyone. Especially the ladies. Prettier than their husbands, each and every one."

The audience outside exploded in laughter.

"But where is my little reward? I don't see it."

A pipe already lit, some packages of *chistamaw*, tobacco, a few wads of chew were pushed inside. In a few moments the *ospokwan*, the pipe, now fully smoked, was thrust back out.

"I believe I hear the first guest arriving," *Mihkināhkw* continued.

There was a loud roar, but the tent remained still.

"Thunder has just come down but I've convinced him that he mustn't come in. He's so rough he's apt to do damage. Just last month he accidentally split the poles into bits and wrecked the tent. I gave him some moose liver and he left."

"What was Thunder's role then?" I asked. Nobody paid me any attention.

The tent began shaking vigorously. "Flying squirrel has arrived," *Mihkināhkw* announced.

Cornelius, who was sitting beside me, explained, "This one, he says one thing but always means the opposite."

Strange grunting sounds were heard which *Mihkināhkw* translated. "The sun will shine every day, the game will be plentiful, and your bellies will be full."

"Which means we're going to have a hell of a winter," whispered Charlie.

The next visitor, the Loon, didn't beat around the bush. "Oh my dears, the north wind is angry and will wreak a beating on your poor hides."

"But what have we done to deserve such punishment?" someone yelled,

"I'm not at liberty to say, but one among you knows the answer."

It better not be me, I prayed. But, thank the Lord, nobody looked in my direction.

"Strong Neck! He's on his way," *Mihkināhkw* yelled, still inside the tent. If they weren't already wearing hats, the crowd scrambled to find something to cover their heads.

"Keep your eyes down!" Shaman Benaouni suddenly thundered.

"He's the only spirit that isn't invisible," Cornelius clarified. "If you look in his direction, he'll kill you." I quickly joined the others and stared intently at the ground.

A hoarse, heavy voice boomed out, translated by *Mihkināhkw*. "I am Strong Neck, mightier than them all. I've come to warn you. Be prepared. This will be a most dreadful winter. The animals have vanished."

Strong Neck was followed by Jackfish, who spoke French so I could understand him. Then Bull, whose manners were as rough as his voice, followed by Hairy Beast who was famous for his bragging – "I never shot a moose or bear, but always pursued them on foot, and cut their throats open with my knife." But this time there was no boasting from Hairy Beast or any of the other spirits. None of the usual wisecracking. No jokes. All those spirits gathered in the shaking tent were sad, predicting the same thing – a winter of frightful want.

The last guest to arrive was *hahasho*, the raven, the trickster.

"Vamoose, you phantoms. What are you doing here when times are so dire? Fly away, fly away," he shrieked. Suddenly there was a whoosh, followed by a great flapping noise from the hole at the top. A mighty rattling, the tent shook violently, then dead silence.

Shaman Benaouni emerged from the tent, looking so sad, so dejected, I felt an unease crawling up my spine. "You've heard them. Prepare as best you can," he told the crowd.

It was all magic tricks, I was sure of that. But I could see from the expression on their faces that the others felt otherwise. They had no doubts the terrible situation described by the spirits would play out that winter. They were so panic-stricken they could hardly utter a word. For the first time in my life, I tasted real fear.

At the end of December, the north wind blew itself into a fury, the snow blanketed down – it whipped our tents for four full days. Charlie was fascinated by the thermometer that I had brought along, and one morning he shouted out, "Minus fifty-two degrees. Cold as a *witigo's* tits."

The fire was kept burning but only barely, as wood was now scarce. Although it had been carefully stacked in a pile and then covered with oil skin, it was now buried under six feet of snow. We all huddled in our wigwams, covering ourselves with anything that was available – coats, blankets, moose hide robes, the few flour sacks the women had kept.

By now the fact that Marguerite and I were keen on each other was accepted by the elders – I suspected my grandparents had hoped that would happen – and they turned a blind eye when we snuggled together.

"I love you, Marguerite," I whispered in English one evening.

"Love! L–O–V–E. Is that how I spell it?" she asked as she wrote the word down.

"I want to marry you, Marguerite."

"Marry. M–A–R–R–Y. Is this how it looks?"

The men had been able to dig out the cache of food buried under the snow, but the meat and fish stored there were almost used up. There was still a little pemmican, oatmeal, dried peas, dried cranberry and some flour and lard. These were carefully rationed. The men' portions were larger than the women's and children's, for everyone agreed that the hunters needed the food to sustain their energy. And, since it was hard slogging for the dogs pulling the sleds through the deep snow, they too had to be fed – at least a little whitefish.

By mid-January we were living on one small meal a day. I was surprised that my stomach no longer grumbled; it had got used to being empty. Uncle Raymond found the carcass of an old bull moose that had obviously frozen to death in the extreme cold. The meat was as tough as dog harnesses, but I thought it tasted as good as the beef Bourguignon my mother made for Father Bonnald.

By the third week in February no other prey had been spotted, not even a rabbit, and there was talk that the sled dogs might have to be slaughtered for food. Everyone knew how stupid that would be. Snowshoeing was slow going, and if you did manage to kill something, how would you haul the remains back to camp?

To add to our grief, Charlie was driving us all crazy with horror stories. "Those *witigos*, they come in all sizes and shapes. Some of them look ordinary, like you and me. They're the most dangerous because they sneak up on you, and they get you before you know what happens. Other *witigos* – they're monsters, tall as the tallest jack pine, so heavy the earth shakes when they walk. They never wash, so they stink, their teeth are all rotten, and their nails are long like ragged claws. Their skin is most often a black colour. They have huge heads and, of course, no lips since they've bitten them off. And starving! They're always starving and the only meat they'll eat is human flesh."

Of all the fantastic stories I had heard in the last year and a half, this was the most ridiculous. I couldn't help mocking him.

"And where do these charming creatures come from?"

Grandfather looked at me as if I was an imbecile, but Charlie answered with patience.

"All these *witigos*, they were humans who went crazy whilst they were starving and ate human flesh. Once that happens, there's nothing can be done but you gotta kill them dead. When *witigo* comes around, you start calling on your *pawachi-kans*. The one with the strongest *pawachi-kan*, he does the killing because he'll have the most power. That one wrestles with *witigo*; sometimes they fight so fiercely they fly right to the top of the trees. And if *witigo* shouts louder than the human, then he wins, and everyone is a dead duck.

"Even if *witigos* lose, they're hard to kill. Their hearts are made of ice, you see. You try and burn them, but the water that melted keeps putting the fire out. And you do have to burn them or they'll come back and eat you."

I understood that the story contained an important message — cannibalism was taboo. But Charlie's retelling was irritating when we were all so hungry. There was nothing left to eat now but a little flour and a bit of lard to cook it in. If some game wasn't found soon, we would starve to death. I noticed Marguerite's round face was gaunt, but she was not so lethargic as to stop copying out vocabulary – hungry, starving, famished, ravenous.

Finally, one morning in mid-February, a delegation consisting of my aunts Charlotte and Louisa, and my cousins Lucy and Rita, cornered Grandfather in his wigwam. "Chief," Lucy said, "we admire you and love you, but sometimes you are stubborn as Raven. We are all starving. Our children cry all the time, their bellies are so empty. We must go to Pelican Narrows. There will be food there for sure."

Grandfather wouldn't even consider it. "To beg the white man on our knees? Not as long as I'm alive. If we perish, at least we will go as proud Indians."

The women were obviously disgusted. They turned their back and walked away. I hoped that they would persuade their husbands to rebel against the edicts of my ridiculous, and cruel, grandfather.

The next day Cornelius said he'd go looking – maybe some big rabbit would come bounding along his path. Once outside he let out a shout. There against the setting sun were silhouetted two dog sleds. Each was pulling a line of toboggans piled high with freight. As the caravan approached closer, the shapes of the two mushers and one passenger came into focus, but the travellers were so bundled up against the cold, none of us could make out who they were. When the convoy finally came to a stop, a figure slowly emerged from a pile of robes. I found myself in the arms of Father Bonnald.

The mushers, Joseph Canada and Leon Highway, quickly unloaded the freight. There was plenty of pemmican, but, although everyone was starving, there was no rush to make a meal of it. Everyone remained calm. Prayers were said, thanks given. A few questions politely asked. How had the priest managed to find them at this time of their need?

"I said a prayer and I'm here," was all he would say. I found out later that the scarcity of game had forced many Woodland Cree to seek help in Pelican Narrows. Only Grandfather had been too proud to do so. Father Bonnald had learned our approximate location from the others.

I was looking forward to a long chat with Father – maybe I'd tell him about Marguerite – but he was exhausted from the brutal trip and fell asleep right after dinner.

The next morning the Blackfish and Charboyers were waiting to meet with him the minute he finished his breakfast. They gathered around, but Grandfather stood a way off, refusing to join the group. He had to accept Father Bonnald's charity or he'd have had a full-blown revolt on his hands, but he wasn't happy about it. I wondered if he had abandoned his plan to blow up Pelican Narrows. By the sour expression that played on his face, I suspected that he somehow blamed the weather and vanishing game on the white man too.

There were now enough supplies to last until spring when food would surely be more plentiful. But my relatives insisted that I return to Pelican Narrows with the priest. Not only was I one more mouth to feed, but, at such dangerous times, they'd no longer accept the responsibility for my wellbeing.

"I'm not going," I blurted out, "not unless Marguerite comes with me."

Father Bonnald didn't raise an eyebrow, didn't show surprise. He had been afraid something like this would happen.

"And who is Marguerite?" he asked.

I sang her praises until I was sure I had convinced him of how much I loved her.

"You realize, Joe, that this will end any chance of studying at the Collège de Montréal."

By the pleading look in his eyes, I knew that I was about to break my beloved teacher's heart. I said nothing. Finally he sighed, "Maybe some things are just not meant to be."

CHAPTER THIRTY-THREE

JOE PUTS HIS ARM AROUND Izzy's shoulder. It's such a relief to be able to tell his story to someone. They move towards each other, about to kiss, when they hear something. They both groan as Gilbert Bear comes stumbling out of the bush.

"Joe, you have to come. The boss is calling you. Mr. Lewis the writer got so pissed, he wandered off and ended up on the beach. Said he wanted to go for a swim, but while he was taking his pants off, he fell on his ass. Now his feet's in the water and he won't get up. They think you can talk sense to him."

"You can tell Mr. Arthur Jan that I'm off duty. I'm about to suffer a week of babysitting that drunk and that's more than enough for me."

"Mr. Jan's going to be awfully mad."

"You know what? I don't give a damn. Leave us alone."

After Gilbert goes away, Izzy asks, "What's the matter? I thought you were looking forward to this trip."

"There's something wrong with the whole business, something really shady is going on. Remember I told you that my *pawachi-kan* visited me? Well, it happened only once. Two night ago Thunderbird came into my dreams and screamed at me, 'You're an idiot if you get mixed up in this business. Evil, all evil.' Then she flapped away."

"Maybe you shouldn't go then. Maybe these warnings mean something."

"I've given my word and I won't go back on it. But this will be the last time I work for Arthur Jan. He's so greedy, he makes me puke. Exactly the kind of white man Grandfather Blackfish loathed."

He nestles his head against Izzy's shoulder. "Now I'm going to tell you not only my secret but also how my heart was broken."

St. Gertrude's Church, all dressed up in spring flowers, was packed. All the Cree families showed up. Father Bonnald officiated and Florence and Russell Smith were there too, representing the white folk. The Blackfish and Charboyer clan had made the trip, all except, of course, for Grandfather – he wouldn't be caught dead in the village he hated so much. My bride was so young, so radiant, so beautiful, dressed in a deer skin dress she had beaded herself. As Father Bonnald read us our vows, there was regret in his voice and tears welled in his eyes, I was surprised at this because by that time, everyone, including him, had fallen in love with Marguerite Settee.

My mother admired her artistic talent, oohing and ahing over the birch bark box Marguerite had made for her. It was beaded in an intricate design of blue, red and yellow. "It's done so beautifully, I don't know how you managed it," Mother exclaimed.

Once Father Bonnald discovered Marguerite's obsession with reading and writing, he too had warmed to her. He drew up a schedule of study – French, mathematics and history this summer; Latin, science and literature the following year.

"Don't you think she should have time just to relax and learn our way of doing things," I had protested. But Marguerite interrupted, insisting, "I will begin my studies at once."

The world came to Pelican Narrows that summer. First, two veterans of the Great War, Angus McCallum, and Jamie Bird, both of them fantastic sharp-shooters, arrived home. Intact, thank goodness. The stories of their harrowing adventures in France thrilled everyone.

With fur prices soaring, white trappers showed up by the dozen. We didn't like them, we thought they were irresponsible and unscrupulous. Still, there was something foreign, something exotic about them. Louise Bird ended up marrying Don Pomeroy, an American from Montana.

When word leaked out of rich zinc, copper and gold deposits, prospectors flooded in like a swarm of mosquitoes. And when Dominion Land Surveyors were assigned to the north country, Pelican Narrows became one of their staging points. Tents popped up everywhere. The place was actually bustling.

During the summer, I was hired on for many different jobs, and earned some good money. By now I had decided that full-time hunting and trapping were not for me. I would combine my newly learned savvy in the bush with the education I'd received from Father Bonnald. I began drawing up plans for a winter transport business. Mother, though, never stopped reminding me of my obligation – I had promised to spend one more winter with my Cree relatives and I must do so.

Mother had volunteered to move into the rectory, so we newlyweds had the little cabin to ourselves for the summer. It didn't take Marguerite long to sweep and clean the place, and she was an efficient if not brilliant cook, so she spent most of her time either working on Father Bonnald's assignments, or beading deerskin "as soft as lard" which she planned to make into a vest for me.

"So, you will always remember me," she said with sad eyes.

"Why would you say that? We will never be apart."

"You never know," was the reply that wrenched my heart.

I knew that her parents had died suddenly in a boating accident when she was only four years old, and put her fatalism down to that. Still it bothered me. I vowed that no matter what, I must make her feel safe.

Our reunion with the Blackfishes and Charboyers was a joyful one. They all adored Marguerite, and had come to respect me, if somewhat grudgingly. By marrying one of their own, I had become one of them. Even Grandfather smiled a little. There was no mention of hand grenades or Pelican Narrows being blown up. I was thankful for that, but, of course, that wasn't the end of it. Forget about strychnine poison or bombs – those were white man's weapons.

Grandfather had decided that the massacre must be conducted in the old-fashioned, Indian way, with hatchets, knives, bows and arrows. But also firearms. "Our people have been using guns for so many centuries, they're as much ours as the white man's," he said. We were to wear war paint and feather headdresses. "We will wait for a moon-less night. You will be our guide, leading us along the paths to the white bastards. Then we will slaughter them in their beds." I was revolted by what he was telling me. If anything came of it, I would have to contact Father Bonnald. Meanwhile, I hoped that it all was just another pipedream.

That autumn, the hunting returned to normal. My shy cousin Leon, now seventeen, had turned out to be a superb shot, and he killed the first moose of the season. We all congratulated him. But all of us hunters did well. I bagged two woodland caribou, the meat of which was considered the sweetest in the world.

Marguerite and I were given a rare privilege, we were assigned our own wigwam. It meant more work for both of us, tearing down the household as we travelled and setting it up again, but we liked the privacy. Our lovemaking was beyond anything I had dreamed of. Marguerite's ecstasy was greater even than mine. Some mornings I awoke thinking that I would die of happiness.

Her studies had advanced so that I could now read to her in English, and I had brought a few books I thought she might enjoy. Lewis Carroll's *Alice's Adventures in Wonderland* was her favourite.

"A rabbit hole, what a wonderful place to be," she said. "But would there be enough to eat?"

One morning at daybreak, three weeks after we started out, I was shaken awake by Grandfather Blackfish. "Important business this day," he barked.

I hadn't noticed the night before – too tired I guess, but a makeshift trail had been cut through the bush. We men, all six of us, walked single file, one behind the other, until we reached what looked like a small hill but turned out to be a roughly-hewn shed covered with branches. There was a door of sorts which Grandfather pulled open. What was inside shocked me.

Stacked in one corner were a half dozen rifles. "Three Enfields, a Winchester, and two Remingtons," Uncle Raymond explained. "The handguns – a couple of Colts, a Lancaster and two Smith & Wessons. That one over there? That's a Lewis automatic machine gun, designed by the Americans but used by the British. All materiel left over from World War One. Your grandfather somehow got his hands on them."

These were the guns, as well as our hatchets, knives and bow and arrows, we would use to slaughter the white people, all eight of them, residing at Pelican Narrows. But not right away, thank God. The real event would take place in the spring. Today would be a trial run; a chance for us to get a feel for our weapons.

Each of us armed ourselves with one rifle and a pistol. We marched single file along the path until Grandfather sang out, "Ready!" We dropped onto one knee, steadied our guns. "Aim! Fire!" Followed by silence. This was only a pretend exercise as Grandfather's rifle was the only one equipped with live bullets and he didn't want to use them up.

The fifth time we all knelt as ordered, but rather lazily, as all of us except Grandfather were growing tired of this charade. Suddenly there was a rustling sound and the shrubs quivered. We couldn't make out what was there, but it's shadow loomed large. A moose or a bear probably. Grandfather fired. A blood-curdling scream rang out.

We raced over. On the ground, blood pooling on his chest and in his grizzly beard, lay an old white man. I bent over him, but his eyes had already glazed over. In a few seconds he was dead.

I recognized him immediately. Once a year Daniel Whitton showed up at Pelican Narrows to trade his fur catch for provisions at the Hudson's Bay post. I remember seeing him scrambling out of his canoe, a large man with an enormous white beard and long hair tied back in a pony tail. He was surprisingly neatly dressed for someone who was known as the Mad Trapper. Then, about five years ago, he disappeared into the bush, never to emerge again. It was thought he was dead until Xavier Morin had spotted him, approached him, spoke a few words with him. Hunting for rabbits and any other creatures, fishing, picking edible plants, he was managing quite well, thank you. And he definitely wanted no company.

The soil in these parts is so thin, it was hard to find a suitable place to bury the body. Finally, some boggy land near a stream was deemed suitable. Charlie and I set to work digging the old man's grave. As we rolled the shaggy figure into his last resting place, I thought, the first victim of Grandfather's revenge. For a massacre that happened two hundred years ago. How ridiculous! How evil!

Izzy's mouth has fallen open, her eyes are bulging. "Did you tell anyone?" she gasps.

"No, I didn't, and no one ever questioned Daniel Whitton's disappearance. I knew when the truth came out that you would despise me. I wouldn't blame you one bit if you tell the authorities."

"It was hardly your fault, Joe. After all you didn't pull the trigger."

"I might well have if my rifle had been loaded. I will say this for myself, though. I made a pledge right then, that the moment I got back to Pelican Narrows, I would straight away tell Father Bonnald what was going on. Warn him and everybody else. But that never happened. Do you want to hear why?"

"Yes, of course. Go on with your story."

One evening, at the beginning of December, stretched out before the fire, I happened to pick up Marguerite's notebook. By now her handwriting was neat and legible. "Baby, infant, child, tot, toddler" I read. "Have you got something to tell me, wife of mine?" I asked.

"I've made a decision," she replied. "If it's a girl, we'll name her Clara after my great grandmother. If it's a boy, he'll be called George after your late father."

I thought to myself, what have I done to deserve such incredible good fortune?

Later, when I forced myself to remember, I realized that the Spanish flu struck on the very day that Marguerite had told me this good news. I was the first to fall ill– probably I caught the sickness from the returned soldiers I met that summer – and passed it on to the others. The symptoms were the same for us all – a sudden exhaustion so overwhelming you took to your bed, fierce diarrhoea –you tried at first to make it to the latrine, but soon gave up and used the bucket if you could – vomiting your guts out, a cough so intense you were sure your ribs were cracking, a headache so excruciating you wanted to die, sweating until you soaked the blankets through, and then shivering with cold until your teeth rattled. Luckily, maybe because I was young and strong, I recovered quite quickly, and so could help the others.

I ran around doing what I could, delivering cups of water, mopping foreheads, emptying pails of throw-up and shit. But I knew that my efforts were basically useless. People either died or they didn't.

Great Grandfather Blackfish was the first to go. This wasn't a surprise since he was so ancient. Then Aunt Charlotte passed, followed by my seventeen year old cousin, the crack shot, Leon. I carried the bodies outside so they could freeze. They'd be buried as soon as the ground could be worked. I had no time for tears.

Marguerite seemed lethargic, but I was so busy with the others, all I could do was keep a watchful eye on her. The first warning was the blue-black patches on her round cheeks. I could do nothing but hold her as blood gushed from her ears, mucus flowed from her nose, the frothy liquid boiled up from her lungs. Of course I knew what it meant. For an hour I cradled her in my arms. Finally she whispered, "Love, spelled L-O-V-E," closed her eyes, and died.

Grandfather, too, was sick – within minutes he would be gone – but he managed to grab my hand as I walked by, and gasped, "Do you understand now, Grandson. The white man brings us only death. Unless we fight back, we as a people are doomed." I didn't give a damn what he said. As far as I was concerned, my life was over.

The dawn is breaking a pale red and yellow.

"I have to go," whispers Joe. "It's only a few hours before we leave."

Izzy looks up at him. She is weeping uncontrollably.

FLORENCE'S FAREWELL BREAKFAST

Sunday morning

CHAPTER THIRTY-FOUR

FLORENCE SMITH HAS FINALLY MANAGED to escape the square dance and is making her way home. It's 4 a.m., and the sky is the colour of lemon juice.

The moment she steps in the door, she's accosted by her husband's raucous snoring. How infuriating! It was Russell who, with great fanfare, invited everyone to a Farewell-to-the-Famous-Author breakfast, but it will be she who ends up doing everything. It's been like that her entire married life.

There she was, eighteen-years-old, the naive daughter of a hard-bitten prairie homesteader. Russell Smith arrived on the scene an up-and-coming employee of the Hudson's Bay Company, dapper, cheery, certainly the most eligible bachelor around. Everyone was astonished that, with all those pretty girls hanging on his every word, he had chosen plain, big-boned Florence. She thinks now it was probably her strong arms, muscled from years of labouring on the Saskatchewan farm, that attracted him, because, from the moment she pronounced, "I do" all those years ago, she's done all the hard work.

She knows the post's inventory like the back of her hand. The guns, the kettles, the frying pans, the dog harnesses, the whips, the snow shoes, the toboggans, the tea, the HP sauce, the canned beans, the baking powder, the beads, the thread, the fancy ladies' hats — she can locate them with a snap of the fingers. Not only does she keep the books, and very well too, but manual labour isn't beneath her, manhandling the heavy press used to bale pelts for shipment, for instance.

There's an ancient birch bark canoe strung from the rafters of the store, proudly emblazoned with the HBC's crest, a talisman of the Company's glory days, and this Russell conscientiously keeps free of dust and bat droppings, but that's about all he does. It's just as well they don't have children. All Florence's energy goes into looking after her husband.

Something else is rankling her this morning. Sinclair Lewis is a drunk, a fool, a clown. And, judging from the conversations she's had with him, he has no understanding of the Cree way of life. Yet he is threatening to churn out a novel about his "exotic adventures in the Canadian north." The people of Pelican Narrows will be slandered for sure. So why are the Smiths celebrating The Great Writer? Because Russell thinks it will impress the idiot Indian agent. He bows to authority, no matter what. And, no question, she too must do her duty.

Yesterday, Florence had asked Lionel Bird to take her by motor canoe to Angus Highway's little farm and there bought several dozen eggs and a few quarts of fresh milk. She takes these from the icebox and, from the pantry, flour, baking powder, salt, pepper, sugar. She also plans to retrieve from the storehouse the ingredient that makes her pancakes famous – a cup or two of Russell's homemade beer. She's about to start mixing the batter when she hears a loud bang at the dispensary door. Oh drat, she thinks to herself, just my luck.

What greets her is two drunken Indians, their faces a bloody pulp of black eyes, swollen lips, scraped cheeks. In English that they don't understand, she demands, "What now, you numbskulls?" In Cree she says, "Okay, tell me what happened."

There had been a brawl, a real dust-up, instigated by Bibiane Ratt and Sinclair Lewis.

"Any white man can drink any goddamn Indian, any half-assed half-breed, under the table," The Famous Writer had challenged. The two other white men there, Arthur Jan and Bob Taylor, had winced.

"You gotta be kidding!" Bibiane scoffed.

The two sat down with jugs of homemade hooch, and the contest was on. Soon every adult male in Pelican Narrows was engaged in what The Famous Author slurred, "is our interesting little experiment in eugenics."

"You're lucky you're both not dead," butts in Florence.

"Yah," says Gordon Ballendine. "One of the guys yells, 'An Indian could do any damn thing better than white scum.' Fists started to fly then. Redskins and whities – all were drunk, ready to fight. I got punched maybe a dozen times. It was too bad."

"And, of course, you two just sat there with your hands under your asses."

The men attempt a guilty smile but their puffed up mouths make this impossible.

As Florence cleans off the matted blood, applies antiseptic, stitches the wounds, she thinks, it used to be so peaceful here in Pelican Narrows. People were nice to each other. Now the booze has come, and we, Indians and whites alike, have descended into hell.

After the two leave, Florence decides to sneak off to the beach for a smoke – and to hide. Doc Happy Mac is officially off duty and there's bound to be more beaten-up party-goers showing up on her door step.

She plunks herself down on her usual log seat, lights her pipe. Artemis and Athena curl up at her feet. She loves these pugs – they're the only creatures who seem genuinely happy just to be alive. It's beautiful outside, the thin, milky light playing tag on the waters before her. She has so much to do, and she's already exhausted from staying up all night. If only Sally were here to help.

Florence had visited her yesterday, and there she was, as usual, lying in her bed, her face to the wall. Florence couldn't help but yell, "You stop this nonsense, Sally Sewap. Everyone misses you. I miss you. Your son misses you. Father Bonnald misses you."

But, of course, the priest would miss her. Sally had been his slave her entire adult life. She is rebelling at last. Yesterday morning, Florence had been set to deliver the lecture she'd been rehearsing for a month. "Father Bonnald you must get rid of that annoying brother of yours. His ridiculous dithering has driven Sally mad." But the priest was nowhere to be found.

"And that might have been my last chance," she sighs.

For the first six months after the Smiths' arrival at Pelican Narrows, Sally and Florence had hardly spoken to each other. Sally was the housekeeper of the Roman Catholic priest, and a Cree, so that pretty well ruled out a friendship with the store manager's white Anglican wife. Then one night a fire had broken out in the HBC store – containers of Kerosene had mysteriously blown up. Florence had assumed that Bibiane Ratt was responsible but, as usual, nothing could be proved.

The blaze was contained without too much damage being done, but Russell, in his anxiety to save the antique HBC canoe, had defied the smoke and flames until he himself was ablaze. Florence had doused him with a bucket of water, and carried him over her shoulder to safety. She treated the blisters that quickly formed on his chest and arms with Percival's Lotions. This did no good; his pain was excruciating. He screamed so loudly that Florence thought his heart might give out under the strain.

Just after midnight, there was a knock on the door and in walked Sally Sewap with her medicine pouch. She patted a mixture of swamp tea and larch pine all over his body, and soon he was able to sleep, at least a little. The next day she forced a purgative down his throat. "That'll remove the smoke particles in his lungs," she insisted.

He coughed and spit and swore, but within days Russell was well enough to walk around.

A week later Florence walked over to the Catholic rectory and presented Sally with two bars of scented soap imported from Britain as a thank you gift. The two women struck up a conversation, discovered that the healing arts were a common passion, and soon became fast friends.

Bit by bit Sally unveiled her trove of herbal remedies. A potion made from the inner bark of the speckled alder bush relieved sore, itchy eyes; the root of the rattle-pod, when chewed and the juice swallowed, alleviated stomach ache; pitch of the black spruce mixed with grease was used on skin rashes, scabies and burns. Every ailment imaginable found relief in some concoction: berries, flowers, leaves, roots, bark, moss.

The two began trekking into the bush, searching out rare specimens – the Wentworth girl often tagged along. Both women loved the sounds of the forest so few words were exchanged. They didn't need to speak, they were in perfect harmony.

One day in mid–August, four years ago, Sally announced that she had permission from Father Bonnald to visit her family. An old aunt was fading; Sally must say goodbye to her. "She's been important to me all my life. She's a medicine woman, a very famous and wise one, and I want to thank her for all she's passed on to me."

When Florence asked if she could go along, Sally looked dubious – would the elderly shaman want anything to do with a loud, curious white person? Probably not. Finally, though, she had given in, not so much because Florence had begged like a dog, but because the hunting season was upon them. No one else would go with her.

The trip took twelve days. The two women paddled south on Mirond and Corneille Lakes, then down the rock-strewn Sturgeon-Weir River, enduring dozens of portages – around the Birch, Leaf, Snake, Spruce, Rat, Two Mile and Crooked rapids. They crossed the huge Amisk Lake to Sturgeon Landing – this was where the new residential school was scheduled to be built. Sally wouldn't even glance at the spot. From there it was another three days, often in driving rain, until finally they arrived at Cumberland House.

Since Sally's aunt lived some ways from the village, they had to walk another half day through heavy bush. As they finally approached the plain little cabin, late in the afternoon, Florence suddenly felt uneasy. Supposing the old woman ordered her off the

property? She was famous for being a loner, refusing to have anything to do with the Blackfish or Charboyer clan. What should
Florence do? But Betty Cheechoo, or Judique as she preferred to
be called, welcomed them both.

She was a short, rotund woman, with pudgy cheeks, a rose pod of
a nose, and small, bright eyes. Her long hair, still black although
flecked with gray, was worn in braids down her back giving her a
youthful air. Where Sally got the idea that her aunt was fading
Florence had no idea. The moment they walked in the door she
began a lively discourse on her interpretation of Cree philosophy
which didn't stop until they left.

The world, Judique believed, was a perpetual battlefield where
forces of good and evil were forever struggling for supremacy.
Humans, poor things, were caught in the middle. It reminded
Florence of the universe populated by all those eccentric Greek gods
and goddesses she had come to admire so much. Zeus zapping the
world with lightning bolts would fit right in.

According to Judique, nothing happened by chance, everything in
the universe was interrelated. Although the medicine woman made it
clear that events were not predetermined. They could be altered
through intervention. People were victims of fate only if they couldn't
interpret the patterns playing out around them, and act on them.

"If tragedy strikes, say a man's young wife dies while giving birth,"
Judique said, "it means that man's lost his knack of reading the signs.
His *pawachi-kan* had deserted him for some reason. Or, maybe some-
body with a stronger, more dangerous *pawachi-kan* blinded him."
When the terrible small pox had struck, for example, she blamed it
on the Indian being too fascinated by the white man's enticements.
The guardian spirits had been ignored.

Shamans were smarter and craftier than other humans – their
pawachi-kans, who were the colossals of the spirit world, made sure
of that, coaching them to divine the future through dreams and signs.
The intricate workings of the universe were *not* a mystery to a healer

like Judique. Curing illnesses, or predicting where game animals could be found, or foretelling the sex of an unborn child were all a result of her mediation between human and gods.

Of course, there were good shamans and evil shamans. The latter might persuade a foolish *pawachi-kan* to do something destructive — kill a human on whom the shaman sought revenge, for example.

"My *nikawis* is definitely a good medicine woman, a holy one, really," Sally interjected.

The old woman frowned at her — surely everybody knows *that*. She continued, "We humans are but little white clouds being scattered here and there by the wind. The Great Creator gives wise people like me the power to look into the heavens and understand how best we can survive the never-ending storm that rages between *mitho-kikwi*, good, and *machi-kikwi*, evil."

Judique talked nonstop for a week, pausing only for a smoke and to nibble on some bannock and smoked fish. Now and then she'd snooze for a few hours. Sally eventually got bored and went berry picking, but Florence's attention never faltered.

In the hut there was only one chair, rickety with part of the seat webbing missing. It was this dais from which Judique held forth. Florence had to perch on the hard little bed, her back aching, her legs numbing. The old woman applauded her fortitude. "If you had been lucky enough to be born a Cree," she said, "You might have been a shaman, even a great one."

"Well," thought Florence, "maybe I will never be able to forecast how an irritable spirit feels on a particular day or how it will take revenge on whoever offended it, but maybe I can become a soldier in the universal battle between Good and Evil."

On her return to Pelican Narrows that fall, she organized a band of disgruntled Cree men, about a dozen in all, most of them wardens at St. Bartholomew's Church. She named them Warriors Against Wickedness. Since then, for a good three years, they have regularly gathered late at night on a plateau not far from Father Bonnald's grotto, and, under Florence's strict command, they have marched. She had learned a lot from an uncle who was a sergeant during World War One and had never stopped talking about how he drilled his men almost to death. Her bark echoed through the bush. "Parade, turn right. About turn. Turn left. Company retire."

They were a straggly, undisciplined group, with only one real soldier amongst them. Harold Bear was a veteran of the Great War, had the bullet wounds to prove it, but he was now so discombobulated by his experience that he could give no leadership, only staggered about trying to follow Florence's orders. Her army sometimes laughed out loud at her commands, her pretence, and yet she knew they were sincere. The last vestiges of Cree life are crumbling away like sand dunes before a raging storm, and they will do anything to stop it. Tonight they tackle their first assignment. General Florence Smith knows that they will do well.

But Florence didn't forget another of Judique's important teachings – helping others was the true Cree way. She persuaded Sally that they should open a dispensary/clinic in a lean-to built at the side of the Hudson's Bay store. Sally provided Indian remedies, Florence, the hands-on knowledge she had acquired through Red Cross courses.

Yesterday afternoon Florence had proudly shown Doc Happy Mac around. "My Lord, you girls are amazing," he exclaimed. "Everything from pulling teeth to healing fractures. Hope those Indians appreciate you."

What the doc wasn't told was that Sally has given up on life and Florence is stuck with the entire load. Well, soon somebody else will have to take over.

CHAPTER THIRTY–FIVE

FLORENCE GLANCES UP at Arthur Jan's house. There's no sign of life. Arthur's likely down at his dock, getting ready to leave. She climbs the path leading up the hill towards his place, Athena and Artemis puffing beside her. Even before she gets there, she can smell the gasoline. The Warriors Against Wickedness have properly carried out instructions. She heads towards the back of the house.

Jan is the only person in Pelican Narrows who keeps his house locked, but then, as he points out, he's the only one with anything valuable to steal. What he doesn't know is that Mavis Custer, his housekeeper, always leaves the kitchen door open. Out of spite.

The light is dim inside, but Florence can see well enough to make her way towards the jewel box that is in his parlour. Sitting on a sterling silver tray atop the bureau, twinkling in the pale sun, is Arthur's collection of George II ale glasses, circa 1750, exquisitely engraved with hops and barley. She picks up one of these and smashes it hard on the floor. She laughs out loud, heaves another, then another, until the entire lot lies in sparkling pieces. Artemis's and Athena's eyes bulge even further from their heads.

Florence walks out onto the porch and opens the windows. She lifts the cloth off the parrot cage, unlatches the door. "There you are, you ridiculous creature. Vamoose!" The bird looks at her with beady eyes, but doesn't move an inch. "It's for your own good, you stupid thing."

Florence returns to the parlour where she spots a decanter of brandy surrounded by lovely crystal snifters. She pours herself a shot and plops down on the sofa. Her memory of the last time she was in this place, four years ago, still fills her with rage.

Several Pelican Narrows girls had gone missing. Searches were organized, but turned up no sign of them. The village went into mourning. About a month later, Leonard Sewap was in Moose Jaw, trying to raise money for a fish processing plant. One afternoon, he spotted one of the missing girls walking along the street. He followed her to one of the brothels that were flourishing in that randy city. When he confronted her and eventually the others, they refused to come home. They explained they wanted a more exciting life than dull old Pelican Narrows could provide.

Bibiane Ratt had been seen chatting them up the afternoon before they disappeared so their parents were sure that he had something to do with their running off. But this was never proven.

One Saturday morning, Florence was arranging some wild flowers on the altar of St. Bartholomew's in preparation for the next day's service. Annie Custer, the Wentworth's housekeeper, was washing the floor.

"Mrs. Smith, could I talk with you for a moment," she had asked.

Florence replied, "Of course," and Annie poured out her story. Her second daughter Helen had always been an irritable, frustrated kid, the trouble-maker among her six siblings. She was now in open revolt, refusing to obey any of the rules Annie and her husband, Alphonse, laid down, particularly the eight o'clock curfew. She was seen late the previous evening talking with Bibiane Ratt, and by this morning she hadn't come home. Her few clothes were gone. Could Mrs. Smith help in any way?

Florence had a pretty good idea of what was going on. Russell had insisted the rumours were nonsense, but she was sure there was something to them. Bibiane was bribing the girls with a lot of money, supplied, of course, by Arthur Jan.

Florence ran up the hill, puffing like a steam engine, and barged through the Arthur's kitchen door. Following the shrieks and grunts, she walked straight into the bedroom. Even now she gasps at the obscenity – the girl's outstretched arms and legs tied to the four posts of the bed with rope, the man's skinny, white rump pumping up and down like a mongrel dog fucking a bitch in heat. Florence marched over, grabbed Arthur by his hair, and pulled him off.

"What do you think you're doing!" he screamed as he struggled to free himself. "She's here of her own free will!"

"Thirteen. That's how old she is, Arthur Jan. Even in this primitive society, that's unacceptable. If it's with my dying breath, I'll see you pay for this."

Helen lay naked, crumpled on the bed. Florence untied her bonds, wrapped her in a blanket, and half carried her to her family's cabin. There it was discovered that her back and behind were covered with welts, her arms and legs with bruises.

"Mr. Jan beat me with a whip," she whimpered. "Again and again, and I couldn't get him to stop."

Florence was ready that very day to travel to the RCMP depot in Prince Albert to have charges laid, but, to her dismay, Russell refused to make the arrangements.

"I'm telling you the only thing you'll accomplish is to harm the girl's reputation even further," he had insisted. "Jan will persuade the authorities that he had no idea of her age, and that she came willingly. Even pleaded with him to have sex. Who do you think they'll believe? A young native girl or a respected man of business, a Justice of the Peace!"

Florence kept arguing with her husband until Alphonse Custer showed up. "Please, Mrs. Smith, forget this whole thing. Helen has learned her lesson."

Florence was horrified. "You're saying Arthur Jan should get off Scot free? He was responsible for the disappearance of all those others girls, you know that."

Alphonse nodded his head, yes, but said not another word.

"Well, the least you can do is give me your reason."

"Okay, but it's a sad story. I owe Mr. Jan a lot of money. Advances on next season's catch. I've never been able to pay it back, and it's piled up year after year. If you go ahead with this complaint, he'll take everything I own."

Florence gave up then, but she has never forgotten. Today, Arthur Jan will finally receive his just desserts.

CHAPTER THIRTY-SIX

IT'S NOW FIVE A.M. and the sky is turning egg-yolk yellow. Since the Treaty Party is eager to leave, guests will be arriving soon. Florence scurries down the hill and is relieved to see bustling on the beach. Russell is lighting the fire under the makeshift griddle. The coffee is being prepared. Annie has arrived with bannock and scones. All is well. The first stage of the plan can be set in motion.

Florence yells to the group, "I'll be right back, I'm just going..." then mumbles something unintelligible under her breath. She throws a couple of sausages into the bush, and Artemis and Athena dive after them. Good, now she can escape.

She walks along a path which circles behind the HBC store. This is where the tents of the Treaty Party have been set up. No sign of activity there. She's surprised Bob Taylor hasn't sounded the bugles by now – everything is done with such precise routine under his watch. A meaner, more petty and narrow-minded man would be hard to imagine. And to think, as the Government's representative, he personifies Canada in the Indian mind.

She continues down a cliff to a small bay where her canoe is tied, hidden behind willows that lean over the water. She unties the little craft, and, with surprising nimbleness for a woman of her bulk, settles herself in the bow.

She paddles close to the shore, praying she won't be seen.

She passes St. Bartholomew's rectory. No stirring there yet. Annie has already left, so there's nobody to wake them. Poor Ernst Wentworth. He is a sincere man yet, try as he might, he's so ineffectual. A joke of a missionary really. Good thing he doesn't know how the Indians laugh at him behind his back. And Lucretia, that ridiculous wife of his. The Queen of England isn't so pretentious. She's obviously got herself ensnarled with Arthur Jan. Well, she'll pay dearly for that. A broken heart, for sure.

How these two could have produced an offspring as splendid as Izzy Wentworth is beyond Florence. She's seen so much of Izzy over the years that the girl has become like a daughter. But, of course, there's the rub. Izzy is what Florence might have had. Often, when she catches sight of the girl running here or there, her hair spinning like golden candy floss, that terrible time comes flooding back.

After years of working as a clerk, Russell had finally been promoted to a manager. Located where the parkland merges into boreal forest, the post he was assigned to had been doing poorly for decades – the Company would close it down a year later – and the house was small and shabby, a cabin really. Florence didn't complain. At last her husband was getting ahead.

The baby, Katie, was four months old, a wisp of a thing with her little tuft of blonde hair, pale skin and green eyes. Florence couldn't understand how a strong, big-boned woman like herself could give birth to such a tiny child prone to every kind of illness. Katie, though, had made up for the trouble this caused Florence by being so sweet, so cheery.

That year, spring arrived early, melting the snow and ice a month before the usual time. Russell decided he would take the pelts that had been traded so far to the main depot in Prince Albert. He'd be gone a few days. Would Florence be able to manage? She nodded her head yes, but felt uneasy, especially when she discovered that he had forgotten to cut more firewood.

That night, a cold snap descended, freezing the melt into hard, ragged ice, sharp as a razor. In the morning, she had to chisel out her front step so the door would open. She managed to get to the shed only to discover that there was barely enough wood for the day's cooking and heating. Well, tomorrow she would have to chop some more herself.

In the evening the temperature dropped to minus 20, the wind raged, a blizzard descended. Florence knew she had to get to the woodshed, but when she opened the door, she couldn't see two inches in front of her nose, and she realized that if she took another step, she'd be lost.

The firewood already stored in the house was quickly used up. Florence tried to keep the baby warm, wrapping her in blankets and coats until her little head could hardly be seen. Hour after hour, she held the infant against her chest.

By midnight, Florence's nose and hands were so cold she thought they might snap off. Katie's cough grew worse. One minute her little forehead was beaded with sweat, the next her teeth were rattling she was shivering so hard. She refused to suckle. At three a.m., she gave a tiny whimper and closed her eyes forever.

Florence knew she shouldn't blame Russell – how could he know that a blizzard was on the way? But deep in her heart she thought that if it had been her, she would have found some way to get home. To rescue them. That he was as devastated by the baby's death as she was didn't ease the tension. Whatever love had been between them vanished. The tragedy did teach Florence one never-to-be-forgotten lesson – she must rely on no one, she must always take command.

What is she doing, letting her mind wander like that? On today of all days she must stay focused.

She glides past St. Gertrude's. Both priests are probably still in their beds; since Sally took ill they've had to fend for themselves. Of the two brothers, Ovide is definitely crazy, but Étienne is pretty strange too. His parishioners adore him, Florence acknowledges that, but he is so aloof, so sad. Like a doomed character in a Greek tragedy. Oedipus or Agamemnon, perhaps.

"This is a man who doesn't pray very much," she thinks to herself.

Father Bonnald treats Sally's son as if he were his own. Which is probably okay. Joe seems a fine young man even if the priest has turned him into an introverted egghead, and a loner. Izzy claims she loves him. Florence can only imagine what the Wentworths will think of that. An Indian, and worse still, a Catholic! What a row there'll be. Izzy will fight back, Florence is sure, but it won't be pleasant.

Florence is now approaching Cornelius Whitebear's dock. She spots the chief sitting on a log, bundled in a blanket. Despite his illness, he's managed to get there, just as he promised. Her heart begins to pound. After all these years, he's still the only man she has ever truly loved.

When she married Russell, she gave up her Lutheran faith and joined the Anglican Church. It seemed a peculiar religion – Florence still thinks of Henry the Eighth and all his wives every time the hymn 'All God's people come together, worship the King' is sung. But it has served her well. Everywhere Russell was transferred, and this happened often, there were Anglicans to welcome them.

When the Smiths first arrived at Pelican Narrows, Reverend Wentworth was still trying to undo the damage done by that old reprobate, Canon James Mackay. He had turned to Cornelius Whitebear for help and the chief did his best to lure the Cree back to church. "Just got to show them kindness and respect and they'll be faithful," he had suggested.

He'd been so nice to Florence, shaking her hand and smiling that big, rubbery grin of his. He was such a spectacularly handsome man, tall even for a Cree, with a mighty, broad chest, huge muscular arms and thighs – like shanks of a moose, Florence thought – a head of thick hair, cut short so that it stood up like a porcupine quills, black-as-midnight eyes which conveyed every conceivable emotion, and a wide mouth forever in motion.

She fell instantly in love with him and she was sure he felt the same way about her. Not that anything sinful ever happened. Quite the contrary, they were entirely proper. This was not Florence's idea – she would have leapt into bed with him if he had nodded his head in that direction. To her sorrow, he kept her at bay. The relationship between Chief Whitebear and his wife could hardly be called passionate, but Dolores Whitebear had been a good mother to his eight children, and he honoured her for that.

What Florence admired most about Cornelius was his audacity. He was the most outspoken, the prickliest, Indian she had ever met.

Being an Anglican in a sea full of Roman Catholics, he laboured under a major handicap. Nonetheless, he had been elected chief of the Peter Ballendine Band eight times in a row. The reason was obvious – he had valiantly fought for his people in a battle that had come to mean life or death. He told Florence, "The government is determined to swallow us like the whale did Jonah, and vomit us out after we've been made into obedient, little white people. We are to be assimilated, never mind that we were here first, and that we like being Indians."

During the sixteen years Chief Whitebear was in office, petitions, requests, pronouncements flowed from his pen, landing on the desks of bureaucrats and politicians. Hundreds of them every year. And he was not afraid to confront an officious twerp like Bob Taylor, demanding that promises made by the government be kept. The Chief was never rude, just persistent. Taylor referred to him as "the Cree bulldog" in his reports.

The Indian agent and his bosses would have loved to get rid of a man that was so knowledgeable, diligent and obstinate, the most dangerous kind of trouble-maker, but they didn't dare. Chief Whitebear was too beloved, not only by the Peter Ballendine Band but by every other tribe in the north.

The officials needn't fret any more, thinks Florence. What they hadn't been able to accomplish, nature has. Cornelius Whitebear is mortally ill.

"All set, Chief?" she asks as she wraps the blanket around his shoulders.

He nods yes. Florence notices that he looks even more frail than when she had last seen him three days ago. She practically picks up the lanky man, now nothing but skin and bone, and helps him into her canoe. Then she paddles towards Arthur Jan's dock.

Florence has gambled that his workers will be at the HBC breakfast stuffing their faces, and she is right. No one's around. As she had foreseen, the three canoes are parked at the dock, one behind the other. They are already weighted down, ready to travel to The Pas. There, the precious cargo will be loaded onto a train bound for New York City.

She has brought rope which she uses to carefully attach the bow of one canoe to the stern of another, until all three are tied together. She then helps Cornelius over to the lead canoe – a motor is attached at the back – and settles him in the bow. She fetches the drum that has been hidden in bushes nearby, and hands it to him. He places it between his knees. "I'm ready," he says in a steady voice. Florence turns around, puts her hands on his shoulders and kisses him – full on the mouth. Then she climbs into the boat and starts up the motor. "Here we go, Chief," she says.

CHAPTER THIRTY-SEVEN

IT'S SIX A.M. On the beach in front of the Hudson's Bay store, Russell and Annie are busy as bees tending the griddle while everybody else mills about.

The kids are all there, boasting about how many pancakes and chunks of bacon each has shoved into his or her mouth. Their parents have filled their bellies as well, and are now standing around, cracking jokes.

Bob Taylor is walking back and forth nervously. As soon as Arthur Jan and Sinclair Lewis leave for the south, The Treaty Party will set out in the opposite direction, and he is eager to pack up. Where is his crew?

Happy Doc Mac stands encircled by Marguerite Linklater, Madeline Ballendine, Flora Michel, Helen Bear and Juliette Bird. They giggle at everything he says.

Ernst Wentworth paces about, upset that he still hasn't yet been able to confront his daughter. He just can't believe that she's become involved with that native boy. She's given him as wide a berth as she can manage. Right now, in broad daylight, she is standing on the far side of the beach, holding hands with that Indian, Joe Sewap, her lover.

Lucretia Wentworth flaps about like an excited Sandpiper trying to catch *her* lover's eye. Arthur Jan avoids her. He has decided that he'll dump the scrawny clergyman's wife. There's a curvaceous blonde show girl waiting for him in New York, of that he's sure. Curiously, his side-kick Bibiane Ratt is nowhere to be seen.

Father Bonnald is waving at Joe, trying to get his attention. He wants to tell him that the water is low at this time of year on the Sturgeon-Weir River and he should look out for rocks hiding just beneath the surface.

Claude Lewis is sitting on a washed up log, contentedly smoking his pipe and writing his daily letter to his wife. His brother, having boozed the entire night, is passed out on the sand. The Famous Writer is about to miss the spectacle of a lifetime.

First the whir of the engine is heard. Then a loud, slow, solemn drum beat. The people on the beach look up and spot the three canoes attached by a rope, one following another like a circus parade. Who is that sitting in the stern of the lead boat, steering the little motor? Of all people, Florence Smith! Is that Chief Whitebear in the bow? He's deathly ill. So what's he doing there?

Abruptly, the lead canoe turns sharply to the right until its bow almost touches the stern of the third boat. Chief Whitebear some-how manages to catch hold of a rope and attach the two. Now the three boats form a distinct triangle

Florence stands up. She's holding what looks like a torch. Now it's lit – the flame can barely be seen against the brilliant, sparkling water, but the greyish smoke is clearly visible as it rises. Like a men-acing fairy, she begins waving an incendiary wand, first over one canoe, then the second, then the third. Suddenly the entire flotilla is engulfed in a hellish inferno.

Florence disappears, but in the undulating flames the Chief can be made out. He sits motionless.

Within minutes, there's nothing left except wafts of smoke and traces of gasoline spreading circles of pink, green, and yellow on the water's surface.

The spectators stare stupefied until a boom resounds through the forest, and a little girl calls out, "Look there! Look up!" Everyone turns around. Arthur Jan's house has exploded; a fireball is wafting up to heaven.

Days later **Bibiane Ratt's body** is found in the bush. The Mountie who is sent to investigate can't believe his eyes. The victim had been tied to a tree, his legs and arms stretched wide, his head secured upright by his Assomption sash which has been looped around his neck and then tied tight to a branch. The bullets which tore into his torso had been fired from many angles. If the Mountie hadn't known better – nothing like this ever happens in Indian country – he would think that a firing squad had performed an execution.

Arthur Jan rummages through the rubble of his destroyed house, but finds only the left arm of the "Young Sultan Wearing a Mask" Höchst Porcelain, 1775. He collapses on what used to be his doorsteps and weeps.

Meanwhile the entire Cree population of Pelican Narrows gathers at his store. Since there's no one to serve them, they have a wonderful time. Hours go by as calico dresses, beaver traps, boxes of tea, bottles of HP sauce, kegs of Bibiane's homemade liquor, are pilfered. This doesn't upset the proprietor. Arthur Jan has fled Pelican Narrows, never to be heard of again.

Florence Smith manages to swim to The Island where she will live with the dogs until the Mounties complete their futile investigation and leave. When, weeks later, she returns home, nobody blinks an eye.

Waiting to greet Chief Cornelius Whitebear is his *pawachi-kan*. Loon collects his corpse in her wings and lays its down carefully on the bottom of the lake. She then gathers the scattered bones that had tumbled out the boxes when the canoes burned. She places them atop The Chief. They will rest forever together. The ancestors will stay home. As Loon says, a displaced soul is better than no soul at all.

ACKNOWLEDGEMENTS

While this book is a work of fiction, it was inspired by a number of first-hand accounts of events in Pelican Narrows in July 1924. In particular: *Arthur Jan's Memoirs*, self-published in 1960; *Sinclair Lewis & Mantrap: The Saskatchewan Trip* by Claude B. Lewis, Main Street Press, Madison, Wisconsin, 1985; the reports of W.R. Taylor, Indian agent, to the Department of Indian Affairs during the 1920s; the reports of *Missions de la Congrégation des Oblats de Marie Immaculée* 1919-1930; and *The Diocese of Saskatchewan, Synod Journals* 1920s.

Secondary sources include *The Vicar Apostolic of Keewatin, Canada*, by Mary Agatha Gray, Librairie Beauchemin, 1939; *Grateful Prey: Rock Cree Human-Animal Relationships*, Canadian Plains Research Centre, 2002; and my book, *Bitter Embrace: White Society's Assault on the Woodland Cree*, McClelland & Stewart, 2005.

I am indebted to my editor, Dave Margoshes, who provided such valuable insights and advice. I would like to thank Peter Gordon Ballantyne of the Peter Ballantyne First Nation, Pelican Narrows Reserve, for his help, and also Gail Greer, Henry Jerzy and Kathleen Brooks for their much-appreciated encouragement.

ABOUT THE AUTHOR

MAGGIE SIGGINS is the author of twelve books including *Canadian Tragedy: The Story of JoAnn and Colin Thatcher*, which received an Arthur Ellis Award for crime writing and *Revenge of the Land*, which won a Governor General's Award for Nonfiction. *Riel: A Life of Revolution; In Her Own Time: A Cultural History of Women*; and *Bitter Embrace: White Society's Assault on the Woodland Cree* all won the City of Regina Best Book Award and were named a *Globe and Mail* Best Book of the Year. *Canadian Tragedy* and *Revenge of the Land* were made into four-hour miniseries broadcast on CBC and American networks. *Scattered Bones*, is her first book of fiction.

Maggie has also written-produced more than twenty documentaries for her company, Four Square Entertainment, of which she is vice-president, creative. Her films include the award-winning *Stage, Screen and Reserve: The Life and Times of Gordon Tootoosis*, the eight-part series, *Scarred by History* and the acclaimed *A Cruel Wind Blows*.

Maggie lives in Toronto with her husband Gerald Sperling and two dogs.

FSC

www.fsc.org

MIX

Paper from
responsible sources

FSC® C016245

ENVIRONMENTAL BENEFITS STATEMENT

Coteau Books saved the following resources by printing the pages of this book on chlorine free paper made with 100% post-consumer waste.

TREES	WATER	ENERGY	SOLID WASTE	GREENHOUSE GASES
13	**6,181**	**6**	**414**	**1,139**
FULLY GROWN	GALLONS	MILLION BTUs	POUNDS	POUNDS

Environmental impact estimates were made using the Environmental Paper Network Paper Calculator 3.2. For more information visit www.papercalculator.org.